HEADS

HEADS

An Entertainment

EDWARD STEWART

The Macmillan Company, New York

*This book, with all its frailties
and follies, is with untellable gratitude
dedicated to
the Reverend Father Perry M. Smith,
to his spiritual insights
and devotional practice.*

Friday, June 16

It was the best sort of deathbed scene; they were all being brave. There lay the mother, pretending not to be dying; there stood the son, pretending not to be weeping. And there, lined against the walls, were the spectators, pretending not to be whispering.

"Willoughby," the woman said, drawing her son closer with the feeble touch of a finger.

"Yes, Mother?"

"Two things you must remember." The drugs had eased the final pain—in fact they had made her talkative. She alone among those in the hospital room did not seem to realize that these were to be her last words. "All our lives," she said, "we are part of a tradition."

"Yes, Mother."

"It's a pity you didn't know your father better."

"I loved my father."

Her head rolled back into a valley in the pillow. "Two things you must remember."

"I'll remember, Mother."

"Remember to continue."

He nodded. Now she gripped him with ferocity, and her voice became harsh as a ratchet.

"Two other things."

"Anything, Mother."

"Never begin a letter with the word *I*, and never . . ."

She did not complete her injunction. The head rolled sideways, and the hand released him. The doctor hurried to the bed, felt for her pulse, and buttoned up her pink woolen bed jacket. She looked as though she had died healthy. There was a bloom on her cheeks, and her skin was as smooth as a twenty-year-old girl's. No one who did not read the obituaries the next day would have guessed her age.

"Ladies," the doctor said to the nurses, "that will be all." They scurried from the room, whispering. The doctor folded the woman's hands across her stomach. "She was a good woman," he said.

"They say she wasn't," the young man replied.

"She tried her best. You know, Willoughby, it's early to judge. When you're older . . ."

A rabbi was waiting in the hallway. The young man told him "It's over" and left the hospital to murmured condolences and whispers.

The world expressed shock and respect at the news of her decease, but the bright acres of flowers sent to the funeral expressed relief. The sympathy cards were few and short, and most of them began with the word *I*. Willoughby glanced at them and filed them away in shoeboxes. Two shoeboxes held the lot.

The funeral service was Unitarian. She had wanted to be

cremated rather than buried, and she left a note in a wobbly hand asking that her ashes be scattered over the stage of Vienna's light-opera house, the Volksoper. Willoughby ignored the request.

He never moved from the house where they had lived. He never had visitors, or visited. He got a job and stayed a bachelor, and grew older. His mother's reputation grew dimmer, and when people spoke of her, it was no longer in a whisper, but with nostalgia, as though she belonged safely to another era.

Twenty years later, the anniversary of her death fell on a Friday. A dog happened to be murdered the very same day. If there was any connection at all between the two events, only one person knew for sure.

Winnie was waiting in the woods, hidden behind a bush, watching. Scarcely a hundred feet away the ax was chopping wood into fence posts. On the upswing it threw a splash of sun against the side of the barn; on the downswing it sent a muffled report into the afternoon. Its rhythm was regular as a metronome. It was a good ax, a reliable ax. Winnie could see that.

The dog saw Winnie, but it didn't bark. Winnie had a way with animals.

A bluish haze thickened over the distant glimpse of horizon, and black-bellied clouds were mounting the hills, weaving with the stealth of spiders. They crept forward silently, in no hurry to pounce. Winnie had been observing them for half an hour, glad that they were there. The cicadas crackled overhead like electric cables, and the swallows spiraled over the lake like a funnel of soot dropping from the sky.

The farmer had been pitching hay from the wagon into the barn loft for two hours now. He paused to pass his forearm over his glistening brow. The ax kept chopping.

The cicadas died away, leaving only a twitter of birds. The air was growing darker. A breeze riffled through the leaves and exposed quick glints of silvery green. The swallows scattered into the trees, and the dog barked a warning.

The boy said, "Cloudburst." With a last swing he planted the ax in the log. The farmer nodded and tossed his pitchfork into the hay. He spread a tarpaulin over the wagon, and the boy followed him into the house. The first leaden drops fell, and the dog went mewling into the barn.

They had forgotten the ax.

Winnie waited until the rain came, then ran through the slapping opaque sheets, shielded from the view of any observer. The ax was firmly lodged in the log, and it was a struggle to loosen it. A growling at Winnie's feet indicated that the theft was not going unnoticed: the dog was circling, defiant, cocky.

"Get outa here, ya mutt," Winnie said.

The animal pawed Winnie's trouser cuff, then fastened its teeth into the cloth. Winnie gave it a bash with the ax handle, smack on the muzzle. The animal backed off.

"You be careful," Winnie warned.

The dog began yelping. Winnie gave it a last caution, palm flattened. When it started to howl, there was no choice: Winnie raised the ax.

"You're asking for it, ya mongrel." Winnie swung downward.

The forelegs bucked first, then the hindlegs. The carcass rolled to the side, jerking, but after three quick spasms the convulsions subsided. A foot away, from a rain puddle, the head watched silently.

Winnie shouldered the ax, ran into the trees, and arrived drenched at the car on the other side of the woods. The drive home took eighteen minutes. It was cheaper and simpler than buying an ax in a hardware store. Those salesmen always asked questions, and they always remembered.

The black suitcase was the only one large enough. Winnie strapped the ax to the bottom and piled clothes on top. The bag, fully packed, was almost too heavy to lift, but Winnie managed. The airline people seemed to think it odd that anyone would want to keep such a large case under the seat, but Winnie told them that it contained valuables.

Winnie called from a telephone booth in the terminal. A woman with a Spanish accent answered and said that the doctor was at work.

"Could you give me the number?" Winnie asked.

"I don't know the number," she said unhelpfully. "It's in the phone book. Manhattan University."

Winnie dropped another dime into the phone and asked the woman at information for the number. Two minutes later a secretary came on the line.

"Dr. Langsam is at lunch," she apologized, as though it were somehow her fault. "Can I take a message?"

"Yes, if you'd be so kind. This is Mr. MacAndrew, Winnie MacAndrew—a classmate."

"Yes, Mr. MacAndrew."

"Would you ask Dr. Langsam if he could meet me for a round of squash at six-thirty at the Eli Club?"

"I certainly will, Mr. MacAndrew. Can he reach you anywhere?"

"I'll be on the court waiting for him," Winnie said, quickly depressing the cradle. Ignoring the blandishments of porters, Winnie hoisted the bag, walked to the taxi rank, and hailed a cab.

Dr. Langsam took his time. The hush of a funeral had fallen on the building. The hall was deserted now, and as he passed closed doors, he could hear the muffled drones of section men and assistant professors explaining the examinations to their students. Dr. Langsam knew that only 50 percent taking the exams today were going to pass, for as chairman of the department it was his duty to set policy.

The long gray passageway, bordered with the rows of boxes in which the students' papers were returned to them, always reminded Dr. Langsam of the corridor leading to the

gas chamber in Dachau. Not that he had ever been to
Dachau, even as a tourist; he had only occasionally speculated about it.

He stopped at the box labeled *G* and pulled out an examination booklet marked *Thomas Glazer.* The red gashes of a
section man's pencil obliterated the greater part of four
essays. He could not remember which of the mob Glazer
was. The only music student of that name whom he had
ever known had committed suicide the semester before last.
The boy had had trouble identifying the isorhythmically
disguised *cantus firmus* in an anonymous thirteenth-century
motet and, unable to bear the thought of life without a
master's degree, had jumped from a fourth-story window of
the gymnasium. Naked. Dr. Langsam remembered the photograph of the body lying shattered on the sidewalk. Wondering why music majors had such scrawny physiques, he returned Thomas Glazer's doomed effort to the *G* box and, in
deference to the hour, quickened his steps. His heels echoed
crisply, like shots from a rifle.

The examination was being held in the small conference
room behind the library stacks, since only four candidates
had lasted out the semester of Musicology 203 (*Idiosyncra-
cies in the Notation and Transcription of Polyphonic Works
for the Lute: an Historical Approach. Knowledge of Tabla-
ture Presupposed. Monday, Wednesday, and Friday mornings
at 9 A.M.; additional meetings Saturday, 2 to 4 P.M., at discretion of instructor. Required of all doctoral candidates; rec-
ommended to candidates for master's degrees*). The janitor
had dismantled the conference table, stacked the dismem-
bered bits against the wall, and installed four rickety school
desks. The four candidates looked up uphappily as Dr. Langsam breezed into the room.

"Sorry to keep you waiting," he apologized cheerfully. He
handed the four copies of the exam—it was a dilly—to the
monitor, a lethally proportioned giant who looked more like
a prison guard than a university employee. "A word about

the test." Dr. Langsam struck a stance at the front of the room.

"Once the examination has begun, none of you will talk. Should you have any problems or questions, you will raise your hand, and this gentleman . . ." Dr. Langsam wondered where they found such apes. "This gentleman will take care of you. Part One—you have your choice of essays. Write on one subject only. Misspellings and poor punctuation will count against you."

Dr. Langsam's glance fell on a wiry-haired student; his skin was bright red, doubtless from an attempt to cure acne under a sun lamp. Dr. Langsam looked away from the reproach in those unhealthy eyes.

"Part Two—this gentleman will play you a record." Fleetingly, the doctor wondered if the man could run a phonograph. "He will play it three times. You are to discuss the music in the light of what you have learned this semester. Are there any questions?"

The girl student blew her nose. Her hands were not steady. Dr. Langsam doubted that her night of cramming and black coffee was going to do her much good. He could not abide female Ph.D.s. He walked to the door.

"And lastly, this country needs trained musicologists. Good luck to all of you." He gave a nod and slammed the door behind him.

As he ambled down the corridor, the departmental secretary called to him. He leaned into the office. "Yes, Miss Jones?"

The old woman's ringless fingers were playing with the margin release of her typewriter. "There was a call for you— a Mr. MacAndrew."

"I know no Mr. MacAndrew," Dr. Langsam stated.

"He asked if you would play squash with him today," she persisted.

"That's ridiculous. I haven't played squash for years." Surely the old bag had reached the age of forcible retirement.

She was seventy if she was a day, and he had suffered close to fifteen years of her senile, garbled message-taking. Now that he was chairman of the department—well, he might just bring the matter up at the next faculty meeting.

Miss Jones lowered her eyes, as though she had read his mind. "He did say squash, sir. Winnie MacAndrew. Says he's an old classmate."

"A classmate!" Dr. Langsam guffawed at the improbability of it. He had cut the umbilicus to his alma mater the day of graduation, a sparkling June fourth some twenty years ago; he had dropped his college roommate at the very first mention of fund raising; and he had abandoned his fellow graduates to their double martinis and commuter trains with nary a twinge of nostalgia. Aside from communications with the editors of the alumni report, he had nothing whatsoever to do with Eli University.

"I have no classmates," Dr. Langsam said firmly.

Miss Jones sniffled. "I'm only telling you what I heard him say."

"Perhaps if you'd stop hearing things and start paying attention to your typing you wouldn't make mistakes like this." Dr. Langsam thrust a copy of the Musicology 203 examination under her chin and jiggled it.

Miss Jones took frail hold of the page and squinted. "Where's the mistake? I don't see any."

Dr. Langsam had not seen any mistake either. "Maybe you'd better get your eyes checked, or hire a proofreader. Good day, Miss Jones."

"Air conditioning may be fine for people," Dr. Langsam said, "but it's murder on harpsichords."

"Is that so?" The other man in the elevator opened his evening paper and lifted it as a barrier between himself and the doctor.

"Quite so." Something—perhaps the resolution to fire Miss

Jones—made Langsam feel chatty. "You see, the finest harp-sichords are built of unseasoned Bavarian peach wood . . ."

"Uh huh," the other man agreed, though Dr. Langsam had not finished. The newspaper trembled as, somewhere on the other side of the headlines, a page turned.

The elevator stopped on the nineteenth floor, and a woman wheeled a baby carriage in and pushed the first-floor button. The doors whooshed shut, and the elevator kept going up.

"I pressed the down button," the woman said.

"The elevator will go down," Dr. Langsam assured her with a smile, "after it's finished going up."

The woman frowned at him as though he were trying to kidnap her, or as though she didn't think his little joke was funny, or perhaps as though she disapproved of bald pro-fessors wearing dark glasses and polka-dot bow ties. Security was worth a little inconvenience, Langsam thought of telling her. After all, he had lived in countries where a man risked his life stepping out of the bomb shelter to urinate. There was no denying that conditions had improved.

Dr. Langsam got out on the twenty-ninth floor. "Now you can go down," he told the woman. As the doors sliced off her frown, he saw the elevator begin to rise.

The professor tiptoed down the furry-carpeted, beige-lit corridor, past metal doors painted to simulate oak and alpha-betized A through Q. The inner walls of Madison Towers East (the building overlooked the west shoreline and drive of Manhattan, but probably had derived its name from its location east of New Jersey) were not much thicker than those of the honeycomb that he demolished daily with his morning coffee; and during heat waves, the concerted buzzing of air-conditioning units in every window on every floor was like the droning of a hive of insects.

Humming a snatch of the fourth Brandenburg, the profes-sor felt in his pocket through pennies and souvenir Empire State buildings and miraculous medals for the key, and nodded at a little girl hauling a Bergdorf Goodman bag of garbage toward the incinerator closet. Dr. Langsam unlocked his door and stepped into his bachelor flat.

Mrs. Garcia had cleared the breakfast dishes from the little mahogany table; she had straightened the music on the harpsichord and fluffed the pillows on the love seat; she had angled the blinds to keep the afternoon sun from fading the needlepoint screen (parakeets and chivalric knights woven into the flowing hair of Rhine maidens); she had removed the dead cactus and watered the other three; and she had set his leather slippers beside the leather armchair.

Dr. Langsam was momentarily as happy as a shoemaker waking up to find that a band of benevolent gremlins had done his week's work. Every Friday evening, staring across a vacuum-swept carpet over an unlittered harpsichord through polished glass doors at a candied-apple sun bobbing below the New Jersey skyline, he pondered the mystery of Mrs. Garcia's intervention into the litter of his affairs; and silently he blessed her.

He stooped over the hall table and picked up a handful of mail that on first glance seemed to consist only of circulars and bills. "Damned ads," he muttered. Even when he spoke to himself the professor retained a trace of an accent which his ear sadly recognized as un-American, despite the hours he had spent carrying on conversations with long-playing records.

He went into the kitchen and poured himself a martini from the gallon jug that Mrs. Garcia left in the refrigerator every Friday. Into the glass he popped a clever American invention: three plastic cubes containing frozen water. He licked his pinky dry and glanced about the kitchen to see what surprise his housekeeper had prepared for his supper. He could find nothing in the icebox and nothing in the oven. He was about to rummage through the shelves when a well-modulated telephone bell summoned him. He rushed into the bedroom.

The telephone, a petite pink model which the New York Telephone Company had dubbed "Princess," jiggled when it rang, and if he did not catch it before the fourth ring, it jiggled off the bedside table onto the floor.

He grabbed the Princess on the third ring and dropped into the terry-cloth chair. Lansbury, the cat, screeched; the professor raised a haunch, and the animal wriggled out from under him and dragged itself limping into the living-dinette room.

"Hello, Langsam here," the professor panted.

"Have you been running upstairs?" the Princess demanded in the Bronxish tones of his sister. Frieda had been endowed with a better ear than her brother and had mastered the local dialect within six months of their arrival.

The professor caught his breath. "Just running from the kitchen."

"Don't run," his sister cautioned. "Running you could drop dead."

"Walking I could drop dead!" the professor cried. "Sleeping I could drop dead!"

"Shouting you *will* drop dead," Frieda stated.

"What are you calling for? I'm busy. I have to find my dinner—Mrs. Garcia hid it."

"Probably on top of the bathroom cabinet where that cat can't get at it. What I'm calling for, have you gotten any funny mail today?"

"Bills, bills, bills. And some ads."

"Have you read the ads?"

"What would I read the ads for?" Lansbury peeked in the doorway, then waddled toward the professor. He raised a foot and threatened her away. He sifted through the stack of letters and idly opened a thick envelope "Holy moley," he discovered, "a class report!"

"Does the name Gretchen mean anything to you?" Frieda asked. "I got a steamship ad from a travel company, signed Gretchen Blomquist. Seven weeks ago an airplane ad from a Gretch Smith. Today the employment bureau wanted to send me a G. Johnson for a housemaid. I want you to look through your ads. If there is any Gretchen, you tell me."

But Dr. Langsam was thumbing through the fat red book. "I'm in here! *Langsam, Bertram Amadeus, musicologist.* What do you know, they got my note about the promotion! It says right here, *head of the musicological department of . . ."*

"I asked for your ads."

"Frieda, I am chairman of the department, I don't have time to read ads. I get thirty ads a day. I have exams to correct, theses to read, seminars to organize—I am not superman, I cannot go through ads."

The Princess grunted as if it had expected as little cooperation. "Put your ads in a brown paper bag and leave them with the doorman."

"Always this paranoia! Why do you need to search my ads? I get no dirty pictures, believe me!"

"I am looking for Gretchen."

In the other room, Lansbury jumped onto the harpsichord; the strings rumbled eerily.

"Frieda, my love, twenty-two years we have been living in the land of the free, for twenty-two years you have been finding codes in the telephone book and spies in the morning mail, I will not be bothered with them! You do not understand, I must work thirty-two hours a day, I am chairman of the Musicology Department! Even my college classmates know I am chairman, but you—you know nothing. I must hang up—the cat is walking on the harpsichord."

He found Lansbury whining on the bathroom sink, trying to climb to a bowl of tortillas and chili with guacamole that was balanced on the top of the medicine cabinet. She leaped to the simulated tile floor; he stood on the toilet, hoisted the bowl down, and glimpsed his painfully red face in the mirror.

"You must get more exercise, Doc!" he told himself. "It will never do to have a heart attack now that you are chairman! Stay in trim!"

The professor turned on the television picture without sound, sat in his leather chair, stared at a Doris Day movie, and ate Mrs. Garcia's cold tortillas and chili. He put the guacamole on the floor for Lansbury. After dinner he rinsed his hands, wiped the green off Lansbury's whiskers, and sat at his harpischord. Lansbury mewled at the sour octaves and went onto the terrace.

Dr. Langsam lifted the harpsichord lid and began tightening the culprit strings with a tuning wrench. He had reached contrabass *f* when the phone rang again. He dropped the wrench and ran.

"Hello, Langsam here."

"Bertie, Bertie Langsam," the phone bellowed, "is that you?"

Bertie, the professor pondered. No one had called him that since his college days. "Yes," he said cautiously, "this is Bertie." It began to fit together: the class report, the mention of his promotion, the phone call. They were raising funds for alma mater. He poised a finger over the cradle.

"Well, howdy do, howsa going, what's cooking? Betcha can't guess who this is, haven't seen you in a coon's age!"

"No," the professor confessed, "I can't guess who this is. Someone I know from college, maybe?"

"Betcha g.d. soul, it's your old chum Winnie!"

"Winnie," the professor repeated.

"Winnie MacAndrew, you old Hebe! What's cooking?"

"Cooking?" the professor pondered.

"Now you're cooking with gas! Why haven't you got your ass down here?"

"Down there?"

"The Eli Club, baby, you're late. They're holding the court for us."

"Court?"

"Squash court, Bertie, squash—bim bim, bam bam, the little black ball and the little white racquet—whassa matta, you forget we had a date?"

"I didn't forget, I never knew."

"Well g.d. it all, that little chick up at your office said you were going to be here at six sharp, you didn't get the message?"

"There's been some confusion," the professor fumbled. "You see, I was promoted—I'm now chairman of the department."

"That's A. double O.K., Bertie."

"There are so many messages now. She must have overlooked . . ."

"Doesn't make a bit of difference, Bertie, not a bit. I'll grab a bite and a drink. Why don't you grab a cab and get down here in half an hour? I'll be on the court."

Dr. Langsam was about to explain that the harpsichord needed tuning; but exercise *was* exercise, and there was a squash racquet gathering dust in his closet.

"I'll be there," he said, but Winnie MacAndrew had hung up.

There were no proper sports clothes in the apartment, so the professor changed into plaid Bermudas and a striped T-shirt. He stood on the bathroom hamper and pried the squash racquet from the top shelf of the closet, unleashing a cascade of fifteen-year-old squash balls so tired that they did not even roll, but simply thudded to the floor.

Dr. Langsam took a swing at himself in the bathroom mirror. His form was not bad, considering. He wondered what sort of form Winnie MacAndrew was in, whoever he was. A classmate, he decided, an old drinking pal: *gaudeamus igitur!*

"Lansbury?" Dr. Langsam checked. "Where have you gone?"

The professor tiptoed to the terrace doors and peeped through. Silhouetted against the New Jersey skyline, Lansbury squatted on the railing and stared with glowing eyes across the street. A barge hooted on the river below.

"You got a sailor cat friend?" Langsam joked. He lifted the cat into the apartment and slid the terrace doors shut.

He glimpsed a pudgy, bald collegiate phantom in the glass, hovering above New Jersey, and after an instant's amazement recognized himself. He decided to wear a raincoat over his Bermudas and T-shirt.

Seven minutes later the doorman was tucking the professor into a Checker cab. "Have a nice trip, Doc," he said and grinned, closing the door and sealing Langsam in.

Trip? Langsam wondered. *Why does he say "trip"?* Watts was one of that new generation of colored people, and perhaps he enjoyed putting "Whitey" on. Langsam was never quite certain that he understood minority senses of humor.

"You came in to sit, or you going somewheres?" The cab driver, whose face was eerily reminiscent of a split melon, flashed a snarl over his shoulder. An old man, bitter, like so many New York cabbies.

"The Eli Club, Park Avenue and . . ."

Before Langsam could finish giving the address, the cab lurched forward, throwing him back against the seat. The high-rise buildings tumbled by, ablaze with lights and television sets, and the cab wheeled south onto Broadway. There was a jam of taxis and black Cadillacs at the Lincoln Center for the Performing Arts, and constellations of jeweled dowagers sparkled on the sidewalk.

The driver pulled the cab to a halt, grumbling, and Langsam peered at the license and photo pasted on the dashboard. Mordecai Blatt was the troubled man's name.

"*Vie fiel an zeiga?*" Langsam asked pleasantly, leaning forward to offer a packet of mentholated cigarettes.

"Seven thirty-five," the driver snapped, ignoring the offer and the Yiddish.

Langsam settled back into the seat and lit himself a mint-flavored smoke. A ten-cent tip, he decided exhaling.

Mordecai Blatt must have read the professor's mind in the rear-view mirror, for he pulled to a stop almost a block away from the Eli Club, on the wrong side of the street, and flicked off the meter. "Can't go any closer," he said. "It's a one-way street."

What does he mean, a one-way street? the professor asked himself. *He can't let me off at the door, like any other passenger? The street suddenly changes direction?*

"How come?" Langsam challenged. "How come that *garbage truck* can go further and we can't?

"Look, Mac, I gotta go home. This is my turn-off."

Langsam handed the man a dollar bill—a nickel tip—and stomped out of the cab. A passing motorcycle almost clipped the squash racquet from his hand. Langsam took his bearings on the town house across the avenue, squatting like a bloated toad among the glass skyscrapers, and plunged through the traffic.

The doorman was no help either. "MacAndrew?" he queried, a nasty red-faced leprechaun.

"Winnie MacAndrew. He's expecting me for a game of squash." Langsam produced the racquet as though it were a safe-conduct.

"You're a member?" the doorman asked dubiously.

"I am an Eli graduate," Langsam stated, "and Winnie Mac-Andrew is a classmate of mine and a member of this club. I am his guest. He is holding the court, and I am late, and if you don't mind . . ."

"Can't let you in like that." The doorman shook his head. "No pants."

Langsam flung open his raincoat. He gave his Bermudas an instant to baffle the old bureaucrat, then strode into the vestibule of the Eli Club. It was tall, cool, dark, and empty as a cathedral. No need for air conditioning, Langsam reflected enviously. Imagine how a harpsichord would sound in here!

As he waited for the elevator, a sound caught his attention. He squinted his ears. Someone was singing. Light music, something post-Schubert. The professor drifted closer to the sound. Now, as a door was flung aside and a tipsy debutante wobbled into the vestibule, the melody burst into the open: a

tenor and a baritone, in vibrant Pythagorean harmony, pro-
jected the refrain across the hushed clubhouse:

I'm on the look-out for love,
I want the love I've never known.

"Love," the professor whispered, smiling; the oldest song
in the world. Holding the door open with his sneaker, he
peered into the darkened auditorium.

Sometimes I wonder
Whether I'm under
A spell that has held me forever alone . . .

A gulf of heads, faceless in the dark, separated Langsam
from the floodlit stage where a young man in evening clothes
and a young man in an evening gown crooned to each other.
The song reached its gentle cadence; the youth in the gown
stretched out an arm to his companion, and they turned and
bowed to the warm applause. Amateurs. A chorus of boys in
can-can skirts filtered onto the stage, and the two pianos in
the pit struck up a catchy bit of ersatz Offenbach.

"Squash courts, sir?"

The elevator man was staring at Langsam's racquet. The
professor nodded and entered the elevator. The bronze grill
of a door clanged into place, and they were airborne.

"Tell me," Langsam asked. "That operetta—is it a Rice
Pudding show?"

The elevator man nodded.

"I was in one of those once," Langsam remembered. "I
played a boy."

The elevator man glanced at him. "Is that so."

"Years ago. Twenty years ago. Tell me, what's this year's
show called?"

"*On the Rocks.*"

"Is it good?"

The man shrugged. "No worse than any of the others."

"You've seen them all?"

"Every damned one—for thirty years."

"Oh—then you saw mine. I wrote the music. It was called *In the Bag.*"

"Can't say I remember." The door lumbered open. "Fifth floor. Squash courts."

"Well, it was twenty years ago," Langsam smiled. He stepped out of the elevator and into his past. For a moment he almost believed himself back at the old Audubon Street squash courts of his undergraduate days. The same mammoth, vaulted ceiling two and a half stories above his head; the same intersecting claps of racquets and squash balls and feet, invisible behind the court partitions; the same pungent, unmistakable odor of black rubber and honest sweat. Langsam's heart beat faster, and he was two decades younger. He shifted his weight lithely and poised his racquet, still encased, against an imaginary serve.

"Help you, sir?" The court keeper, an ancient fellow, came toward Langsam, a huge ledger clutched under his arm. Langsam explained that he had a date with Mr. MacAndrew. The man ran a trembling index finger down a column of beautifully penned names. Langsam noted with surprise that he wore an Eli class ring. "MacAndrew, Winston?"

"That's right," Langsam said. He shifted weight again and leaned into the ball. *Swoosh!*

"And you are . . ."

"Dr. Langsam, Bertie Langsam."

"Oh yes," the man's voice creaked, "we've got you down here. Would you care to leave your mackintosh? Mr. MacAndrew is on court six."

Langsam left his raincoat with the keeper and sprinted down the corridor. Court six was the last door on the right. He leaned an ear against the wood and listened, hoping to catch his opponent's practice volley and gauge his ability. But the court was silent, and such thuds and thumps as Langsam could make out were echoes from other parts of the building. Glancing up at the ceiling, he saw that the court was illuminated—hence, occupied. He raised a hand to the door and knocked.

The door was opened by a blond man whom Langsam had an odd feeling he knew.

"Well well, so you finally made it, how's it going, Bertie?" Beaming an incredibly white smile, the man crushed Langsam's hand. "Haven't seen you in a coon's age!"

"No," Langsam said, "that's true." Langsam dropped the racquet case to the floor and took a practice swing at the void.

The man watched Langsam, smiling. For hair so blond and eyes so blue, Langsam would have expected a taller person. His opponent was below average height; in his bulky sweat clothes he looked strong, stronger than Langsam certainly. He surprised the professor by pitching a squash ball at him from out of nowhere, like a magician.

"Go ahead," the man invited, "practice a little."

Langsam leapt into the ball and swung; the ball continued on its way. "I haven't been on a squash court," he explained, "in twenty years."

Beneath the sweat clothes the man had the bones of an ex-football player, the expanding flesh of an athlete who had spent a decade too many without working out. Langsam could imagine him drinking gimlets with clients, advising old ladies on investments, shuffling papers in some Wall Street office, still being called "kid"—and answering.

"Me neither." The man grinned. "Not since we graduated."

"We were classmates?" Langsam asked.

"Housemates." The man pitched another ball. Where did he get them from? "You remember me, don't you?"

The question distracted Langsam, and he missed again. "I know I know you, but . . . well, there were lots of undergraduates at Eli."

"Too g.d. many." The man smiled.

A ball that Langsam had not even seen struck him in the chest. He smashed after it with his racquet, stupidly and vengefully. On the other side of the partition invisible players struck up a volley with all the clamor of a pneumatic street drill. "Practice serve?" Langsam shouted.

Though he was smiling, the man could not have heard, for a squash ball struck the professor in the ankle. Langsam swung but merely hit his own foot.

"Practice?" Langsam screamed.

With a gesture, the man offered Langsam the court. Langsam threw a ball into the air, lost sight of it, but by some freak of coordination managed to hook it on the tip of his racquet and lob it onto the front wall. The man kicked the ball back to Langsam.

"Have another go," he cried.

Langsam managed a halfway decent serve, not bad after twenty years of no practice. The man ignored it. Langsam's heart began to thud. "You did ask me here to play squash, didn't you?"

"Yes." The man's smile was catlike, as though he knew something that Langsam didn't, as though the professor's fly were unzipped. Langsam glanced down at his Bermudas.

"Ready?" the man undid his racquet case. The handle struck Langsam as oddly thick.

"You do have a regulation racquet, I take it?" Langsam challenged.

The man nodded, but Langsam was not at all reassured.

"I'd like to see it," Langsam insisted.

"You'll see it." The man loosened the four screws of the case and dropped the trapezoidal wood frame to the floor. Less and less did the racquet look conventional; in its velvet hood, it had an almost wedgelike shape.

Langsam stretched out his hand. "May I have the racquet, please?"

"Most certainly." The man then did something oddly unsportsmanlike: he swung the racquet, smashing Langsam's hand against the wall.

"Stop that!" Langsam cried. A patch of red was dribbling

down the side of the court as though someone had hurled a ripe tomato. Langsam saw that his thumb was gone. He cried "Help!" and the neighbors started up their volley again.

Langsam ran, his hand so paining him that he could scarcely fumble with the lock. He yanked the door open, but the man kicked it shut.

The racquet, unveiled, had a massive steel head. The blade was polished brighter than a mirror, and as it flew toward him, Langsam clearly saw his own two eyes blink. Then, lighter than air, he bounced across the court. Or rather, he realized with fading comprehension, part of him had bounced. Some eight feet away he saw the rest of him, encased in a T-shirt and Bermuda shorts, stumbling against the wall, hands groping blindly for some kind of support. The ax swung again, cleaving him in two, then in four. He seemed to be in twenty places at once.

It was an odd feeling while it lasted.

Saturday, June 17

SHOES ASHINE, hair combed, not a spot on his Harris-tweed vest showing, Greg Archibald flashed a lame smile at the doorman and stumbled into the lobby of the Eli Club. The room—like so many rooms after so many parties Greg had been to lately—was moving in a counterclockwise direction around him. He steadied himself, gripping the back of the nearest leather chair. A wall slammed into him.

" 'Scuse me," a burly Italian-looking laborer said not very apologetically, and the wall moved on. It was a painted flat —the sort of fake Versailles interior that college boys throw together as a backdrop to those annual musicals where the only joke is a team of football bruisers in Marie Antoinette wigs. The wall wobbled precariously through the Eli Club doorway and disappeared into a waiting van.

" 'Scuse me," a colored laborer demanded. He was carrying an armload of silk shirts and blouses with breasts sewn into them. Greg stepped aside an inch and wondered why the workmen didn't use the service door.

"Excuse me. My ear."

Though it made him dizzy, Greg glanced down in the direction of the voice. His hands were still tan from the Nassau sun, though two knuckles were alarmingly white reminders of rings that he absolutely had to get out of hock. Midway between the hands was a head, bald, half turned to glare up at him. Beyond the head was a newspaper, and on the newspaper a banner headline that seemed to say MAN IN THE MOON.

Greg squinted his one contact lens into place—he had lost the other last night—and the headline corrected itself into a man *on* the moon. They could put a man on the moon, Greg brooded, but they couldn't get the hangover out of Scotch.

"You're pinching my ear," the man said.

"Sorry." Greg moved his hand, then released the chair and made a manful attempt to stand on his own two feet. He calculated his route to the elevator. The sofa was ten feet away; he could lean on it a moment, then walk six feet to the table, where he could catch his breath and pretend to look at the *London Illustrated News;* from there it was scarcely three giant steps to the elevator.

At the sofa a man stared at him, and in self-defense Greg pretended to look at his watch. Rolling back his cuff, he discovered that the watch had gone the way of his rings; he fumbled in his pocket, searching for some substitute purpose. All his fingers could produce was the crumpled yellow telegram that had roused him from bed a hideous half hour ago: URGENT MATTER COME TO MY OFFICE EARLIEST CONVENIENCE SIGNED PLIMPTON DANIEL DIRECTOR OF ADMISSIONS ELI CLUB.

Greg's knees went weak for the tenth time. He banished the telegram to the brass spittoon by the elevator.

The office of the director of admissions, a sign on the third floor stated, was number 312. Taking a chance, Greg turned right and followed the corridor up to door number 311. There it stopped. He retraced his steps, managed to locate the elevators again, and started in the opposite direction. A small arrow that he did not think had been there before indicated that he should have gone left to begin with.

Mr. Daniel's receptionist, a young woman in a gray wool sack, was prying a Coca-Cola from a machine by the window. She looked at Greg over her upraised bottle.

"Good morning," Greg forced himself to smile.

She took the bottle from her mouth with a smack. "Morning."

"Mr. Daniel's expecting me."

The woman pressed a buzzer on her desk, and an inner door swung open. A heavy-set man strode into the room. He was wearing a three-piece tweed suit, new-looking and clean, and his handshake had not a hint of a tremor in it.

"Mr. Archibald?" he beamed. The smile was a good sign.

"Greg," Greg said.

"Plimpton Daniel," Mr. Daniel said. "Call me Plimp." With a spacious gesture, he invited Greg into the inner office. "No phone calls, Miss Bernkrandt."

Mr. Daniel drew a comfortable chair up to the desk, indicated that Greg was to have a seat in it, and offered brandy and cigars. The brandy and cigars were a good sign, and Greg decided that he could not have been summoned to discuss the question of dues.

"You're a year behind on your dues," Mr. Daniel said. He waved an Eli-crested lighter under Greg's cigar.

Greg froze his smile into place.

"Which has nothing to do with why I asked you here this morning. Greg—may I call you Greg?—you work in public relations, don't you?"

Greg resisted the impulse to gulp his brandy and merely sipped. "Yes, I work in public relations." The present tense was not too great an exaggeration; it was only seven weeks ago that he had been fired.

"And since it was only seven weeks ago that you were fired, I assume you are—free-lancing at the moment?"

Greg allowed himself a gulp of brandy. "Yes—free-lancing."

Mr. Daniel paced a complete circle around his desk. "We don't want to go to one of the big outfits—too many hands, too many tongues. In situations like this, it's sometimes best to turn to the independents. Like yourself."

Greg nodded. "Yes, sometimes it's best."

"We would count totally on your discretion."

"It goes without saying."

"We couldn't give you much in the way of expenses—or fee for that matter."

Greg waved a hand emptily. "Fee, faw," he smiled. He wondered if Daniel would offer another brandy.

"Another?" Mr. Daniel carried the bottle to Greg's glass and filled it to within a drop of overflowing. "House brand," he explained. "We get it from Mexico."

"Excellent stuff," Greg smiled.

Mr. Daniel lowered himself slowly into his chair. He stared a full minute at the class photographs covering the walls of the office. When his eyes met Greg's, they seemed embarrassed.

"We would be willing . . . to overlook your indebtedness to the Eli Club. In a word, to expunge your unpaid dues."

Greg had the impression that his hangover was going to lift.

"As for the services we would ask in return . . ."

"No problem," Greg assured him. "I'm at your disposal."

"Good. I don't suppose you heard about the incident last night—on the squash courts?"

"Someone was caught cheating?"

"Worse. Someone was beheaded."

"Ah," Greg said as neutrally as possible.

"Thank God for that man on the moon, at least we're not on page one." Mr. Daniel pressed his fingertips together. "I don't suppose you ever heard of Bertie Langsam?"

Greg shook his head. "Can't say I have."

"He was about ten years before your time. Came over from Germany just after the war—refugee. Got a scholarship to Eli, graduated with honors, went on to become one of the country's leading musicologists." Mr. Daniel looked up. "Were you by any chance a member of the Rice Pudding Club?"

The Rice Pudding Club, as Greg remembered it, was little more than a glorified mess hall; the meals were a bit better than in the dorm kitchens, and not too much more expensive. "Wasn't everybody a member?"

"Not everybody, Greg. In his senior year, Bertie Langsam wrote the music for the Pudding show. As a gesture of gratitude, the club elected him a member. He was Rice Pudding's first Jew."

For some reason, the First Jew reminded Greg of the Last Mohican; the Last Mohican reminded him of the Last Supper and the fact that he had not eaten since two nights before. In the street, a drill started; Daniel raised his voice.

"There was opposition. A lot of the old guard were distressed—there were even threats. But the show was one of the biggest smashes in Rice Pudding's history. It was called *In the Bag*. Maybe you remember some of the songs. They were popular for about ten years."

"Can't say I remember."

Mr. Daniel took a deep breath, as though the most painful part of the business were approaching. "As you know, the Pudding takes its show on tour around the country. Two nights a year, every winter, they play here at the Eli Club. Last February they were such a success that—well, frankly, we haven't seen anything like it since *In the Bag*. They were such a success that the alumni invited them back for a week's engagement in the summer. Sell-out. And yesterday, some time during the show, Bertie Langsam was decapitated upstairs on the squash court."

Greg helped himself to another brandy.

"We don't know who did it, or why. The court was reserved in the name of a graduate, class of 1892—but he's in a rest home, and frankly, we don't see how he could have done it."

"You're not asking me to find out who the killer is," Greg said. "I'm a lousy detective. It took me half an hour to find your office."

"All we're asking from you is a little bit of pub rel." Mr. Daniel poured himself half a brandy and took it in a swallow. His pale gray eyes fixed on Greg's. "You see, Greg, there's an outside chance that this was a grudge killing."

"I should think so. Somebody hated Langsam."

"Not Langsam, Greg: *us*. We're afraid someone wants to embarrass the Pudding—or the Eli Club—or possibly Eli University."

"Sort of a roundabout way to do it."

Mr. Daniel rose, slower this time, and paced another ring around the desk. "Sometimes it's easier to kill a scapegoat than an institution. Sometimes one stone can hit a lot of birds." Daniel leaned down toward Greg. "Don't you see what it could mean—Pudding's first Jew is Eli's first homicide."

"Doesn't need to mean anything."

"But we have to be certain. And that's where we need you. There's a police detective working on the murder. We want you to keep track of him, keep tabs on everything he uncovers. We've got to have warning if it looks like anything ugly is turning up."

Greg tried to purse his lips intelligently; it looked pretty ugly to him already. He wondered if the killer had played a game of squash with the head.

"At the first soupçon, the first whiff of anti-Semitism— you've got to alert us."

Greg uncrossed his legs and nodded. "You mentioned expenses."

"Fifteen dollars a day. I'm sorry, our emergency fund allows us nowhere near what we'd like to pay."

"And a year's credit at the club bar."

"All right." Daniel held out his hand. "I'll accept those terms."

Greg shook Plimpton Daniel's hand. Fifteen dollars a day, he calculated, was well over fifteen times what he was earning at the moment.

"Now if you'll come upstairs to the courts . . ." Daniel indicated the doorway with his hand. "I'll point out the detective to you."

"I believe," the witness stated, "that the word was *help*."

In his thirty-five years of reading mysteries and his twenty years on the force, Inspector Stanley Breeze had never met a man whose vowels wrenched his jaw so far sideways. It hurt just to listen to him.

"You heard someone scream *help*?" Breeze persevered.

"Not exactly a scream, just a call for help—but I didn't think anything of it, I mean *help* is the sort of thing you say instead of *oh shit* if you drop your squash balls or miss a serve or do anything dumb like that. Sort of an in-joke around the club."

"And then?"

"This—*thump* on the wall. But I mean you hear thumps all the time on a squash court, someone's always thumping something, especially on the walls. Then the thumping started on the floor. More like thwacking, come to think of it. Odd, I thought, so I finished the volley and peeked into the hallway."

"And you saw . . ."

"Nothing really, just a fellow coming off the court next door."

"Could you describe him?"

"Well, he was average height, lightish hair, clean-cut chap —wearing sweat clothes. They were freshly laundered. Rather a dapper-looking fellow, I'd say."

"Had you ever seen the man before?"

"Can't say. He was the type of fellow you'd think you knew if you saw him anywhere. I mean, he just looked like an Eli man. A little heavy-set, but an Eli man. You'd say hello to him."

"And did you say hello?"

"Oh yes. I said, 'Hello, anything wrong?'"

"Did he answer? Did you notice anything about the voice?"

"An ordinary voice—like anyone's. He said 'Cheerio.'"

"Is that a usual sort of greeting?"

"It could be."

"Was he carrying a racquet?"

"He was carrying something—it could have been a racquet."

Their answers all came down to the same thing: *maybe, possibly, I couldn't say for sure.* Breeze wondered if they were closing ranks to protect one of their own; he felt tired, and he wished he weren't involved. He thought of his month's annual vacation; he reminded himself that in twenty-five years he would be able to retire on half-salary and devote himself to any hobbies he had by then acquired. He thought of his sister and two nephews, his only relatives in the world, and his pen pal in Iceland with whom he exchanged monthly letters and whom he would never meet. He remembered a goldfish that had died when his work took him away for two weeks.

"Did any of you see the man?" Breeze asked. His eye traveled the circle of witnesses. Except that they stared down from different heights, their faces were identical in their bland lack of expression They even dressed the same— around each neck the same green tie with the gold pattern of ivy-covered squash racquets; on each hand the same class ring. And on each face the same mute disdain.

Breeze could understand their attitude; he was used to it. If he had been a tall man, he might have considered himself passable in appearance, and others might have agreed. But on a man whom any boy and many women towered over, the deep-set eyes and eagle's nose and immense forehead were almost deformities. Breeze had not grown an inch since early adolescence, and even then he had been shorter than his playmates. At eighteen he had despaired of any sort of physical stature; at thirty he had given up despair and merely loathed his reflection in mirrors.

"No—didn't know him," the murmur went around.

"But you . . ." Breeze turned to the doorman. "You let him into the club. Why?"

"He looked right. We can't check everybody on a Friday night. Especially when there's a show."

Breeze turned next to the court keeper, a pale old man who looked as though he were barely staving off leukemia. "And you gave him a court?"

"He looked like the sort that comes here every Friday to play squash. Sure I gave him a court."

"Did you see him after his game?"

"Yes, he thanked me for the court and he tipped me five dollars. We chatted a little. Don't remember what about."

"Was he carrying a weapon?"

"Looked like a squash racquet to me. But it was in a case, I couldn't see."

"He wasn't nervous or in a rush?"

The keeper shook his old head. "Nope."

"Did you see whether he took the elevator or the stairs?"

"Nope. Mr. Evarts here . . . " The keeper inclined his head respectfully toward the gentleman on his right. "Mr. Evarts asked me if there was a spare court, so we went down the row knocking on doors. That was when we found what's-his-name, the body. By then MacAndrew was gone."

Breeze appealed to the group. "Did any of you see or hear this MacAndrew actually play squash or even hit a ball? Do we know for sure that he plays the game?"

The murmur went around the circle, "Everyone plays squash." But no one claimed to know for sure.

Breeze wanted to scream. If he was to believe these people, an eighty or ninety-year-old alumnus, at present ensconced in an oxygen tent in a rest home, had donned sweat clothes and popped into the clubhouse last night to ax the head off a complete stranger, a middle-aged musicologist whom nobody knew and who had no business being in the club in the first place. Simultaneously an assortment of undergraduates in the dining room had been staging a standing-room-only reprise of the college's annual drag show, an event that for some reason was considered both musical and funny. At the precise instant of decapitation, ten unmusical alumni had been batting squashballs on the neighboring courts and had apparently no more than paused in their volleys at the sound of the victim's shouts and the fall of the ax. The murderer had wrapped up his gear, chatted with the court keeper, and meandered into some other part of the building. No one could remember his leaving the clubhouse, and the closest thing to a weapon anyone had seen was the murderer's squash racquet.

At the sound of a door swinging open, Breeze turned toward court six. A blond head and big shoulders bobbed into view. Bernard Kluski smiled right and left at the collected witnesses and hurried with the longest strides he could manage. He was barrel-chested and looked like a toy soldier in his uniform, but he was close enough to Breeze's height for Breeze to trust him and, occasionally, to like him.

"Find anything else?" Breeze asked.

Kluski unfolded a handkerchief. "A thumb," he stated. Breeze looked and saw that it was indeed a thumb. The witnesses craned forward in unison curiosity; there was a sound like group retching, the first honest reaction Breeze had caught them in all morning.

"Come have a look," Kluski invited. His eyes glittered blue and his teeth gold. He held the door, and Breeze followed him onto the court. Six men in business suits were spraying white dust onto every square inch of wall, searching for fingerprints. The chalky air echoed with their coughs. Kluski crouched and pointed at a seven-inch slash in the floor. "See that?"

Breeze suppressed a cough and nodded.

"And that?" Kluski rose, pulled Breeze through a dust cloud, and nodded toward an eight-inch scratch on the wall. "Same stroke."

"How do you figure that?" Breeze asked.

"Geometry. The axhead penetrated the floor. The hole defines a plane." Kluski opened his billfold and set it edgewise into the hole in the floor; it tilted slightly, like a miniature sail in a breeze. Kluski gestured from the billfold up to the wall. "The plane intersects the wall there—at the scratch. Conclusion—one stroke."

"So what?" Breeze said.

"The ax was the length of a squash racquet, right? Now to swing an ax the length of a squash racquet, and to hit the wall there and the floor there in one fell swoop—you have to be between five foot five and five foot eleven."

"That doesn't exactly narrow it down," Breeze observed.

"It rules out one suspect. Winston MacAndrew, class of '92—the one in the rest home. He's six foot four."

"Call him a suspect?" Breeze said. "He's been in and out of an oxygen tent for the last three months."

"So?" Kluski shrugged. "At least we know it was someone else."

Three hours, Breeze counted; three hours they had been on the court hunting for clues. He glanced hopefully at the team of print men. "What about the fingerprints?"

"About three hundred different sets," Kluski said brightly. "A lot of people play squash."

"You're not going to photograph them all."

"Why not? It won't take more than a day."

"Do me a favor," Breeze said. "Just get the prints from the doorknobs and leave it at that, okay?"

Kluski frowned; his eyes met Breeze's. "All right," he relented. He snapped his fingers at the print men. "Okay, boys, take five." The men laid down their spray guns and filed coughing off the court.

"Where did you find the thumb?" Breeze asked.

"Under the ventilator. You don't happen to know if the Jews are like the Greek Orthodox, do you?"

"I don't happen to, no. Why?"

"If you're Greek Orthodox, all of you has to be buried in the same place. I was thinking, maybe we should get this thumb up to the synagogue before they start the funeral."

"The funeral's Monday," Breeze said. "No rush."

The court door swung open and a fat ball of tweed leaned in. "I say, gentlemen, any idea how much longer you'll be needing the courts?"

Again, Breeze wanted to scream: the fat man's hand was on the doorknob. "What's your name?" Breeze demanded.

The man jerked backward, as though Breeze were a rabid little terrier. "Plimpton Daniel, director of . . ."

"Kluski, fingerprint him," Breeze ordered. "He probably just ruined the only clue we had."

Plimpton Daniel lifted his hand from the doorknob and stared at his fingers. "I apologize if I've . . ."

"It's all right." Breeze pushed him off the court. "Keep this floor clear, will you?" he shouted to the guards at the end of the corridor. "Witnesses only." He singled out a new, unauthorized face in the crowd. "What are you doing here?"

"Just looking," the stranger beamed. Breeze sized him up in a glance: fairish hair, five foot ten, mustard stains on his vest, early thirties, dead drunk.

"Why don't you just look somewhere else?" Breeze suggested.

Breeze's sleeping habits had about as much routine as the cases he worked on. Only in the long view was there any pattern to them. One night in three he didn't go to bed at all, but slept an hour or so at his desk at the station or in the front seat of his car, in the booth of an all-night diner or in the coach of an early morning train. Other nights there were narrow beds in cheap hotels, when his work took him out of town, or the sofa in his two-room flat that was supposed to turn into a bed and that had sheets some weeks and other weeks didn't.

When he was in hotels, Breeze never slept: he spent the night sipping ice water and staring at the ceiling, battling off old memories and trying to keep his mind on present problems. He had come up with some of his best solutions in hotels. When he was home, he generally opened the sofa at ten. Sometimes he fell asleep within an hour. Tonight it took forty minutes, and then the phone awakened him.

It was Kennedy, his boss. The voice always reminded him of a bullfrog. "Breeze," it croaked, "have you solved it?"

"Solved what, sir?" Breeze glanced at the unfinished crossword puzzle on the floor by the bed.

"The murder, what else. You don't think that old fellow did it, that Winston MacAndrew in the oxygen tent, do you?"

"No sir, I don't."

"Why not?"

"He's over ninety, for one thing. But I'm going to check it out, just to be on the safe side."

"Guess you'll have to come up with something better then."

There was a click, and the phone went dead. Kennedy was like that. In twenty years Breeze had come up with no explanation of the man. Some of the fellows in the department said he was related to the mayor, some said to the Machine, some said to the Mafia. Breeze preferred to think of him as a voice on the telephone, a bad dream. Some day, Breeze decided, he would change his phone number and forget to tell the boss.

Sunday, June 18

GWENNIE HAD NOT actually left the house when the phone rang, but since she feared a call from Mr. Charrington of Charrington and Graves, counselors at law, and since she was about to mail them a letter of instructions with regard to her husband's possibly imminent death, she told Emelina to say that she had gone to the mailbox; it had taken her almost the entire morning to put the letter together, and she had no wish to see her labor made superfluous.

Emelina caught her on the flagstone terrace. "That was that nice Mr. Jackson, ma'am, at the rest home."

Gwennie stroked her nose with the corner of the envelope. "If Winnie's dying, he's dying. If he's not, he's not. What more can they want with me? What did Mr. Jackson say?"

"He wants you to call back right away."

Gwennie deliberated. "Very well, I shall . . . in a while."

She turned her back on the servant and crossed the lawn. She noted that the tennis court needed fresh chalking and a good weeding. She paused to toss an acorn into the goldfish pond and watched the fish scatter like little red sparks. She followed the white gravel drive through the apple orchard as far as the rhododendron hedge and Route Five. She opened her mailbox. There was nothing in it but a dead frog. Little boys were always roaming Route Five leaving dead things in the mailboxes.

Gwennie scooped the frog out with her letter and let it drop onto the macadam where some car would squash it. She left the letter in the box and turned the red flag up. Twiddling her fingers at a brown rabbit hiding under a bush, she started back through the orchard.

She was at the goldfish pond dropping acorns when the sound of a motor made her turn. A blue car was winding along the drive. She crossed the lawn to meet it. The car slowed to a stop.

"Have you lost your way?" she smiled.

A large, dark Caesar profile appeared at the driver's window. "I'm looking for Mrs. Gwendolyn MacAndrew."

"Really? What for?"

"I'd rather discuss that with Mrs. MacAndrew."

"I'm she. Who are you—police?"

"Yes ma'am." The door opened, and Caesar got out. He took off his hat and was even shorter. "I'm Inspector Stanley Breeze. New York City Police."

Gwennie liked the name and she rather liked the man. She sensed that with a little prodding he might play chess with her or allow her to feel sorry for him. She offered her hand. "How do you do. Shall we walk?" She indicated the garden. "What color rose would you like?"

"White," the little man said without an instant's hesitation.

Gwennie broke off a white rose and fitted it into his buttonhole. It was too white and too large and made him look even darker and smaller, but it lent poetry to his rumpled drabness.

She led him to the strawberry bed. "Would you like a strawberry?"

"If you're having one."

"No, I'm not," she said, "but if you'd like one don't be afraid to say so."

"No thanks, strawberries give me a rash."

"I'm sorry." Gwennie gave him a tour of the asparagus bed, the petunias, the sweet peas, and the potatoes.

The inspector nodded. "Very well laid out. Nothing clashes."

"Can you stay to lunch?"

The inspector looked at his watch. He had a little white wrist.

"We're having roast beef," Gwennie coaxed. "There's lots of it."

"You're very kind, Mrs. MacAndrew." He gave her a pathetic smile. "Yes, I'd enjoy staying."

Gwennie led the way to the porch, to the sofa suspended by Indian chains from the ceiling. She tapped the space beside her, and the inspector sat. Gwennie began swinging gently, and the bells on the chains tinkled.

"Is your husband confined to his nursing home?" the inspector asked.

Gwennie nodded.

"I tried to visit him," the inspector said. "They told me he was asleep and couldn't be disturbed."

"That means he was in the tent," Gwennie said. "Oxygen. He's in and out all the time. Poor Winnie."

"I was told that I'd need a court order or your permission if I wanted to visit him."

Gwennie turned a speculative gaze on the inspector. "Do you want to visit him?"

"I may need to."

"Then you have my permission. It's silly to bother with a court order. I'll warn you though, he's not much fun. He has to sit in a wheelchair, when he's not in that tent, and it makes him gloomy. And when Winnie's gloomy he thinks everyone else should be gloomy, too. It always depresses me to see him."

"You mentioned a wheelchair—is he paralyzed?"

"More or less."

"Do you have any children?"

Gwennie could not see the connection, but she supposed there was one, somewhere. "A daughter, somewhere."

"No sons, no Winston MacAndrew Junior?"

"No such animal," Gwennie smiled. "Is that all you've come to ask me?" He was silent. "Would you like to play chess?" she suggested.

"I don't play, thanks. Does your husband have any enemies?"

"Don't we all? I daresay Winnie had his share. They're probably mostly dead though."

"No living enemies? No one who might want to blacken his reputation?"

"Winnie's reputation is pretty black already." Gwennie tempered the confidence with a smile. "I can't imagine anyone wanting to waste the time." She saw the inspector staring at the floor; his feet hung two desolate inches above it. "I'm not helping you," she apologized.

His eyes lit on her mournfully. "A young man signing your husband's name at the Eli Club squash courts in New York beheaded a musicologist."

"My word." Gwennie gave a little gasp. The dinner bell rang, and she led the inspector into the dark, high-raftered dining room. They took their seats at a table smothered for the occasion in silver and crystal and linen.

"My mother left me this house," Gwennie explained, with a glance up at the ceiling where bats and spirits sometimes hovered. There were none at one in the afternoon, however. They began their watercress soup. Gwennie listened to the inspector's story, sipping from the edge of her spoon.

"Winnie used to play squash," Gwennie said. "He was on the Eli varsity and the 1903 Olympic team. People used to know his name—as much for the athletics as the banking swindles. He was a legend—some time ago."

The little man put down his spoon and looked at her almost beseechingly. "Mrs. MacAndrew—is it beyond the realm of credibility that your husband might have had a hand in this?"

"I'd be very surprised if he's been on a court in half a century," Gwennie said. "Of course, you never can tell. I'll be going up there soon; I'll ask him—just to be sure."

Like a life rope, the bell pulled Breeze out of a dream. He sat up in bed, realized the phone was ringing, and lifted the receiver before his head had quite cleared.

"How's it coming," Kennedy wanted to know. "Found the killer yet?"

"No sir, not yet."

"What the hell you been doing?"

"I'm working on it, sir."

"I haven't been satisfied with your work lately, not satisfied at all. Get on the stick."

With a click, Kennedy was gone, and Breeze, dismissing him, went back to far more urgent matters.

Monday, June 19

It was close to four o'clock in the afternoon, his third day of expenses, that Greg awakened in a double bed that was not his own. Recognizing neither the monogram on the sheets nor the girl next to him, he felt under the pillow for his contact lens, wedged it into his left eye, and blinked.

"Howdy," Gillian said, sliding slowly into focus. She was a Bengali girl; he remembered meeting her in some discotheque or other just before closing. She was sitting on the edge of the bed running a stiff bristled brush through dark hair that must have been at least six feet long. With a whiplike toss, she threw the mane over her shoulder and leaned down to kiss him on the tip of his nose.

"You could use a shave." Her hand was soft on his cheek. "There's an electric razor in the loo."

Greg crawled out of bed on all fours, and when he managed to stand, was surprised to find himself in flowered surfing trunks. "Are these yours or mine?" he asked. They matched her slip, or sack, or whatever that sheet was she was wearing.

"They're yours now," she said.

"Thanks. What the hell is that thing you're wearing, a curtain?"

"No, it's a bed sheet." She stood up and showed him. She was scarcely five feet tall, and her hair dragged on the floor like a bridal train.

Greg groped his way into the bathroom. The faucets were little gilt gargoyles. He ran cold water into the sink and splashed his face. The electric razor was in the cabinet. The cord was entangled with a little gold wristwatch that said five after four. He hesitated, then dropped the watch into the pocket of his new trunks. A loan, he promised himself, till he got his own watch back.

Shaved and smelling of her lemon soap, he staggered in a more or less straight line back into the bedroom. "I'm late for a funeral," he announced.

"Who died?" She helped him into his shirt—the collar was gray—and into his tweed trousers; the last ghost of a press had vanished from them. "Somebody famous?"

"A musicologist. Bertram Langsam."

"Who he?" She slipped the tie under his collar and knotted it.

"He's the gent what lost his head on the squash court."

"Ugh. Why are you going to that?"

Greg buttoned his vest, all but the bottom two buttons, which were missing. "Because I've never been to a Jewish funeral."

"I know a better one. Teddy Rothschild's giving a thing for the Transatlantic Review at five-thirty. Want to come?"

Greg slipped into his jacket and shook his head. "Have to go to this one. Part of my job."

"I didn't know you had a job."

"I won't have if I miss this."

"Then I'll come with you."

"Dressed like that?"

She knotted the sheet around her waist and crisscrossed two folds over her shoulders. "No one will know the difference."

They ignored the cabby's grimace at the West Side address and settled into the taxi. The cab lurched through traffic like a bronco trying to throw them; by the time Greg had finished explaining his job, they had reached their destination and Gillian was frowning thoughtfully.

"Funny they'd hire you," she said. "You're not a detective."

"It's not a question of detection, it's pub rel."

"What would happen," she asked, "if you did some snooping on your own?"

Greg handed the cabby two dollars and held the door for her. "Why should I tire myself?" They headed west along the sidewalk, searching the numbers above pawnshops and grocery stores for the address of the synagogue. "They just want me to keep an eye on a cop."

"But why couldn't you burrow around and ferret out the whole shmear yourself?"

Greg stopped to compare the number above a shop window with the address in his engagement book. They were the same. "Why should I want to ferret anything out?"

"Lots more lovely money that way."

"What makes you think so?"

"My natural duplicity. It sounds to me as though Eli University is about to come into a big fat endowment and is scared of losing it."

"Possibly." Greg grimaced at the shop window. Raincoats, guitars, and electric Madonnas were for sale. "This doesn't look like a synagogue."

"There's a star of David." She pointed to a display balanced between two concertinas.

"But it's for sale."

She shrugged, angled her head upward, and took a backward step. "Yes, there's the sign."

Greg craned his neck and squinted. The place was called Congregation Beth Rico. Gillian opened the door. Greg hung back a moment, fighting down an ancient superstition he had about pawnshops. Inside someone had mounted a cardboard sign on an easel, welcoming the visitor to the Neighborhood Religious Center. A shaky red arrow pointed to the rear of the store.

Greg followed two paces behind Gillian, his eye roaming the shelves of alarm clocks, typewriters, fifth-hand suits, fake jewelry. A subdued babble of voices and wails rose up as they approached the back room. Gillian pulled the bamboo curtain aside, peered in, then tugged at Greg's sleeve. He squinted into the gloom.

It looked more like a stockroom without stock than a synagogue. A Japanese lantern, badly singed and from the smell of it about to go into a slow burn, muffled the glare of the one dangling lightbulb. A circle of wobbly light caught the edge of a wood coffin and the bald, bowed head of a man wearing an antimacassarlike shawl. From time to time he looked upward; his eyes seemed to trace a crack in the ceiling, and he made a spitting sound that might have been Hebrew, or possibly, just plain spitting.

"He was a good man." An embroidered cap sat on but did not subdue the woman's gray, unruly hair. Her eyes were bright, and she clenched Greg's hand. "You knew Bertram?"

Greg hesitated. "Slightly," he whispered. "Same alma mater."

"I'm Frieda, his sister."

"And this is Gillian." Greg could not remember her last name.

"You knew Bertram?" the woman asked.

Gillian shook her head. "Read about him in the paper."

"Yeah? Do me a favor, honey, will you? Stand over there." The woman pointed to a row of empty shelves. "We're orthodox."

Gillian accepted her banishment cheerfully and stood in the

corner adjusting her sheet. The woman shifted her beanie
with one hand, as though to balance it better. "Good turnout,"
she whispered. "Better than I expected."

Greg nodded. He counted eight men in the room, excluding
himself and the corpse. Of the two short ones, he recognized
the dark-haired as the detective he was to keep an eye on.
The blond-haired, he supposed from the way they were
whispering, was an assistant. Another man was wearing a
priest's collar; two others were holding rosaries.

"Bertram didn't have many friends," his sister whispered,
"but the few he had were loyal. I got a sympathy telegram
from the musicology department where he worked."

"That's wonderful," Greg whispered.

"And that man there, that priest? He's a classmate of Bertram's, he came all the way from Long Island."

Greg brought the priest into focus: a pink-faced man with
rosebud lips and a baby's bonnet of luxuriant graying curls.
He appeared to be paying close attention to the growlings
at coffinside.

"He told me he knows Hebrew," the woman confided.

"Are these all Bertram's friends?" Greg asked.

"I don't know everybody," the woman confessed. "They're
friendly, that's all that counts in this world."

The bald man aimed his gaze out into the gathering. "Bertram Langsam," he concluded, "was a fine man, a good man,
a gentle man. He will be missed. In the words of the immortal
William Shakespeare . . ."

"That's Rabbi Blake," the woman said. "He's a fine rabbi."

A breeze fluttered the newspaper dangling across the one
window in the room and ushered in a smell of chili powder.
Coughing, the rabbi moved out of the draft and mingled with
the standees.

"It is over?" Gillian asked.

"That's that," the woman nodded. She took Greg by the
arm. "You want to meet some of Bertram's friends?"

"Certainly," Greg accepted.

"I'll introduce you to Father Fields," the woman said. But Father Fields was in conversation with the rabbi, and at the mention of his name he gave them only the most cursory of nods.

"Then you don't believe in an afterlife?" he was asking.

"We do not." There was a cutting edge to the rabbi's voice, as though more were being discussed than theology.

"I thought perhaps," Father Fields faltered, "what with the *aggiornamento* of the last few years, Judaism might have . . . changed."

"Judaism does not need aggiornamentos and afterlives. We try to make do with this life—and do well with it."

"Sometimes, in this life, we make mistakes," Father Fields said, as though apologizing.

"Sometimes," the rabbi replied, not accepting any apologies today.

"After all, man is mortal—he may not have time to repair his errors."

"In that case," the rabbi said, "he would be wiser to behave himself."

Father Fields swallowed but kept smiling.

"If I were a Buddhist," the rabbi said, "I would say Bertram Langsam, dying as he did, was paying for errors committed in one incarnation or another." There could be little doubt which incarnation the rabbi meant; and the smile on Father Fields' face wilted. "But I'm only a rabbi, and all I can say is that Bertram Langsam was a man, and time and chance happeneth to all men."

"Time," Father Fields muttered, squinting at the rabbi. "Chance." He pursed his lips, then brought his voice up from his stomach with suddenly renewed vigor. "Still, I should imagine that there are areas of agreement between our faiths."

"Possibly," the rabbi said.

"I'll bet there are, too," the dead man's sister interrupted. "Do you all know each other?"

The rabbi glanced at Greg and Gillian.

"Friends of Bertram's," the woman stated. "You're all friends of Bertram's, so that makes you friends of each other."

"A friend of the Bertie's?" The priest sounded interested.

"Didn't actually know him," Greg apologized. "Same college."

"I was a classmate," the priest said, a little wistfully. For a moment he appeared to be lost in a memory, unaware of the rabbi's chisel-sharp stare. "What house were you in?" the priest asked.

The question was standard, as were the questions that inevitably followed, and Greg gave the automatic answers that he had a hundred times at a hundred gatherings, some no more festive than this. He noticed that the dead man's sister had dragged the rabbi away and was introducing him to the inspector and his assistant. The rabbi kept glancing back at the priest, and once—when their eyes met—the priest reached a forefinger under his collar.

"You'll have to come out to Syosset," the priest said. "Saint Mark's Episcopal. My church."

"Fine," Greg said.

"Things are in a little confusion for the moment; the rector retired and I've . . . taken over."

"Congratulations," Greg said.

"But any time after next Tuesday we could have sherry— or dinner." The priest turned to Gillian. "You, too, of course."

"Of course," Gillian smiled.

Greg shifted position in the conversational group to get a better view of the room. He observed that the inspector had done the same. "Odd place," Greg remarked.

"As I understand it," the priest said, "this is a neighborhood religious center—serving several faiths."

"Things seem to overlap a little," Gillian said.

"All in the spirit of the times," the priest smiled. His forehead was sweating.

Two men in overalls hoisted the coffin to their shoulders and negotiated their way to the door. The crowd in the room had thickened, and the place hummed with Spanish. The priest glanced at his watch.

"Looks like there's another service." With an air of magnanimity, he placed a chubby hand on Gillian's bare shoulder. "After you, my dear."

The mourners were clustered like exiles in the anteroom. The rabbi had put on a torn raincoat and a taxi driver's cap and was shuffling restlessly while the dead man's sister shook hands all around for the tenth time. "Thanks for coming, Bertram would have been grateful," she told Greg.

"He was a fine musicologist," the priest assured her, "and a fine man."

"You don't need to tell *me*," she said. "We used to telephone every day. He left a cat, you know. Poor thing won't eat."

"It will work out," the priest assured her. "And if I can be of any help, just give me a ring. Saint Mark's Episcopal, in Syosset. Ask for the rector."

"I'll do that," the woman nodded.

In the next room a chorus of voices rose in a Spanish translation of "Rock of Ages."

"Bye bye now," the woman smiled crookedly, then went to accept the sympathies of the detective and his assistant. The priest held the door, and Greg followed Gillian onto the sidewalk.

"Remarkable woman," the priest said thoughtfully. "Rather reminds me of Naomi in the Old Testament."

"Or a television character," Gillian said.

The priest turned. "I beg your pardon?"

"I mean the *gemütlichheit* was a little thick in there. And since when do women wear yarmulkas?"

"What's a yarmulka?" the priest asked, interested.

"The thing on her head," Greg said. He had been curious about it, too.

The priest shrugged. A taxi passed the curb, and he leaned abruptly down to the driver's window. "Penn Station," he said.

"I'm taken." The driver shrugged a shoulder toward the rear of the cab. A man in dungarees was attaching a U-Haul-It trailer, and two others were sliding the coffin into place.

"Terribly sorry," the priest said, blushing. "I'd better try up the avenue." With a wave and a "Cheerio!" to Greg and Gillian, he bounced quickly up the sidewalk. From the rear, there was something penguinlike about him.

"Breeze should be out in a minute," Greg said. "Care to tail him with me?" The coffin rattled as the taxi pulled away.

"No thanks," Gillian said. "I'm catching the tail end of my party." Then her eyes narrowed, and she clutched his elbow and whispered, "Turn around."

Greg turned. A figure in a tattered raincoat and a taxi driver's cap was moving up the sidewalk, fleet as a shadow.

"He was standing in that doorway," Gillian said. "He's following the priest."

"Odd," Greg said. His eyes met hers. He felt tired in the legs, weary in the shoulders, empty in the stomach, and dry in the mouth. He wanted to go back to some nice girl's comfy pad and curl up in a bathrobe and sip bourbon and have his back rubbed. He didn't feel up to exertions.

"Very odd." There was a nudge, an impatience in her voice.

"I suppose I should go after him," Greg said wearily. "It's rather obvious, isn't it. The Eli Club is worried the police will find out something embarrassing about this murder. Implication, something embarrassing exists. I've been hired to keep an eye on the police. Implication . . ."

"If you got a jump on the police and dug up the goods yourself," Gillian said, "you'd win the gratitude of the Eli Club. Cash gratitude." She gave him a smile that was all white-on-brown. "And you could split with me." She touched Greg's arm.

"How do we know the rabbi isn't just running to catch a bus?"

"Because there's no bus in sight." She kept her grip on Greg's arm and steered him to the corner. The priest was a block ahead. He stopped at a newsstand, bought a paper, and ducked into a subway entrance. "Ten to one," Gillian said, "the rabbi takes the same subway."

The raincoated figure broke into an unmistakable run and disappeared into the subway entrance.

"You have a point," Greg said.

"Call me tomorrow, love," Gillian smiled, "and tell me about it."

Greg had not run for ages, and he suspected from the pain in his chest and the stares of little half-dressed children that he was not doing a very good job of it. As he puffed to a stop at the newsstand, another button popped off his vest—third from the bottom—and his shirt, off-white since its last visit to the laundromat, bulged into view.

He slapped down a dime and ripped a paper from the old lady's hands and plunged down the stairs into the subway. He dropped a token into the slot, but the turnstile, unbudging, buffeted him in the gut. He pushed again. It was jammed. He muttered a little curse. A train pulled into the station. He vaulted the hurdle, disentangled his shoe from the turnstile, and ran toward the car. He made it just before the doors slammed shut.

He was not tall, but he found himself towering over a Red Sea of dyed hair. He ignored a dozen female voices giggling in Spanish and opened his paper. On page one was a gory picture of the late Bertram Langsam as discovered by the Associated Press on the squash court. The accompanying banner headline was in Greek.

Holding the paper a foot before his face, like a mask, Greg pried his way through the giggling ladies to the front of the car. He made out the rabbi several yards ahead in the crowd. The door to the next car opened and shut again, and the raincoat bobbed in and out of view. When Greg caught up with it, the raincoat was on a Negro, a conventioneer with his name pinned in a cellophane envelope to the lapel of his business suit. The man looked up at him oddly. The train pulled into the station, and Greg saw the priest on the platform, face buried in a copy of the *Village Voice*.

"Excuse me." Greg forced his way out of the car. Father Fields paused at a candy machine to smile at his reflection and brush a gray curl away from his forehead. Greg flattened himself against a pillar. His eye caught a wisp of tattered raincoat hiding behind the next pillar; a moccasined foot was tapping on the platform, and a taxi driver's cap dangled from a half-visible hand.

Greg walked with careful nonchalance to a bench, took a seat between two toughs in leatherette jackets, and opened his paper wide. Glancing to his right, beyond photographs of a Harlem trunk murder, beyond the neighbor cleaning his nails with a switchblade, he saw three steps, a hallway, and a door labeled *Men Hombres*. It was to that door that Father Fields strolled.

The priest folded his paper, tucked it under his arm, and dropped a coin in the pay lock. The door creaked open; he entered; the door creaked shut.

Greg turned a page of his paper.

It was several minutes before the door opened again. When Father Fields stepped out, he was no longer wearing his black shirt front or clerical collar, though a bulge in his jacket suggested where he might have hidden them. In his striped, open-necked shirt he had the air of a graduate returned to a reunion. He took the three steps in a jump, stopped again at the candy machine, and threw himself a chummy grin, and went to the trackside to peer at the approaching train.

The priest got into the third car; the rabbi hurried into the second, leaving Greg no choice but the fourth. Through the connecting door he watched Father Fields study his *Village Voice*. At Columbus Circle the rabbi, cap pulled down over his face, entered the priest's car and took a seat in the corner. Father Fields did not even glance at him.

At Times Square the priest got off the train and sprinted up the steps to Forty-second Street. The rabbi followed. When

Greg reached street level, they were several yards ahead of him in the crowd. Women in cowboy boots and boys with teased hair made up the bulk of the population, but there were milling soldiers and drunks and policemen. The priest gave a dime to a pandhandler, and smiling, approached the ticket window of a double-bill grind house.

ALL NEW SHOW, the marquee blinked: EDGAR ALLAN POE'S THE BLOOD DRINKERS ALSO MURDERS IN THE RUE MORGUE IN COLOR. Greg moved up to the panel of stills and pretended to study them.

"Could you tell me," the priest asked the henna'd lady at the ticket machine, "which film is on now?"

The woman pointed an emery stick at a typed sheet of paper taped to the window. The priest peered at it; his uncertainty seemed to deepen. Finally, with trembling hand, he gave the woman a dollar.

Greg held back in a throng of dirty-smelling teenagers while the rabbi bought a ticket and went in. After thirty seconds Greg went after them.

Father Fields tiptoed to the balcony as though he hoped to surprise the film in something naughty. He took a seat in the front row, apologizing to sleepers and possibly corpses whom he did not seem to be disturbing in the least. The rabbi sat two rows directly behind him, and Greg sat on the side where he could keep an eye on them both.

Halfway through *The Blood Drinkers* the priest went out and returned balancing a jumbo soft drink and a large sack of popcorn. During *Murders in the Rue Morgue* he covered his eyes, but peeked through his fingers as an ape with a straight razor dispatched a bordello full of Parisian cocottes.

After the capture of the ape, when it was clear that there would be no further murders, the priest left the theater and crossed the street, where another double bill was showing: *The Flesh Eaters* and *It Came from Dimension Four*. Greg had a headache at the end of the show, and he noted that the rabbi was chain-smoking.

Father Fields now paused under a marquee proclaiming THE DIRTY GIRLS and OLGA'S MASSAGE PARLOR. He consulted his wristwatch but did not go in. He hailed a taxi. The rabbi hailed a taxi. Greg hailed a taxi.

The taxis lurched to a stop bumper to bumper at Pennsylvania Station. Greg fumbled for money and managed to fumble longer than the rabbi, whom he could see in the taxi ahead trying to fumble longer than the priest. They got out of their cabs at fifteen-second intervals, and the priest led the way through underground corridors to the ticket window of the Long Island Railroad.

"One way to Syosset, if you please." Father Fields pocketed his ticket, bought a movie magazine at the newsstand, and ambled down the ramp to track nineteen. Greg took a seat at the rear of the priest's car and buried his face behind a shield of Greek newsprint. It was only as the train was pulling out that he realized they had lost the rabbi.

Breeze had killed the evening at home with a crossword puzzle. It was close to midnight when the phone rang.

"I don't suppose you've found the killer yet," Kennedy said.

"I'm following up a few leads."

"I don't want hunches and fancy hypotheses, Breeze, I want the killer."

Killer, Breeze thought; six letters down. He filled in the squares. "I promise you," Breeze promised, "no hypotheses," although he could already feel the stirrings of one or two. Tomorrow, he decided, he would talk to the dead man's sister; alone. She struck him as a fake.

Tuesday, June 20

WINSTON MACANDREW, for whose MacAndrew she had forty-three years ago traded her father's Saint-Simmons, was Gwennie's lawfully wedded husband. She loved him as dearly as any woman of sixty-four loved any man of ninety-seven: she felt something for him that was midway between condescending affection and affectionate condescension. But as she stared at him, swaying in the rocking chair, shrouded in a Mohawk blanket, she experienced an almost telepathic certainty that the inside of his head was murky, like morning five o'clocks, and she felt murky just seeing him.

"Hello Winnie," she smiled.

Lately, on her few and growing fewer visits, the idea had pestered Gwennie that Winnie felt for her neither affection nor condescension, but simply—in his unfathomable murkiness—nothing; a bottomless boundless topless nothing. She took an uncomfortable seat on the forward half of an aluminum chaise lounge.

"I met a detective yesterday," Gwennie said.

"Well, well," Winnie said. His voice had the tinny resonance of an old Rudy Vallee record.

"This detective was wondering if you knew a man called Langsam."

One-thirty A.M. was an unorthodox hour for tea on the sun porch, but clouds were chalking over the eastern sky, and it was a good idea to enjoy the moonlight while it lasted. The attendant had arranged a tray of teabags, hot water, lemon slices, and the dried toast that Winnie subsisted on.

"This detective is nuts," Winnie said.

"They found Mr. Langsam—chopped up—on the Eli Club squash court."

"You're nuts. People called Langsam don't play squash, and they don't get into the Eli Club."

"But he did get into the Eli Club. That's what I'm telling you."

The paper napkins flapped in the breeze. Gwennie steadied them.

"I've been in the Eli Club thousands of times, and I never heard of any Langsams on the squash courts." Winnie gave his chair a quick rock. "You're nuts."

"I wish you'd stop saying 'nuts,' Winnie."

"If you're driving yourself nuts, I'm going to tell you so. I don't believe in evading issues. And frankly I think you're getting nuttier and nuttier. I think you're spending too much time with this detective."

"He stopped by the house thirty minutes to tell me that Mr. Langsam had been chopped up."

"He's nuts."

"He's not nuts at all. Poor Mr. Langsam was in all the papers. Why even that man you play chess with, that nice attendant, told me he'd read about it."

"Mo Jackson has absolutely no grounds for saying such a

thing. Mo Jackson is trying to encourage your manias by inventing stories. Mo Jackson wants to drive you nuts. Watch out."

"I believe Mr. Jackson. He's got a good mind."

"He's a hundred years old and he's senile."

"He's ninety-eight. He told me so. He's quick-witted and he's nimble for his age."

"For his age he ought to be buried. He's a gerontosaurus."

"He called you a pterodactyl."

"Calling's easy." Winnie gave the chair another rock. "I'll bet he couldn't spell it."

"He's not as stupid as you think. I'd like to see you throw around meta . . ." Gwennie tried to remember the word, "phors like that when you're ninety-eight."

"Metaphors hell. He wouldn't even know those big words if he hadn't swiped my crossword puzzle dictionary. The only thing you can say for that man is that he's got a memory like the petrified forest."

"Why do you hate Mr. Jackson?"

"I don't hate him." Winnie raised a book in front of his face. "Tell this detective friend of yours that no one was chopped up in the Eli Club. The chopping happened at the Yale Club, and the pieces were brought over in a brown paper bag."

"How do you know?"

Winnie's smile was visible under the book. "I have my sources."

"What sources?" Gwennie asked, but he did not answer, pretending to be deaf. She wished she had stayed home; there was a good horror movie on television. She liked the midnight horror shows. They convinced her, temporarily, that the most terrible horrors were invented; that monsters and murders and madness were worse than the receding reality of the world, the dying of thought, the loss of movement in a limb. But at one-thirty in the morning, the light or dark of a storm-brewing sky showed things in a gloomier and truer perspective. Gwennie saw Winnie for what he had become—a misanthropic skeleton sustaining itself on a crust of zwieback in the shade of an oxygen tent. And seeing him, Gwennie knew that whithersoever Winnie went, she would not be more than thirty years behind.

"Trouble with you," Winnie smirked, "you watch too damned many horror movies."

"Perhaps," Gwennie said. She believed in awaiting the execution of Our Father's will and all, but she prayed that He had not in store for her too many more years; she prayed that she would not one day wake up to find herself turned into a Winnie. She hid her trembling lips behind the teacup; her teeth chattered on the rim.

"I always mean to cut down on the movies," she said. "But something always comes up and it just seems easier to turn on a horror film and take a peek now and then. They make me forget. I can't really explain it, they make me feel more secure."

"Those horror flicks," Winnie said, "are driving you nuts."

Gwennie began to think of moving. It was chilly on the porch. She finished her cup of tea. "Winnie, you haven't answered my question."

"Have some fresh tea, honey." The skeleton leaned a long way forward, dropped a new teabag into Gwennie's cup, and poured a stream of no longer hot water.

"Did you know Mr. Langsam?" Gwennie persisted. "Did you . . . see him?"

"Sit down," Winnie advised.

Gwennie felt wobbly, so she sat down again to catch her breath and balance. She accepted the cup and swallowed without tasting. "Did you go to the Eli Club squash court and chop up poor Mr. Langsam?"

"When would I have done that?" Winnie asked.

"I don't know." Gwennie felt herself flushing; impatience, perhaps. "Last week some time."

Winnie smiled a half mouthful of teeth. "I was in the oxygen tent last week."

"Then you didn't chop him up?" Gwennie asked.

"I refuse to answer," Winnie stated.

"Why?"

"Why should I incriminate myself?"

"But you said you were in the oxygen tent."

"Well," Winnie reminded her, "there are no locks on those things."

"Then you chopped him up," Gwennie said.

"I didn't say that."

"You implied it."

"What I imply and what I say," Winnie smiled, "are not the same kettle of tea. And what I do is another cup of fish altogether."

Gwennie rose again to her feet. "I'm sorry, Winnie, I'm not up to it, not today." She hurried into the building and found the attendant leaning on the water cooler.

"Nice visit?" he asked. His smile had more teeth than Winnie's, and his eyes were kinder.

"So so." She lowered her voice. "Mr. Jackson, tell me something. Those oxygen tents—do they have locks?"

Malagueña eased herself onto a stool at the end of the row; the sailor next to her watched as she arranged her billowing skirt. She took her time. It was important for the hem to hang evenly.

A young waiter with a dopey expression was sponging spilled slop off the counter. His hand stopped at Malagueña's place. "What's yours?" he asked drowsily.

"Pan con libertad."

"Huh?"

Malagueña scanned the row of posters across the top of the stand. "Coconut papaya," she said. She sipped it slowly through a straw and whirled in her seat every now and then to keep track of the travelers going by. The sailor spun around and left.

Malagueña felt in her pocket. *Mierda.* Nothing but the

twenty-dollar bill. Pretending to swat a fly, she clamped a fist down on the sailor's tip. She slid the dime to the edge of the counter, caught it in her lap, then flicked it into her skirt pocket. She sipped the last of her juice, then loudly dropped the dime onto the counter.

"Fifteen," the waiter said.

"*Chinga tu madre, maricón*," Malagueña replied. She rose from the stool and joined the rush of people crowding across the station. She paused at the newsstand to peer at the headlines. A woman was blocking her view.

"*Que carajo mira esta cabrona tortillera*," Malagueña muttered. She reached around the woman and, without paying, lifted a newspaper.

"I saw you," the woman said. She had dark hair like Malagueña, but her perfume smelled worse and her face was more wrinkled and her make-up had cracks like dried mud.

"*Que le pasa, calabaza?*" Malagueña snapped righteously. The blind newsdealer turned an interested ear.

"I saw you steal that newspaper." The woman tapped the headline with a finger that flashed glass jewels.

"*Ay ay ay ay*," Malagueña began humming. She opened her paper.

"Oh yeah? Hey mister, this Spick stole a paper."

Malagueña folded the paper and jammed it into her skirt pocket. The woman grabbed her arm and twisted.

"You Rickans think you run the city. Come on, give." Her face was blotching scarlet under the white powder. Malagueña swung her free arm against the old *vaca's* stomach, twisted her knuckles hard into the flab. The *puta* doubled over and staggered against the stand and sent a pile of city editions cascading to the floor.

The loudspeaker blared a train departure. Malagueña clamped a hand against her thigh and walked swiftly.

"*Ay, ay, ay, ay*," she sang, "*Corta y no llores . . .*"

She pushed past an old couple searching for tickets at the gate and strode down the ramp.

> *Porque cortando alegras,*
> *Hachita linda, los corazones* . . .

Hachita linda—it was a pretty little ax, a reliable ax. It pressed against her leg warmer than any lover.

"Tengo un hachita en el bollo, y es mas sabrosa que cualquier pinga."

They were good friends and constant companions, Malagueña and her ax. Humming, she stepped into the Jamaica train.

It was close to two in the morning when Father Fields had to change trains at Jamaica. He paced the station platform wondering what connection there could be between the emerald isle of the Caribbean and this soot-caked homonym where thrice weekly he awaited the pleasure of the last train to Syosset; if Roquefort cheese could bring suit against the usurpers of its name, why not the Jamaicans?

A railway employee came along the track swinging a lantern, squinting at the rain-dampened rails like a philosopher in search of an honest man. Father Fields leaned down to call to him: "I say, do you happen to know if the Syosset train is on time?"

"Ten minutes late," the man said. Clearly, the lateness or punctuality of the trains made little difference to him.

Father Fields pondered the decline of service in the Western world but decided not to ask why the train had to be late, as indeed it was thrice weekly. Instead he resolved to put the time to good use. He hurried down the stairway at the end of the platform, locked himself into a toilet stall in the men's room, and reattached his black rabat and collar.

Today he was wearing one of the linen collars; they rarely stood more than two wearings, and tonight was a second wearing. The collar would go into the laundry basket as soon as he got back to the vicarage. Much could be argued against linen collars, but they did not chafe, like the plastic.

Father Fields emerged from the stall, a priest again, and

considered himself in the sink mirror. He straightened the collar, smoothed the inevitable wrinkles out of the rabat, and patted his graying forelock into place. He cupped his hands to the cold water faucet and had himself a refreshing sip of aqua pura. An old man came into the bathroom. Father Fields yielded the sink with a smile and wandered back up to the platform.

The Syosset train was eighteen minutes late pulling into the station and, once Father Fields had seated himself in the forward car, another seven minutes dawdling before it finally pulled out. Calculating forty-two minutes to Syosset, Father Fields opened his movie magazine and began reading for a third time the article on Jackie Kennedy.

Twice a cold splash of air struck the back of his neck; twice he turned in his seat and saw that the new occupants had joined him and his two companions in the car.

The first newcomer was a fair-haired young man with an unbuttoned vest and mustard stains on his suit; he sat toward the rear of the car and buried his head in an ink-smudged newspaper. If the headline had not been in a foreign language, Father Fields would have taken him for an Englishman of sorts.

The second newcomer was a different kettle of fish, a woman with torrents of jet-black hair tumbling to her shoulders and obscuring half her face. In a quick glance Father Fields could make out one dark eye, a magnificently aquiline nose that would have been at home on an archbishop of Toledo, and lips redder than ripe tomato. Something in that single visible eye struck him—a look of confusion, perhaps, as though she were a foreigner unable to comprehend American trains. She walked along the aisle, her skirt rustling up a gale, and seemed to be looking for something in one of the seats. More discreet than curious, Father Fields returned to his magazine.

The rustling drew near. From the corner of his eye he discerned a purple skirt sliding into a seat diagonally behind him. He skimmed the same line of type three times be-

fore dropping the magazine to his knees. Two thoughts had
dawned on him in quick succession. First, he knew the
woman was watching him. He could sense in the very hush
of her breathing that her eyes were fixed on a point in the
nape of his neck. Second, he knew that somehow, from
somewhere, he knew her. And from the quality of her silence
—strained, alert—he could tell that she knew him.

It was one of those curious convictions that, more often
than not, turn out to be totally false. The conductor came
down the aisle punching tickets, and Father Fields had a
legitimate excuse to glance once more over his shoulder. The
woman said she was going to Huntington—she pronounced
the word without an *h,* and she held out a twenty-dollar bill
in a way that suggested she had no idea of its value. Grumbling, the conductor gave her a punched ticket and from the
wad in his pocket peeled eighteen bills change.

"Is long?" the woman asked.

"Seven stops." The conductor held up as many fingers.

The woman nodded, but Father Fields suspected she did
not understand. He reversed himself and decided he couldn't
know her. She didn't speak English, and English was the only
language he did speak. And where could they have met? He
had traveled only in England and the Scandinavian countries, and while there was no suggestion of the Nordic about
her, there was a definite, pungent hint of Latinism.

Demonstrably, then, they had never met; and even if they
had, they could never have spoken. So they had to be
strangers. The deduction was borne out by the fact that she
was staring not at him, but through the window at housing
developments whizzing by in the night.

"Ticket, Father?" the conductor asked.

Amused, Father Fields held up his ticket. The conductor
probably took him for a Roman priest, like so many people
with no notion of the Anglican and High Episcopal church.

"Thank you, Father." The conductor tipped his cap and
went back up the aisle.

Father Fields opened his magazine again, but something

pulled his eye to the side: a movement across the aisle
perhaps, a finger tapping on a window pane, a low-heeled
foot sliding out from under a purple skirt? He glanced,
guiltily and quickly, pretending that he had turned to flick
a mote from the shoulder of his jacket. Her head was bowed
toward the window; she had not moved.

Father Fields tried to read, but a certainty nagged at the
corner of his mind; a spark of recognition had leaped that
aisle. She had felt it, too, or she would not be sitting so still.
She was waiting for him to speak. He was positive of it.

He turned to his own window, as though to watch the
housing developments, but actually to find her reflection.
There, with a start, he met her eyes; she was staring at him
in the glass. Ghosts of trees and houses flew between them
as his jaw dropped. He wheeled in the seat, raised his hand
in apology, and was about to excuse himself and ask where
they had met. His forehead knotted into a confused frown.

"Padre," she whispered, coming across the aisle. She slid
into the seat beside him.

"Do you know me?" he asked. "I mean, I think we've
met . . . "

She shook her head.

"I don't speak Spanish," he apologized. That was it: she
was Spanish, perhaps Latin American. Yes, now he remembered. Of course she was. Even the smell of roses and lemon
—that seemed familiar, too. But where? Who? The touch of
her hand as she grasped his was like an old friend's, neither
shy nor brazen, merely urgent.

"Speak English?" she asked.

He nodded, and his heart went out to this shaken, homeless
creature. He wondered at the cause of her turmoil; perhaps,
in some way, he could comfort her. At least till Syosset.

"Confess," she began. It took him an instant to recognize
the word. "Confess."

At moments like this Father Fields thought his heart would
leap from his rib cage and go flying about the room. For

certainly she was a Roman Catholic. Weren't all Latins? Who but a handful of the most sophisticated Anglicans ever indulged in the sacrament of confession? She, a Roman, mistook him for one of hers! He had heard confessions, to be sure—several of the ladies in the parish enjoyed kneeling Wednesday afternoons at the makeshift confessional in Saint Mark's to pour out the full triviality of their sins. But they were Episcopalians, Protestants really. He had never in his life heard a Roman confession.

"Confess, padre!" She had slipped, or fallen, to the floor and was holding to his hand as though to drag him down with her. He nodded, but the nod was a stall. He was deliberating.

The Pope, of course, did not recognize the validity of Anglican orders; but the Anglicans, himself included, recognized the Roman succession, and that was the important thing. He sensed, with something resembling a thrill, that he was on the verge of an immoral act—though logically speaking, he could find nothing immoral in it. The woman was in spiritual need; they were both members of the Holy Apostolic Church, he a priest ordained and empowered to administer the sacraments, she a communicant in good standing. Why should the Pope's shortsightedness come between them? He leaned toward the woman and gently helped her back into the seat.

"I can't hear your confession on the train," he said. "I do have a church in Syosset, five stops from here. I'd be happy to confess you there."

"No," she whimpered, teeth clenched. "Must be here. Now. Important."

Father Fields glanced around the car.

"No can wait."

No one, fortunately, was paying attention. The red-headed woman had fallen asleep against her window, mouth agape; the bald man was concentrating on lighting his cigar; and the man with the newspaper still had his nose buried in it.

"Here?" Father Fields reasoned that pidgin might make things clearer. "No possible," he said, spreading his hands in a flattening gesture.

She pulled him into the aisle and tugged him toward the front of the car. He followed. After all, she was in need. And she was—again, the nagging incompleteness of the memory—an old friend. Of some sort.

"Here." She pushed open the ladies' room door.

"Oh no." Father Fields shook his head; no, it wouldn't be right. "Let's try in here," he suggested, and he pushed open the door to the men's room. "After you, *señora*."

She showed not the slightest uneasiness; her sudden calm, in fact, might have bespoken a lifetime familiarity with men's toilets. She locked the door after them. Father Fields gestured to the one seat.

"Please be comfortable, my child."

She sobbed something he could not understand.

"Now now." He stroked her thick black tresses and found them surprisingly soft. She allowed him to ease her down onto the seat, then hid her face in her hands.

Father Fields made the sign of the cross. "In the name of the . . . "

He stopped, remembering that he should not see her. He cast about for the light switch. There was none. He reached up to the bulb over the sink. It was hot; he jerked his fingers back, sublimated a curse, and licked his lips. She reached under her skirt and produced a handkerchief.

"Thank you," he accepted. He unscrewed the bulb. The men's room was momentarily darker. "Now my child." He crouched beside her, bracing himself against the wall. "In the name . . . "

But there was still light, flashing through the window at ten-second intervals. He got up and pulled down the window shade. He felt his way in the dark and crouched again.

"All right, *señora*, in the name . . ."

Father Fields intoned rapidly; no sense prolonging the dull

part. He hoped her English would be adequate to her sins.

Perhaps it was only an illusion, but it seemed that in the dark sounds became sharper. As he recited the preamble, Father Fields was aware of the clacking rhythm of the wheels and could almost have counted the breaks in the rails. He could hear the wind raised by the train's flight through a grove of trees, and he could distinctly make out the ticking of his pocket watch. Yet the room itself seemed oddly quiet, as though it were holding its breath.

She was holding her breath, he realized. He wondered what on earth for.

He finished his part. Now it was her turn. He settled back against the wall. He heard her inhale. Her dress rustled, as though she had reached down to lift her skirt.

"Speak, my child," he urged.

The dress made a hissing sound, and he wondered if it were ripping. High above him came a whistling. It gained in momentum and descent and ended in a paralyzing crunch. The crunch was like a dentist's scalpel scooping at his teeth, but it was at the back of his neck. The banging of the wheels was closer and suddenly deafening, and his head, dancing on the floor in synchronization, was full of thunder. The blade kept slamming down. He would have tried to fend it off, but he could not find his hands.

Greg watched the Spanish woman come out of the men's room, close the door, and return alone to her seat. He counted ten, folded his newspaper, and strolled to the head of the coach. He got himself a paper cup of water from the fountain, and sipping, turned to see if she was watching him.

She was gone.

At first he thought the men's room was locked; but when he shoved with his shoulder the door yielded and he flew into the dark. There was no electric light, and he had to lift the shade to see.

The window was in splinters. So was the priest.

Greg grabbed the emergency cord.

The train screeched like an electric saw slicing a hole out
of the night. It tore to a stop on an embankment that was
safer for turning than parking. A door slid open in the front
passenger coach, and two figures scrambled to the ground.

Greg got to his feet. "Where are we?"

"That way's Hicksville." The conductor pointed his ticket
puncher. "Other way's Mineola."

"Don't let anyone else get off that train," Greg said.

"I ain't got three hands and I ain't got ten eyes," the
conductor grumped. He fell into stride alongside Greg. "Who
the hell you looking for anyway?"

"The head."

"Who needs the head, he's dead, ain't he?"

"Get back and watch the coaches," Greg said. "Look for
a Spanish woman in a purple skirt."

"Are you a cop?" the conductor challenged.

"I can have you arrested," Greg said.

"It ain't like I'm obstructing justice or anything, but I
gotta keep that train moving, we got passengers, and mail,
and there's another train coming in eight minutes."

"Hey, what's wrong with the train?"

A long-haired boy with a fluorescent tie and suede pants
ambled along the track. He was carrying a box under his arm,
and the box was singing.

> *If you loved me*
> *Half as much as I loved you,*
> *You wouldn't love me*
> *Half as much as you do.*

"Get back in the train," Greg said. But it was too late.
Another silhouette dropped from the door, then another, then
more, like a platoon of paratroopers.

"We going to sit here all night?" a baritone shouted.

"I gotta get this train moving," the conductor pleaded.

"Get the names of the passengers," Greg said.

"I haven't got a pencil."

"All right," Greg said. "I'll phone ahead to Hicksville; the police will be waiting."

"Thanks a heap," the conductor said in a betrayed tone. He herded the passengers back into the train.

Greg walked back toward Mineola. Since the men's room had been on the starboard side of the train, he reasoned that the head must have been thrown to starboard. He was right. It was at the dark end of the Mineola platform, a yard or so from the candy machine, looking very much surprised.

It was almost six in the morning. The sun, bloated with the poisons of Manhattan's air, was already peeking over the tenement tops as Rabbi Blake let himself in the back door of Congregation Beth Rico. He stepped over cartons of junk, careful to make no noise that might awaken the janitor.

"What things we do to one another—what a time, what a life!" He was whispering to himself, as people will when they are alone or old, or both. "Running around, hiding in trains . . ."

He whispered melodically, with a sort of cantillation. Hassidic tunes were always going around in his head at six in the morning. Often, like a dog that had to pee, they kept him awake if he did not let them out.

"Who *is* that man," he wondered, stopping on the fifth step of the stairway. "He was at the funeral. Was he following me or Fields?" The rabbi shook his head and went up the stairs. "Why would he follow me? Who cares anything about a tired old rabbi?"

And he was tired indeed—too much running around, too much hiding in trains. He allowed himself a paper cup of brandy from the medicinal bottle beside his cot.

"My dear Fields . . . " He raised the cup, speaking now, his eyes fixed on empty space in the middle of the room: "This is a special occasion. To you, dear Ferdinand." Swallow.

"And to you, dear Bertram." Swallow. He poured another cup. "Which leaves us only one to go." He drank, and a sword of fire went through him. "Lord give me strength. Lord give me ingenuity." He crumpled the empty cup. "Lord give me a *means*."

The movie theater on West 113th Street was showing a triple bill of two westerns and a horror picture, and a pushcart vendor was hawking watermelons and mangoes in the street. There was a sign in the downstairs window of the building: ROOMS TO LET.

The red paint was peeling off the four-story wood building, and the garbage cans under the front stoop were heaped with a week's jetsam; a cat was chewing on the overflow. A woman with a bath towel turbaned around her head was sweeping rubble off the steps onto the sidewalk. She paused to lean on her broom and stare at Breeze.

"Frieda Langsam live here?" he asked.

She scratched her fanny through her bathrobe. She seemed to have a partial paralysis of the left hip, and she had very few front teeth. It was hard to be sure, but she said something like "third floor rear."

Breeze thanked her and climbed the three flights. He knocked on the door, and the eye of an octopus appeared in the peephole and blinked malevolently.

"Police," he called.

A chain rattled, three locks snapped, and the door groaned open. Frieda Langsam, a hairbrush in one hand, blocked his way. "Yeah?"

"I'm Inspector Breeze, I've been assigned to . . . "

"I remember." She shrugged a semi-invitational shoulder, and Breeze squeezed past her into the room. She tilted her palm at a rocking chair, and he sat and immediately wished he had a steadier seat. Frieda closed the door, locked all the locks, and dropped herself onto a threadbare loveseat.

"Miss Langsam," Breeze dove right in, "do you know if your brother had any enemies?"

She brushed her hair with a monotonous, angry stroke, hardly looking at him. "He didn't have an enemy in the world. You saw the funeral, nothing but friends."

"Maybe someone else, someone who wasn't at the funeral . . . "

"Nobody hated Bertram. Everybody loved him. He was a good man, he was a kind man. Nobody had any reason to do anything to him."

"But Miss Langsam," Breeze corrected, "somebody *did* have a reason."

"It's not true," she said.

"But Miss Langsam, your brother was murdered."

The hairbrush stopped. "So he was murdered, you think *I* don't know?"

A television set was going downstairs—something with gunshots and skidding cars and screams and ominous timpani tattoos which kept recurring between commercials. Breeze raised his voice a notch.

"You want to see his murderer caught, don't you?"

"I don't want nothing." The brush started again, deliberately.

"Who hated your brother? Who wanted him dead?"

"No one hated him, no one wanted him dead."

Somehow it all struck Breeze as circular; he wished he could spiral out of the tautologies and contradictions. "You spoke to your brother the day of his death?"

"On the phone," she said.

"Did he have any plans, engagements? Mention anything out of the ordinary?"

"He was looking for his dinner. Mrs. Garcia hid it from the cat."

"Who's Mrs. Garcia?"

"The cleaning woman."

"Did he mention going out to play squash?"

"No, he sounded tired. He never went out."

"Does the name Winnie MacAndrew ring a bell?"

"Sure." The hairbrush stopped. "He killed Bertram."

"Do you know him?"

She set the brush down on the coffee table. "You think if I knew my brother's killer I'd be sitting here yakking with you? I never heard of him till the cops told me. Bertram never said nothing about him. The only friends he had were up at the music school. If he knew this MacAndrew, he was keeping it a secret, and that I doubt, because we didn't have secrets—not from one another I mean. I'm his big sister, I raised him up ever since Mom died."

Frieda took an apple from the fruit bowl and curled her stocking feet up on the loveseat.

"Your brother played squash at the Eli Club often?"

"Never. He wasn't a member."

Breeze leaned forward and almost lost his balance in the chair. He stiffened his legs. "Was there some trouble between your brother and Eli University?"

"No trouble. Everyone loved Bertram."

"Then why wasn't he a member of the Eli Club? Why did he never give to college fund drives or go to reunions?"

"Why should he? He had better things to do. He was dedicated to his work, that's why." Apple chewed to the core, she padded to the kitchenette—at least Breeze supposed it was a kitchenette, though it looked more like a converted janitor's closet with a hotplate. She put on some water to boil. "Sanka?" she offered.

He shook his head. "You're from Latvia, Miss Langsam?"

"Riga," she said, brightening. "You been there?"

"I'm sorry to say I haven't."

She returned with a plastic cup and took her seat.

"Is there anything in your brother's political background . . ."

"My brother," she said, "didn't have any political background."

"He was anti-Nazi, wasn't he?"

"He wasn't anti nothing."

"The Nazis were anti him, I believe. You were both in a prison camp, weren't you?"

"Yeah, but it wasn't political, it was Jewish."

"And you escaped?"

"No, they let us out."

"Who?"

"The Russians."

Breeze could hear the same crashes and car skids downstairs, but the uproar of canned laughter that went with them sounded like a celebration. "How did you get to this country, Miss Langsam?"

"Refugees," she said. "We were on the first boat, soon as the war stopped."

"How did you get your visas?"

"I don't know. We were sponsored."

"Who sponsored you?"

She exhaled a long, dreary sigh. "That 'One Book' group, I think they're broken up now. They were very busy after the war. They sent Bertram to college. They were very nice to him. Me they weren't so nice to. I had to get a job. But Bertram finished his music studies and he did very well."

"Did you know any of the people running this group?"

"Bertram knew some. All I knew was the rabbi . . . Rabbi Blake, he buried Bertram. He was the rabbi in the group, very active. In those days you had to have a rabbi and a priest and a minister, just to show you weren't anti anything or pro anything."

"When did you meet the rabbi?"

"Right after the war, 1945. He was a real organizer. I have great respect for that man. That's why I asked him to bury Bertram."

"You said you and your brother were on the first boatload of refugees. Do you mean that literally?"

"Sure."

"How did you manage it?"

She frowned. "We didn't manage anything, they asked us."

"Is it possible," he persisted, "that someone might have a grudge against your brother, something to do with the war or his imprisonment?"

"No."

"Maybe he . . . cooperated a little with the Nazis? Maybe he cooperated a little with the underground? Wasn't there anything . . . "

"They loved Bertram during the war. They always loved him."

"Who is *they?*"

"Everyone everyone loved Bertram and Bertram loved everybody, and whoever killed him should have their head examined."

"Yes, Miss Langsam, I agree."

After Frieda, Breeze called on Doña Manuela Garcia de Cuenca, Langsam's cleaning woman. She lived on West Eightieth, in a crumbling brownstone with more than its share of rats and roaches. She put a sixty-nine-cent record of merengues on the phonograph and gave Breeze a Coca-Cola.

"No sir," she said, "I don't know no one that would want to kill the doc. He was a good man, he was a clean man, he was always kind to his cat. He was so kind!"

Every time she mentioned the cat she kept breaking down and trailing off into Spanish and then into Togalog. It was a tiring and not very useful meeting. Breeze left his Coke unfinished.

The tabloids on the newsstands were full of an ax murder —a priest beheaded on the Long Island Railroad. Breeze bought a *News* and a *Post* at the subway station and studied the stories. The photographs of the victim, a Father Ferdinand Fields, reminded him of someone.

When he got home he phoned Kluski. A woman answered, and a baby and a television set were howling in the near distance. "Veronica," Breeze said, "it's me, would you put Kluss on?"

"He's watching his show," she said.

"This is important."

Something covered the mouthpiece on the other end of

the line, and then Kluski was on, telling his wife to keep an eye on the television set and give a shout if anything happened. "Yeah?" he said.

"Find out everything you can about a Reverend Father Ferdinand Fields—rector of Saint Mark's Episcopal Church, Syosset. He was murdered last night in Mineola."

"Veronica was telling me about it," Kluski said.

"Get details. Especially get details that link him in any way to Langsam."

"There's a connection?" Kluski sounded dubious.

"That's what I want to know."

"This can wait till tomorrow, can't it?"

"It cannot. Call me back as soon as you have anything."

Half an hour later, as Breeze was working out a crossword puzzle, the telephone bell went off.

"You're dragging your feet," Kennedy stated.

Breeze looked down at his slippered feet. "There are a lot of people to talk to."

"You talk one hell of a lot, Breeze. This isn't the only murder on the books. We get two killings a day in this town."

"When I get through with Langsam we can look into some of the others."

"Yeah, well just be sure you stick to one at a time. What the hell is Kluski doing in Mineola?"

"I sent him."

"That's their murder, Breeze, not ours. Let's just stick to our own. Let Mineola run Mineola."

"The priest's murder may tie in with Langsam's."

"Who says?"

"I have a hunch."

"Any proof?"

"Not yet."

"Breeze, if I give you a chance you'd bring Marie Antoinette into this. Leave Mineola alone—you're working for New York City. You're working for *me*."

"That's a parochial attitude."

"You're damned right. We're on a budget, Breeze, and it doesn't include your flying off on every ax murder in North America. Stay in Manhattan, baby—and wind this thing up. Don't fall behind. That's a warning. I'm watching you, Breeze."

Kluski phoned and said Kennedy had called him off the case. Breeze wondered how fools like Kennedy ever got to the top.

Wednesday, June 21

THE GRAVEL DRIVE led through a spruce grove along three still lily ponds to a small building that would have looked like a scaled-down Alhambra but for the steeple jutting out of its center. Greg passed under the archway, through an arcade, and across a patio where a small fountain gurgled in the corner. He came to a mahogany door gold-lettered *Chapel of Saint Mark Episcopal.* He pushed; it swung open, well-oiled and silent.

The walls were blue; a blue stained-glass window brooded over the altar, blue carpeting led down the center aisle, and the chapel was eight blue pews deep. A dozen candles winked high and low by the altar railing. Greg glanced at the empty pews and went through the side door.

The cemetery looked like a moderately busy day at a

parking lot for tombstones. It was laid out as regularly as the squares on a chess board, with a few vaults spanning double plots and geometrically placed boxwood hedges monotonously breaking the monotony. A frog was croaking *Dies Irae* from the ponds, a bluejay overhead was having an attack of hysterics, and something was making a tapping noise in the graveyard.

A man was crouching at a vault, cementing a step. He had the sleek black hair and ruddy skin of an American Indian.

"Hi," Greg said chattily. "Is the rector around?"

The man pointed his trowel at the vault. "Went in this morning."

Greg gave a somber nod. "Is there a curate at Saint Mark's —pro tempore?"

"Father Justin. He's over in the parish house."

"Could I talk to him?"

"He doesn't talk much sense—but you can try." The man got up to show Greg the way.

Father Justin was in a dark room massaging a handful of beads, strings, crucifixes, and medallions. An enormous old radio with a face like a jukebox's belly threw a yellow-gel halo onto a jungle of gray hair, a mountain of nose, two long-since abandoned coalshafts of eyes, a narrow fissure of mouth. Periodically the radio diaphragm rattled an intelligible phrase of the Rosary, and the old priest rattled with it.

". . . Blessed art thou among . . ." The old man turned in Greg's direction. "Just a minute," he nodded.

He wore a bathrobe over his shoulders and a rug over his knees. He had wrapped his feet in plaid scarves, and over the scarves he had forced fur slippers, each as large as a stuffed turkey. His hands writhed in his lap, speckled, veined, swollen; and when a trinket escaped him, he leaned out of the rocking chair and squinted at the unlit floor.

Greg retrieved a Rosary bead and handed it back to him.

"I can't see much," the old man confided in a wavering

voice, "but I thank the Lord that He's left me enough sight
to see my prayers."

Little cards printed with madonnas and fat babies, and
Gothic-lettered devotions were laid out across a music stand,
and a single Christmas tree bulb sprinkled a pink dimness
over them. The priest raised the bulb to throw more light
on Greg.

"Take a seat."

"Greg Archibald, sir." Greg advanced, one hand extended.
The old man brushed it aside with the merest shake and motioned him to a chair.

"What brings you here? Wasn't to see me, I'll bet."

"I'd like to know if you have any information . . . or opin-
Something—perhaps a troll—peered out at Greg from the
depths of the right-hand coalshaft. "Greg Archibald, is it?"

". . . And blessed is the fruit . . ." the radio rasped.

"You can turn that down." The old man cocked a forefinger at the radio. Greg turned it down. "What do you want
to know about Fields?"

"I'd like to know if you have any information . . . or opin-
ions about his murder."

"Maybe," the old man said.

Daylight trespassing between shutters and drawn velvet
curtains struck the legs of an upright piano, the arms of two
lion-footed stuffed chairs, which faced one another pompous
and empty, the waxed leaves of bushes and palms imprisoned
and drooping in huge pots.

"Sir?"

"He was pushy. Pushing everybody, all the time. Pushed
me out of my job. Wrote a letter to the bishop, got me
retired."

"It's not known who killed him."

"Oh?" The old man smiled.

Sniffling cats prowled the darkness, brushing folds of old
cloth that rattled dry and crisp as archive newspaper, their
coats glistening wet pink where they had too often rubbed

their loneliness against furniture edges. Greg crossed his legs, and his foot came down on a tail. A cat yelped.

"Damned cat," the old man spat. "If cats didn't have souls, I wouldn't have them in the house. Now move forward a little so I can see you."

Greg moved into the pool of pink light. A gadget in the right-hand coalshaft photographed him and clicked shut. "Another man was murdered, a Bertram Langsam. Murdered the same way."

The old man clicked his tongue.

"Father Fields was at Langsam's funeral. I gathered they were college classmates—and friends."

"I doubt anyone was Fields' friend."

"Did he ever mention Bertram Langsam?"

The old man shrugged. "Maybe . . . now and then. You know, whenever he was reminiscing about that damned show."

"Show?"

"He and Langsam and some other fellow wrote some show at college. He's got a record up in his room . . . or he had. Used to play it all the time. Sure is a relief not hearing *that* any more."

"I'd like to see the record."

"Long as you don't play it."

"I won't play it."

The record jacket had a drawing on the front, an apocalypse of champagne glasses, bubbles, pearl necklaces, heads without any discernible bodies attached. Art-nouveau lettering announced *Rice Pudding Club Theatricals, One Hundred Eleventh Production, In the Bag.*

The old man stood on tiptoes to grimace over Greg's shoulder. "In the bag," he spat. "Supposed to be funny. See, somebody puts this body or head or something in a bag. Fields told me the story once. Nasty business."

"Father Fields wrote it himself?"

The old man pointed an unsteady finger at the jacket. *Book by Ferdinand Fields, Jr.*, the lettering continued. *Music by Bertram Langsam. Lyrics by J. Whittaker Duchamp. Directed by Webster Ten Eyck. Choreography by F. Scott Cerise. Costumes by Alicia von Helsing. Set design by Paavo Saarinen.*

Greg turned the jacket over. "Did Fields and Langsam see one another in recent years?"

"Fields didn't see anyone . . . except the congregation. Spent most of his time in this room. Sitting."

It was an odd place for a priest, or for anyone. The walls were bent in under the weight of a mansard roof, giving the room an oppressive pyramidal shape. A light fixture hung from the ceiling; the pink shade was decorated with a white frill that could have come from an old hat, and two Mickey Mice hung at the end of the long cord, fastened by the tails.

"Father Fields decorated this room himself?" Greg asked.

"Painted the walls green," the old man said, "if you call that decoration."

And indeed the walls were green. The green matched the bedspread. Beside the bed stood a bookcase, filled with shirts and underwear that must have just come back from the laundry. Across the room was a rolltop desk, littered with old postcards and bills. Three Teddy Bears, apparently paperweights, squatted on stacks of letters.

The only wall ornament was a horrific martyred saint. The colors reminded Greg of psychedelic art, and the painting, unsymmetrically stretched and framed, could have been executed by Father Fields himself. Beneath the picture a phonograph sat on a stack of books. Greg eyed the machine.

"You said you wouldn't play it," the old man reminded.

"Is it so awful?" Greg asked.

"It's a hash. Take it home and play it if you want, I don't want it in the rectory."

"Thanks, I'll do that."

"My pleasure," the old man said.

Greg glanced over the record blurb. *Schizo, schizoid—
that's the word for this year's Rice Pudding Show, the 111th
in point of actual fact. (You can go to the Pudding Library
and count the 110 distinguished predecessors, if you don't
believe us.) Now what's so different about "In the Bag"?
Well, for a start—unsatisfied with writing, lyricking and com-
posing the bloody mess, the authors have also copped the
leading roles. Crazy? And that's only the beginning . . .*

"Any reason that a rabbi would be interested in Father
Fields?" Greg asked.

"Why not? It's a free country."

*Like its cast, In the Bag is a frenetic study in total schizo-
phrenia. A musical with murders, you say? Well, granted Vic
Herbert and Jerry Kern never wrote a ballad on the rigors
of mortis, but why shouldn't Whit Duchamp and Bertie
Langsam? There's always a first time, ain't there? With this
production, Rice Pudding Theatricals break, or you might
say dig, fresh ground.*

Greg frowned. "Did Fields' work have anything to do
with Jews?"

"He did some kind of shenanigans with refugees right
after the war." The old man picked something from between
his teeth.

*For those who insist on plot or logic, librettist Ferdie
Fields has concocted a lulu of a madcap frolic. He assures
us that the plot is logical, but we'll give a doorprize—starring
role in next year's production—to anyone who can explain it
to us. Well, for better or worse, here goes.*

"Jewish refugees?" Greg asked.

*As the curtain rises, the natives of the island of Elba are
plotting to crash the house party of their most prominent
local resident, international hostess and wheeler-dealeress
Lady Agatha Trashcroft, a former femme of the demi-monde
whose efforts to snag the squash championship cup for her
nymphomaniacal daughter Hortensia open her house to the
Long Island Mafia.*

"Damned right." The old man nodded. "He was always boasting about it. Here, look at this." The old man bent down to pry open a desk drawer.

Agatha's troubles are compounded by the fact that her husband, Sir Lawrence, is devoting his attentions to house-guest Malagueña la Cha Cha del Amor, a Peruvian sun-priestess turned tramp. Henry's extra-marital sacrilege comes to a hair-raising halt when Malagueña meets with a mishap on the squash court. Pity. We leave it to your imaginations just who or what is "In the Bag."

The old man pulled a framed parchment out of the drawer. "See," he said, "it's in Hebrew."

And indeed it appeared to be in Hebrew, whatever it was.

"It's a citation," the old man explained. He pointed to an inked-in smudge. "That's Fields' name. It goes from right to left. Fields read Hebrew, he was real proud of it."

Greg took the citation and angled it to the window light. "Who gave this to him?"

The light of the setting sun came into the room like a bombardment of X-rays. It pointed up bits of rose-bouquet wallpaper under the green wash; beneath the wallpaper, hollows where one beaverboard plank failed to meet another, rectangular patches discolored like skin grafts where once a wall switch had been installed, where three long pictures had hung, where a half-filled bookcase had stood.

The old man shrugged. "The group—the people he was helping. Someone or other."

"But he never hung it on the wall?"

The light revealed cracks in the floor where black paint had failed to smother the grain of the planks, cracks where dust had collected that no broom would ever dispel. There was a shadow where one warped board jutted an inch higher than its neighbor.

The old man shook his head. "Nope—just kept it there and took it out now and then and looked at it. Never showed it to anyone."

"Then how did you know about it?"

Greg touched the board with his toe and found that it was loose. He lifted it.

"Me?" The old man grinned. "I spied on him."

The board came up, two feet long by half a foot wide, neatly separate from the rest of the floor. There was nothing underneath.

"Miss Langsam mentioned a group—'One Book'—you relocated refugees?"

"Yes, we did a little of that after the war."

"Then you were responsible for bringing Bertram Langsam and his sister to this country?"

"No." The shades in the study were half-drawn, as though to separate the darkness outside from the darkness within. A fluorescent desk lamp reached like a long solitary finger over the desk and cast a flickering arrow over stacks of bills, receipts, canceled checks, some still bound in rubber bands. "I was responsible for bringing no one to this country. Those decisions were not mine."

"Who made the decisions?"

"The others. I merely lent my name to the letterhead. They needed a rabbi. It seemed like a good cause."

"Was it a good cause?"

The rabbi raised his eyes to stare a moment at Breeze. His lips parted and his teeth glinted; he fell silent.

The Beth Rico attic had been partitioned into rooms, and this was one of the results. The beaverboard wall was painted green but had gone bluish where rain had leaked from the roof; a thirty-watt bulb hung from the middle of the ceiling— it had a pink shade and a tired white frill and a long Mickey Mouse cord. A bookcase housed a few shaving odds and ends, a stack of clean underwear and socks, a Torah. The day bed was barely wide enough for a child's insomnia. The window, if you bent down and lifted the shade, begrudged a view of rooftops and chimney pots and granite garbage crematoria.

Breeze said, "Miss Langsam told me you knew her brother."

"I didn't know him, I met him."

"Did he have enemies?"

"I knew nothing about his personal life."

"Then why did Miss Langsam ask you to bury him?"

The rabbi's skin was the yellow of old newspaper. The eyes were moist and weary, like the voice, and each word seemed to be a weight. "Come, Inspector," he said. "A transient congregation like ours produces little in the way of, shall we say, income. What little support we have comes from corpses. We do not turn away a cadaver bearing a thousand dollars."

"Miss Langsam paid you a thousand?"

The rabbi's fingers shuffled and intercut a wad of checks as though they were playing cards. They fell together not with a snap, but a sigh. "I split with the undertaker."

"Isn't that high?" Breeze asked. "The funeral seemed . . . simple."

"It was high, yes. Normally I ask for fifty. She wanted to pay a thousand. Who am I to argue?"

"Why did she pay so much?"

"I am not a mind reader. Who knows, perhaps she felt sorry for a tired old rabbi."

"Is that likely?"

The rabbi pressed a forefinger to a nerve under his eye. "Anything is likely."

"Did you know Miss Langsam, were you friends?"

"I met her twenty-two years ago, after the war. And I met with her to discuss the funeral arrangements. All told, I've seen her three times in my life."

"In twenty-two years she must have met some other rabbis. Why did she come to you? You were virtually strangers."

On the rabbi's desk, a cigarette had burned down to the filter; it sent up a needle of smoke from a coffee saucer that doubled as an ashtray, and an acrid chemical smell jolted the air.

"I can't be certain," the rabbi said. "But I suspect I am the only rabbi she ever knew. When she thinks *rabbi,* she thinks *Blake.* She wanted a Jewish funeral. When she thinks *Jewish,* she thinks *Blake.* So she came to me. It's Pavlovian. Besides she was afraid a stricter rabbi wouldn't bury her brother."

"Why not?"

"Reasons." The rabbi frowned. "Interpretation of the Law varies from rabbi to rabbi."

"Is there anything in Jewish law that might prevent a rabbi from burying Langsam?"

"Well, Langsam was not what you would call a . . . very good Jew."

"That's all?"

"It's enough."

Pulling his window curtain curtain aside an inch, Rabbi Blake was able to peek one eye out for a microscopic view of the street. The inspector emerged from the building and with rapid steps more suggestive of impotence than purpose hurried to a police car double-parked up the block. An invisible hand opened the door to him, and he slammed it twice, catching his suit jacket the first time. The car rounded the corner and disappeared from sight. Blake allowed the curtain to fall back into place.

He lit a fresh cigarette, smoked it down to the filter, and drummed his fingers on the desk top. Pushing aside unpaid and unpayable bills, he moved a small wooden chest to the center of the blotter, unlocked it with a key fastened to his watch chain in place of a watch, and spread out the documents as though they were evidence in a trial. In a way, they were.

He handled the older clippings carefully, lest they crumble further. The earliest were twenty years old. *How young we all looked then,* he thought, and he felt sorry for the faces in those pictures, as dated as the captions and the dry yellow paper. Then there was the letter on 100 percent rag paper. It had not aged at all. It was the notice of dismissal from his first congregation, the Gates of Zion in Brookline, Massachusetts. At the bottom of the box, folded very small, was a piece of parchment, hand-lettered in English and Hebrew: his diploma from seminary. He had taken it out of the frame long ago and hidden it away.

There was an amulet in the chest: he had had to sell the gold chain, but he had kept the little golden heart with the letters that spelled *Shadai*. His mother, who had never learned to speak English without an accent and who had paid for his education raising chickens in Rhode Island, had left it to him, a sign perhaps that she preferred him to his brothers, or expected more of him.

Shadai, he thought: *eternal.* And then he thought, *Words; they're just words, scribbled in one alphabet or another.* He wished he had not sold his mother's chain. He could have sold the watch chain instead, but he had not. He smoked another cigarette and pondered the vagaries of human iniquity, his own foremost. Outside, it was twilight, turning to night.

Frieda's phone rang.

"Hello Frieda, this is Erwin Blake, your rabbi."

"Yes, Dr. Blake?" He sounded drunk, she thought.

"I'm not a Ph.D., Frieda. On the other hand I'm not an idiot. The other day while I was washing your brother's corpse . . ."

"You washed it?" Frieda choked.

"You wanted a Jewish funeral, you paid for one, you got the works."

"Yeah, but *washing* it . . ."

"Tradition, Frieda, tradition."

Cradling the receiver under her chin, Frieda pulled a suitcase from the closet. "I'm listening, Professor Blake." She opened the chest of drawers and stuffed essentials into the bag.

"I'm not a professor, Frieda, and I'm not a detective. On the other hand I'm human. If you prick me, I bleed. If you tickle me, I laugh."

"I never tickled you, Rabbi." It was a twenty-foot phone cord, and Frieda was able to haul the suitcase into the bathroom. She decided to take everything from the shelves.

"And if you wrong me, Frieda . . ."

"I never wronged nobody."

"There were certain signs on the body."

She swept the sink and commode clear of mascara brushes and hair nets. "What do you mean, signs?"

"You know perfectly well what I mean. Signs. Indications. You're a careless woman, Frieda."

She decided against taking the powder. The box was almost empty. "Look, Rabbi, I already gave you a thousand."

"The police were interested in the thousand dollars. They seemed to think it a rather large sum."

"Yeah? Well I do, too, and I haven't got any more money."

"It's a bit late for money, Frieda. I want to talk to you. I'll be over in twenty minutes."

Frieda was out of the apartment in three.

From the phone booth on the street corner outside her building, Rabbi Blake watched her climb into a taxi.

Thursday, June 22

"IT's A CITATION," Greg explained. "That's Field's name—in Hebrew. See, it goes from the right to the left."

Gillian dropped her hairbrush onto the pillow and crawled across the bed. She crinkled her nose at the parchment. "What's that stuff after Fields' name?"

"Nothing," Greg said. "I mean, nothing in particular. I don't suppose."

"Fields' name couldn't be that long in Hebrew, could it?"

"Maybe it's like Russian, patronymics and things."

"Why don't you check?" Gillian said.

"Check?" Greg yawned and stretched his fingers overhead. He stared down at his stomach. It was achieving a curvature close to that of the earth.

"Go see the rabbi."

"Why should he tell me anything?"

Gillian retrieved her hairbrush and gave her hair a jerk. "You have a headstart on the police. You'd be a damned fool not to use it."

"I don't see that I have a headstart on anyone."

"You have this." Gillian slammed the parchment down onto Greg's stomach. "Honestly Greg, why do you think he was trailing Father Fields?"

"I haven't the remotest," Greg said, "unless it was to kill him."

"Well obviously he had to have a reason. And maybe he *did* kill Fields."

"I suppose," Greg said.

"Haven't you ever played the horses?" Gillian asked.

"What if I have?" he said.

"It's the same principle here. You've got a long shot. The rabbi was trailing the minister. The minister was awarded a Hebrew citation. Put them together, and what have you got?"

Greg shrugged. "What have I got?"

"There's no telling," Gillian admitted. "But you *could* take the scroll to the rabbi and see whether he gets upset, or acts strange. He might even break down and confess. You know."

"Angel," Greg sighed. "I am not a Green Beret. I know nothing of the fine art of interrogation. If I march in there with this scroll he'll freeze right up."

"Why? Tell him you need it translated. He's a pedant, he'll love showing off his Hebrew."

"Sorry to bother you," the blond man said. "I need a translation."

"This is not the Berlitz School," the rabbi said. "And I'm behind schedule." He recognized the man who had followed him from the funeral. "I have a great many things to look after today, and I'm late for an errand." His suitcase, bulging and half-hidden behind the open door, sat against the wall like a giant eavesdropping device. The blond man, uninvited and announced only by the janitor's knock, had entered the study just as Blake had been about to pick up the bag.

The man held out five dollars. The study was bright today,

and the money twinkled in the window light. The rabbi accepted the bill and tucked it into his wallet, next to the $450 of Frieda's money that he had converted into traveler's checks. "What's the problem?" the rabbi asked.

"This." The man produced an object resembling a framed scroll. The rabbi peered at it.

"It's a brotherhood citation," the rabbi said.

"I'd like to know the exact wording."

The rabbi felt his voice fall back into the old, automatic sing-song: "*In recognition of works to the benefit of mankind, the Brotherhood Sefer Ehad awards its annual citation.*"

"To whom?" the man prodded.

The rabbi squinted. "The lettering is very bad."

The man tilted the parchment toward him.

"Can't read it," the rabbi said. "No *nikkud.*"

"What the hell's a nikkud?"

"The nikkud," Blake stated, again automatically, "are a system of dots and marks placed under the Hebrew consonants in order to indicate the vowel sounds. There are two sets of nikkud: one for the short vowels, and another for the . . ."

"Rabbi, you read the first part without these nikkuds, couldn't you take a whack at the rest?"

The rabbi frowned at the parchment. His lips moved slowly. "Possibly . . . P'raday . . . P'radayninid Pyolodesh. Yes, the surname looks like Pyolodesh. And the other name . . ."

"There's another name?" the man interrupted.

Blake glanced at him. "Yes, the citation is made out to two people." He squinted again. "El . . . yi . . . shio . . . Ben . . . Ha-Elsinik. Yes, it could be Ben Ha-Elsinik."

"This P'radayninid Pyolodesh, that wouldn't be Hebrew for Ferdinand Fields?"

Blake put a finger to his lips and frowned. "Well," he nodded, remembering the five dollars, "that's a possible reading. Pyolodesh, Fields—it's all in the nikkud. It really doesn't make much difference."

"And this Elyishio Ben Ha-Whatsit, could that be something else?"

Blake drew a deep breath. "Could be," he said. "The *bet* lacks a *daghes,* it could be *vet*—but it's a bad job of lettering, it's difficult to be sure."

"Is there anything else on the citation?"

"The eleventh of Av, the year five thousand seven hundred seven."

"What does that mean?"

"It's a date," Blake explained, "in the Hebrew calendar."

Then the man said something amazing. "Why," he asked, "did you hate Ferdinand Fields?"

A smile flitted across Blake's lips. The man was persistent, but Sherlock Holmes he was not. "I hate no one. I walk with God, do justice, and love my neighbor as myself."

"I think you hated him. His name's on this scroll and you know it."

"It's a free country, think what you like."

The man's manner changed, became confidential. "To tell the truth, I couldn't stand Fields' guts either."

"That's your problem," the rabbi said in his most genial voice, "not mine."

"So P'radayninid means Ferdinand and Pyolodesh means Fields." Gillian tossed a foot of hair off the coffee table and tipped the brandy bottle at the cup of espresso.

"It would appear." Greg held a lighted match over the cup, but the coffee did not ignite. "Which would suggest that Elyishio doesn't mean just Elyishio."

Gillian squirted a drop of lighter fluid into the cup, and the espresso burst into a blazing tower. "It seems Hebrew is just a mess of consonants. They use any old vowel any place."

"It seems." Greg was thinking.

"Drink your coffee." Gillian tousled his hair.

Greg glanced at the cup of fire and decided to wait. He picked up the record jacket of *In the Bag* and considered it. "*Book by Ferdinand Fields,*" he muttered.

"Ferdinand Fields is on the scroll," Gillian said, "and he's dead."

Greg nodded. "*Music by Bertram Langsam.*"

"Bertram Langsam is dead."

"*Lyrics by Whittaker Duchamp . . .*" Greg's eye skipped down the column to the costume credit. "*Alicia von Helsing . . .*" He chewed his lip. "Now if Hebrew is just a mess of consonants . . ."

Gillian frowned, then nodded. In her hand, the can of fluid dripped unheeded.

"Elyishio could be Alicia," Greg mused. "*Ben* could be *von*. Or could it? Are *b* and *v* the same letter in Hebrew?"

"They're pronounced the same in Spanish."

"What a linguist," Greg smiled. "And *Ha-Elsinik* could be *Helsing.* And if that were so, what would it mean?"

Gillian kissed him. His heart beat a little faster.

"One man is on the scroll *and* the record jacket, and he's dead," Greg tabulated. "Another man is on the record jacket, and he's dead, too. And one woman is on the scroll and the jacket, and she's . . ."

"She's more than a coincidence," Gillian interrupted. "She has to be. The same two names—in the same two places— there's some connection between that stupid show and that refugee organization."

"Almost seems to be a pattern."

"There's always a pattern. And if you find the pattern you have the key. And if you solve the case you get a big fat raise from the Eli Club. And then . . . " She was smiling her mischievous smile.

"Then what?" Greg's coffee tasted of benzine.

"Then you move me out of here and you move you out of your place and you move us into a penthouse. How does that sound?"

"Your coffee's gone out." She flicked the lighter and ignited his espresso again. "All you've got to do," she said, "is to find Alicia."

"That's not all," Greg corrected. "But it's a start."

The director was perched erectly on the edge of his chair, twisting, his neck craning forward, his eyes large behind their bifocals. "Mmm-hmm," he murmured, emphasizing the growl, which was in no way a reply, with a nod of the head. He was a smooth, lean man: nothing about him bulged except his eyes. His manner was polite enough but upon exploration proved no more accommodating than barbed wire.

"What can I tell you?" the director shrugged. "He studied here, he graduated. That's all."

"And you have no subsequent records on him?" Breeze asked.

"None."

"Maybe one of the instructors would remember him?"

"No," the director stated. "Absolutely not."

Breeze found Kluski at the crime lab. He was hovering over a pan of developing fluid, his face and hands dimly lit by a red lamp. "Well, well, there's old Breeze," Kluski said.

"There's old Kluss," Breeze said. "What've you got there?"

Kluski's horn-rimmed specs were doubling as tweezers, and he was stirring a wad of negatives in the solution. "Photos of the squash court, just playing around with them."

Breeze sat on the edge of the table, hitched up his trouser knee, and permitted himself a sigh.

"Something bothering you, Breeze?"

"I've been checking up on Rabbi Erwin Blake. He's had a funny career."

Kluski straightened up to his full barrel-chested stoop-shouldered height. "How so?"

"Graduated first in his class, had his own congregation at twenty-four. Now, he's running a burial business, and business isn't good."

"Time and tide," Kluski said. He had majored in philosophy at Antioch University.

"Went up to his seminary, and they wouldn't tell me anything. Seems he's sort of a dirty word."

As he moved back from the pan, the overhead light lengthened the shadow of Kluski's nose and gave him the stony look of a priest of some ancient and forgotten religion. "Maybe," Kluski said, "maybe they caught him breaking the Ten Commandments on a Saturday."

Breeze scratched his nose. "Why did Frieda Langsam want him to bury her brother?"

"Because the rabbi's cheap and so's she."

"He said she paid a thousand dollars."

"Then it's simple." Kluski shook his glasses dry and put them on. "He's blackmailing her, or she's bribing him. Now if he told you about the thousand, he's acting innocent. That means he's not. Which means he's putting the screws on Frieda."

Breeze nodded. "Might be."

"And if he's blackmailing Frieda, that means Frieda did something not-quite-right."

"Good point," Breeze agreed.

Greg strode past the secretary before she could even get the Coke bottle out of her mouth. He pushed open the door to the inner office. "Plimp," he announced to the round mound of cotton dozing at the desk, "I'm on to something."

"Oh?" Daniel lifted his head, raised two bushy eyebrows, and revealed a pair of gray eyes as hard as a child's marbles.

"You heard about the other killing—the Father Fields thing?"

"Fields?" Daniel stretched his arms and clicked his tongue. "Ferdie Fields, the guy with the funny laugh? He's dead?"

Greg nodded and helped himself to a chair. "Same business all over again; head chopped off. Fields was at Langsam's funeral. Afterwards, the rabbi trailed him to the Long Island railroad station."

"Oh?" Daniel said.

"Between Mineola and Hicksville a Spanish woman took Fields into the john. Two minutes later, Fields' head was lying on the tracks."

"Who did it? The rabbi?"

"The Spanish woman."

"What happened to the rabbi?"

"I don't know what happened to the rabbi. That isn't the point."

"Now see here Greg, we're paying you good money . . ."

"Listen, Plimp." Greg leaned forward in his chair. "Fields and Langsam collaborated on a Rice Pudding show; it was called *In the Bag*. Remember, you told me about it?"

"So?"

"*In the Bag* was about a head in a bag. A decapitated head."

"So?"

"Who's Alicia von Helsing?" Greg asked.

Daniel did not answer.

Greg opened his attaché case and laid the record jacket and the parchment side by side on Daniel's desk. "She designed the costumes for *In the Bag*—and she shared a citation with Father Fields for Jewish refugee work."

Daniel snapped a pair of half-moon spectacles over his nose and peered at the documents.

"It's in Hebrew," Greg said. "This is her name, right to left."

"I'll take your word for it." Daniel leaned back in his chair, thumbs planted squarely on the blotter. "Frankly, Greg, I don't see what you're getting at and I don't see where it gets you. We hired you to keep track of Breeze."

"If you'll excuse the expression," Greg said, "I'm heading Breeze off."

"If you'll excuse another turn of phrase," Daniel said, "I think you're free-loading."

"Look Plimp, if you ever studied logic in your life, use some now. First, there are two identical murders."

"Langsam was not killed by a Spanish woman."

"The method was the same. And I wouldn't be surprised if the motive was, too. Don't you see what connects the victims? A Pudding show *about* decapitation."

"It was a mistake ever to put that show on," Daniel stated. "I tried to veto it, but they wouldn't listen. No, they said, it'll be the world's first murder musical. Rice Pudding always wanted to be the world's first." Daniel poured himself a Mexican brandy. "I hated that show. The only good thing was Langsam's score."

"To get back to the point," Greg said. "There's a second tie between the two murders. The Jewish angle."

Daniel slapped the glass onto the desk. "I told them, let Langsam write the score, make him an honorary sub rosa member—but don't elect him. They wouldn't listen, and now we've got a Jewish problem."

"Plimp, do you or don't you know who Alicia von Helsing is?"

Daniel nodded. "Danish, Dutch, German, or something. Actress. Big prewar celebrity. She came to the United States, married an American—designed costumes for the Rice Pudding shows."

"And the refugee work?"

"Something she cooked up with Fields. They sponsored a lot of d.p.'s for Eli scholarships. You know Fields, he always wanted to help people."

"Did they sponsor Langsam?"

"I think so."

"So they were responsible for bringing him to this country?"

"And they got about five hundred other people over here, too. It's fine by me, it's a free country. But they wanted Langsam in the Pudding. I didn't mind Langsam, mind you, but I had to think of the other grads—the misunderstandings, the bitterness—the Pudding just wasn't ready, and it's been nothing but one long headache ever since."

"Where," Greg interrupted, "is Alicia von Helsing now?"

Daniel scratched his chin. "Dunno."

"Would the Rice Pudding have records? Maybe she's still designing costumes?"

Daniel pulled a mimeographed sheet from his desk and ran his pencil down a list of names. "She didn't design them this year." He tweaked his nostril with the pencil point. "I'll tell you what, though—her son, what's his name—he's curator of the Rice Pudding Theatricals Library—up at Eli. He'd know."

"What do I get for travel expenses?"

Daniel looked as though he wanted to cry. "Five dollars a day?" he said in a wee voice.

"Ten," Greg corrected. He slipped the parchment and the record back into the attaché case. His hand was on the door-knob when Daniel coughed.

"Look, Greg—this Alicia von Helsing—what the hell does she have to do with the price of eggs?"

"Frankly, Plimp . . ." Greg turned: "I think she's got the answer to the whole shebang."

"Answer?"

"Refugees, ax murders, rabbis, priests—she's right there, in the thick . . . where the action is."

"Action?"

"Like costumes, baby."

"I'm not receiving you loud and clear, Greg."

"Look—in the Pudding shows—who plays the girls?"

"Fellas."

"Dressed up like girls, right? Now if you were a guy, and you wanted to look like a Spanish lady, what would you do? Go to Berlitz, or go to Alicia?"

"Why Alicia?"

"Because she designed the costume for a Peruvian sun priestess turned tramp by the name of Malagueña la Cha Cha del Amor, that's why. And if you had to be Spanish and female in a hurry . . ."

"Greg." Daniel's jaw was trembling. "You said Malagueña? The murderer wore Malagueña's . . . ?"

Greg nodded.

"That was the role," Daniel stuttered. "That was Fredie Fields' role. He was Malagueña."

Greg bit his lips. "Langsam played a role in that show, didn't he?"

Daniel nodded.

"He didn't by any chance play someone called Winnie Mac-Andrew?"

Daniel cracked his knuckles. "Goddammit. He played a sportsman, a squash champion I think. Isn't there a cast of characters on the back of that record jacket?"

Greg shook his head. "Not a word about the characters."

"There've got to be programs or something on file. Hold on, I'll ask my secretary." Daniel pushed the intercom button. "Miss Bernkrandt, would you step in here a moment?"

Over the hoofbeats of television cowboys Bertha Smedley was aware of a rapping on the glass pane of her door. "Just because it says janitorial technician on the bell," she grunted, "they think they can pester you any time they want." She turned the volume up and rocked so that her chair squeaked. Three shootings and one commercial later someone was still knocking.

Bertha leaned back, whisked aside the curtain, and peered through the upper segment of her bifocals. A man was waving a gun at her. He was wearing a cop's uniform and he didn't look like a nut, but you never could tell. Only last Thursday Bertha had seen a TV show where this cop with a split personality . . .

"Yeah?" she shouted over the television.

"Open up third floor rear," the cop said.

"Why the hell should I?" She opened the door a crack and a smaller, dark-haired man shoved a piece of paper at her.

"Search warrant," he said.

"What's she done now?" Bertha sighed. She got her passkey, turned the television sound up full so she wouldn't miss anything, and led the two men upstairs. She held the key well in front of her, as though it were a firecracker that might go off any minute. She had seen this television thriller called

The Eighth Key where a scientist smeared radium on a lock, and when you tried to open the door . . .

Bertha handed the key to the little dark man. "You open."

He shouted, "Anyone in?" and then he opened. There was no reply; the only sounds in the room were the dripping of a sink faucet and the rising and falling hum of traffic from the street. The two men began opening drawers and poking around with their revolvers.

"Looking for anything special?" Bertha asked cozily.

"Nothing special," the little man said. "Where's Miss Langsam?"

"I don't know," Bertha shrugged. "Didn't see her go out. Maybe she's in the john." Bertha banged on the door. "Frieda?" she screamed. When there was no answer she flung it open. In a glance Bertha saw that the john was empty and Frieda was almost out of toilet paper. Frieda was also out of soap, and tooth powder, and toothpaste, and lipstick, and hairbrushes.

"Not in here," Bertha announced.

The little man opened the kitchenette door. Bertha stood on tiptoes to peek over him. The sink was full of water. Scrambled egg scraps and parsley were bobbing around on the surface.

"Funny," Bertha said. She went to the chest of drawers and peered into the top drawer. Empty. She looked in the other drawers. "Frieda cut out," Bertha announced.

"When did you last see her?" the little man asked.

"Last night."

"Anyone been around to see her lately?"

"Not that I noticed," Bertha said. "Except a man, he was here this afternoon. Matter of fact I didn't see him leave, either. Maybe he used the back stairs."

"What did he look like?" the little man asked.

"Bald."

The janitor at the synagogue said that Congregation Beth Rico had disbanded that morning.

"How come?" Breeze asked.

"Rent trouble."

"Where's Rabbi Blake?"

"He moved to one of those hotels down the block. Just for the time being."

There were ten hotels on the block. Rabbi Blake was not in any of the first nine. Breeze pushed a button wedged between two crumbling bricks. The door of the tenth hotel, the Esperanza, gave a death rattle and swung open. He climbed two flights of sagging stairs, narrow as a ship's ladder, and came to a desk where a champaign-blonde octaroon sat filing her fingertips with sandpaper.

"I wonder if I'd find Rabbi Blake here," he said.

"No rabbis here," the woman said without looking up. "This here's Muslim turf."

"Maybe you have a Blake or two?" Breeze suggested.

She shook her head and began applying transparent lacquer to her fingers.

"Maybe somebody checked in this morning? A white man? With a beard and long hair around the ears? And a beaded black beanie?"

"I told you, mister, he's not here."

The voice in the middle of the night did not surprise Breeze; nor did Kennedy's note of gloating. "Well, Breeze, you certainly let those two slip through your net."

"I have a lead," Breeze said.

"You said that Monday and look where it got you. You're up a blind alley and you know it."

"Blake worked for a group that sponsored Langsam and his sister when they came to this country. The group disbanded in 1949. The headquarters were in Oxford, Massachusetts. That's where Eli University is, for your information. And that's where Langsam went to college."

"Call that a lead? God help you, Breeze."

Friday, June 23

HER STOCKINGS had runs, her hair was hanging down in sweat-washed ringlets, and it was only eight fifty-nine in the morning. "Help you, ma'am?" the policeman asked, not bothering to tip his cap.

"I'm waiting for the embassy to open," she said; and from the incredulous arch to his eyebrows she knew what he was thinking: she was an anarchist, a Castroite. He passed along the sidewalk, but she felt that his eyes were still on her, memorizing her low-heeled shoes, her Coca-Cola-stained blouse, her skirt rumpled from a night's tossing on the Washington Greyhound bus.

I'm not an anarchist, she told herself; *he has no right to think that!* And when she saw the little woman in a shawl unlocking the great wooden doors, she ran to the steps, breathless. "I need a visa." She waved the passport. "I need a visa right away."

The woman let her in, and a man with slicked-back hair greeted her in the marble foyer; rather, blocked her way and asked why she wanted to go to Paraguay.

"A rest," she said. "I need a rest."

"Do you wish to go as tourist or resident?"

"Whatever gets me the visa quicker," she said. He took her passport and turned the pages, slowly testing them between his fingers. "Look," she said, "if there's anything wrong with me or my dollars just say the word and I'll go to Chile." She had already wasted the day before tramping embassy row: eight countries had refused her point-blank. Why—just because her name was Langsam? Because she talked Bronxish and looked Jewish? The focus of her hopes had narrowed to Paraguay. Nobody went to Paraguay, they'd be glad to have her. She would even join a kibbutz in the mountains if they wanted; anything.

"You'll have to leave your passport with us," he said.

"Does that mean I get the visa?"

"We'll see," he smiled.

At nine-fifty-seven, three minutes before he usually got to the office, Miss Gibbon arranged her boss's breakfast on his desk: coffee with milk and three sugars, the way he liked it— she had made it herself—and a prune Danish that she had bought the night before and kept in her refrigerator—the delicatessen was always out of them in the morning, and she knew he preferred prune.

At nine fifty-eight Miss Gibbon turned her chair toward the window and watched the street for his arrival. She glanced at her reflection in the pane of glass and straightened her bun. At nine fifty-nine, when she should have caught sight of him rounding the corner from the bus stop, the telephone rang.

"Mr. Barnes, please," a voice said. She did not recognize it. Her boss got very few calls, and in six months she had learned the voices of almost all his business associates.

"Mr. Barnes isn't here just yet," Miss Gibbon apologized, as though it were somehow her fault. "Can I take a message?"

"Yes, if you'd be so kind. This is Whittaker Duchamp. Whit Duchamp, a classmate."

"Yes, Mr. Duchamp."

"Would you ask Mr. Barnes if he could meet me for a round of squash at six-thirty at the Higginson House courts?"

"I certainly will, Mr. Duchamp." Miss Gibbon's ballpoint took shorthand note of the appointment. "Can he reach you anywhere?"

"I'll be on the court waiting for him." The caller clicked off. It was ridiculous, but—thinking about her boss playing squash with a stranger—Miss Gibbon frowned.

Coming into the office, Willoughby Barnes shook his head with a faintly incredulous expression, as though he had momentarily reversed dream and fact and had expected to find himself somewhere else. This always made Miss Gibbon smile. There was still a little sleep in his voice when he said "Good morning," and his thinning brown hair was still matted to his forehead from splashing his face in sink water. He looked like a boy who had just been swimming, and he had patient green eyes that Miss Gibbon could have stared at forever, except when their glance fell on her.

"Did you get to your movie last night?" he asked.

"Oh," she blushed, "I just finished up a few things around the office, then I went home and watched television."

"Tsk tsk," he chided. "All work and no play . . ."

"I get plenty of play," she corrected.

"I don't believe it for a minute." He set his briefcase down on his desk, opened his coffee, and took a sip. He liked the coffee. She could see that from the little leap his Adam's apple gave.

"Don't I seem . . . playful to you?" she asked.

"No," he said. "You seem serious—sometimes too serious."

She felt her face grow warm. "Serious . . . not me, why goodness, I've only been in the theater six months, and you . . . you've made a lifetime avocation of it . . . and your mother before you."

Miss Gibbon could not help glancing over the fireplace at the portrait. It was a full-length study by Kokoschka: Alicia von Helsing as Bertolt Brecht's immortal *Salome of the Stock-yards;* a brooding Nordic giantess with a slaughtered lamb on her shoulder, her Baltic blue eyes flashing scorn at a world's false gods. Miss Gibbon often stared at the portrait, mentally shearing and undressing the actress till she looked something like Mr. Barnes.

"You're manna, Miss Gibbon," he smiled. "You're heavenly, undiluted, two-hundred proof manna. As for me, well, I'm just a Rice Pudding buff . . . I guess I just love the theatricals and all they stand for. Always have."

"Yes." She lowered her eyes. "I know." Sometimes it amazed her that he had even hired her; she knew nothing about wigs, or dress making, or song writing, and yet he had hired her the day she walked into the office. And here she was; assistant to the curator of the Rice Pudding Theatricals Library; co-custodian of the lore and tradition of a golden century.

"Did you have a good evening, sir?"

"Oh yes," he smiled, and said nothing more.

Miss Gibbon was never quite certain what the smile meant. She knew he lived alone in a wood frame house on a declining stretch of Constitution Avenue; and she knew that bachelors had, or were reputed to have, their excesses. But she had never seen him with a hangover, and women never phoned. She suspected, with relief, that the Club Theatricals were his life. Sitting at home in her tub with an apple, she had often pictured him having a good evening with a scrapbook on a loveseat in the parlor, poring over daguerreotypes of old productions. The first musical comedy presented in the nation had originated on the Pudding stage, and men had doffed the

Pood's wigs and bustles to don the gowns of Supreme Court justices and the top hat of the President of the United States. Just as the nation's leading wealth and intellect gravitated to Eli University, the leaders among the leaders came to the Pudding to let off steam in the chorus. A good many years ago Mr. Barnes himself had been in a show, though he never spoke of it; Miss Gibbon had come across the photograph and Xeroxed a copy for her bedside table. In a way, he was a leader of the leaders of the leaders.

It was therefore with hesitation that Miss Gibbon mentioned a subject as frivolous as squash. "Mr. Barnes?" she said.

He put down his Danish. "Yes, Miss Gibbon?"

"There was a call for you . . . a Mr. Duchamp."

Mr. Barnes made an inexplicable face. Instinctively, her finger reached down to play with the margin release of her typewriter.

"He asked if you would play squash with him today."

Mr. Barnes' voice drained of color. "That's ridiculous. I haven't played squash in years."

"He did say squash, sir. Whit Duchamp. He says he's an old classmate."

"A classmate?" Mr. Barnes set his coffee down with finality, as though he intended to drink no more. "Why is he pestering *me?*"

"I told you sir, he wants to play squash. He wasn't really pestering . . . I wouldn't have said."

"I doubt very much that he wants to play any game with me . . . tennis, squash, or badminton." He looked at her with an unkind expression. "What's he after, Miss Gibbon . . . money? Free booze?"

"All he mentioned, sir, was squash."

"Squash," Mr. Barnes said. "Ridiculous. He thinks he can get away with . . ." He was staring at the bookcase now. "Squash." He frowned at the shelves of scripts, as though there were illicit squash balls hidden behind one of the binders. "Wasn't there a letter from Mr. Duchamp a month or so ago?"

"There may have been. I don't remember."

"The file, Miss Gibbon." He was angry . . . angry at *her*. "Look in the file and see if there's a letter." Speaking to her as though she were an idiot.

Maybe I am an idiot, she thought; *maybe I'm an idiot to feel the way I do about Mr. Barnes; maybe I shouldn't let him hurt me like this.* She didn't see why it was at all important, but there was a letter in the file.

"What did he want, Miss Gibbon?"

"A script." She was quoting from the letter, handwritten on YMCA stationery. "A copy of the script of the 1947 Rice Pudding production."

"Squash," Mr. Barnes said. "Squash my eye."

Miss Gibbon swallowed, her mouth had gone quite dry. "I was only telling you what he said on the telephone."

Mr. Barnes approached the desk. "Perhaps if you would stop hearing things on the telephone and start paying more attention to your typing," he said, "you wouldn't make mistakes like this." He held a copy of the Rice Pudding Theatricals Bulletin under her eyes and jiggled it so that she could barely make out the words.

"I'm sorry, sir," Miss Gibbon stuttered. She wondered if he knew what he was doing to her. She took hold of the bulletin and tried to focus on the page of typescript. But the room seemed to be spinning, and she could find no mistakes, not a single typo in the report of the troupe's summer tour. "Excuse me, sir, I don't see anything wrong."

Mr. Barnes was crouched beside the bookcase; he turned halfway around. "Then maybe you'd better get your eyes checked . . . or hire a good proofreader." Mr. Barnes strode to the door and slammed it behind him. He had taken something with him under his arm, but it was not the briefcase, for the briefcase was still sitting on his desk.

Miss Gibbon tried to dry her eyes on her cuff, but her dress was short-sleeved. She gave up the attempt, laid her head down on her arms, and let her eyes water into the blotter.

When she glanced up several minutes later, the undergraduate president of the club was standing in the doorway. He had a gentle face, and he looked concerned.

"Anything the matter, Miss Gibbon?"

"Oh no," she said quickly, forcing a smile. "Just hay fever."

"You should take an antihistamine," the undergraduate president said. He turned and was gone.

Miss Gibbon began shuffling papers. The sound filled the room, like oxygen, and she was able to breathe regularly again. She separated the papers into meaningless bunches and slipped paper clips around them. She did it all so quickly that anyone seeing her from the doorway would have taken her to be the most efficient secretary in the building.

She shuffled the bunches, then spread them on the desk like cards in a game of solitaire, wondering what to do with them next. She stared at them as though they might offer a solution to her problem. She did not think an antihistamine would help, unless overdoses were lethal.

She did not know how long the man had been standing in the doorway when she looked up and saw him. He was smiling, as though they were friends, and he came into the room with his hand extended. She tried to smile back, but the muscles at the corner of her mouth were recalcitrant and could only manage a little tremble.

"Well well," he said. "Don't get up, don't get up."

"Oh?" Miss Gibbon sat down again.

He was a blond man, and the mustard stains on his vest made her wonder if he were some kind of panhandler. He pulled out a chair and sat down, grinning and staring directly into her eyes in a way that almost made her nervous.

"Let's be friends," he proposed. "Everybody needs friends."

"Well yes, I suppose," she said.

His hand gripped her stealthily, as though he wanted to slip the school ring off her finger. "Archibald," he said. "Greg Archibald."

She realized it must be his name. "Gibbon," she said softly, unable to avoid his eyes. They were very green. "Millie Gibbon."

Breeze knocked on the open door, and a red-eyed woman looked up from the desk where she had been gluing stamps to envelopes. "Excuse me," he apologized, "the graduate center said you might be able to help."

"Oh yes?" she said, then removed a six-cent stamp that had clung, he supposed by accident, to her tongue.

"My name's Stanley Breeze. I'm with the . . . " Breeze opened his wallet and waved the badge at her. "We're investigating the murder of one of your members."

She covered her mouth.

"His name was Bertram Langsam."

She glanced at him peculiarly.

"Did you know him?" Breeze asked.

"Not really, but . . . "

"He wrote a musical in 1947: *In the Bag.* I was told you'd have a script and publicity photographs, that sort of thing."

She jerked her head affirmatively. "Oh yes, we certainly would." She got up, almost tripped over the leg of her chair, and went to a bookcase to peer at a row of bindings. Despite her shield of lace and cotton, or perhaps because of it, Breeze could not remember ever having seen a more vulnerable-looking creature. He instinctively felt sorry for her.

She gave him that peculiar look again, and he wondered if he looked half as remarkable to her as she did to him. Einstein, he vaguely remembered, had established a reciprocity in these phenomena. "You're the second person to ask me about him today," she said.

"Is that so?"

"Someone is doing a biography. He was here this morning." Her voice became a little shrill. "Who *is* Bertram Langsam? I mean, why should anyone write a whole book about him?"

"He was the dean of American musicologists." Breeze noticed the portrait over the fireplace and frowned.

"That's Alicia," she said.

"Ah?" A gold frame enclosed a nine-foot blonde woman wearing Mother Courage rags and an oddly self-satisfied expression. There was a lamb on her shoulders. Breeze wondered if it was symbolic. "Miss von Helsing?"

"She's considered a pretty great lady around here."

"She worked with refugees," Breeze said, "didn't she?"

"Yes indeed, she worked with *everyone*." The woman pulled out a volume, grimaced, and replaced it. "If you're interested in her, I recommend Mr. Barnes' book."

"Mr. Barnes?" Breeze asked.

"Her son. He wrote the book." She pointed to a solitary little black book propped on the desk against a green elephant bookend.

"Ah." Politely, Breeze opened the book to the title page: *Alicia von Helsing: A Memoir*.

"There are some clippings in it," the woman warned. "Please don't lose them." She crouched down at another shelf. "That's very funny, the script should be here . . . right here." She waved her hand at a three-inch empty space. "None of them are here."

"None of them?" Breeze said.

"There's a contest every year." A note of pride crept into her voice. "Sometimes we have as many as eight scripts submitted." She squinted at the space. "I don't understand why anyone would walk off with the 1947 scripts." She put her forefinger to her lip. "Mr. Barnes did take something when he left." She stood up, shaking the wrinkles out of her tweed skirt. "No, there wouldn't be any reason."

"Where is Mr. Barnes?" Breeze asked.

"I suppose he's at home. I could call and check."

Breeze gave her a nice smile, his nicest. "Would you?"

"Feeling tired, bitchy, run-down?"

"Now that you mention it, yes."

"Just can't seem to get started in the morning?"

"I can barely move." As if by way of explanation, the old woman tapped the white-wall wheel of her chair.

"Scientific research has shown that breakfast is the most crucial meal of the day. Don't cheat yourself of the vitamins that you need to feel your radiant best all day long—start your day with . . ."

"Where's my pad, Tasha? You're lying on it—now scat." The old woman waved the cat away, seized the pad of paper and waited, ballpoint pen in hand, while a bottle of pills spun across her television screen.

"Vimbo!" the electronic voice exulted.

"My my, doesn't that medicine look wonderful, Tasha?"

The bottle jerked to a standstill, and the old woman squinted to take down the spelling from the label. The cat arched its back and crept under the chair to doze.

"In bottles of ten, twenty-five, and fifty tablets. Giant economy size of five hundred for run-down families. Get Vimbo!"

She spelled the name out in block capitals, tore the sheet from the pad and folded it. She added the paper to the pile that was gradually lifting the plaster statuette of Blue Boy off the top of the television set. She gazed mournfully at the cat clawing the rug in its sleep and wondered if the medicine worked on pets.

The clanging of the telephone bell interrupted her wondering. She took her cane in hand, lifted herself from the chair, and shuffled into the hallway. The phone was sitting crooked on the little table. She lifted the receiver, her eye still fixed on the television screen.

"Hello?"

"Could I speak with Willoughby Barnes?" a woman asked.

"Maybe." The old woman laid the receiver on the table and waited ten seconds. "He's gone out," she informed the telephone, breathless.

"When are you expecting him back?"

"How should I know? Call back in an hour." She lowered the receiver, but it kept talking. Out of curiosity she put it back to her ear. She realized from the opening shot of a monster emerging from a lagoon that she had seen the television movie twice before.

". . . Gibbon, from the Rice Pudding Library," the telephone was explaining, or apologizing.

"Oh yes," the old woman said, encouraging the phone into further confidences. "You're a friend of Willoughby's?"

"Well, yes, we work together."

"And what was your name again?"

"Millie Gibbon."

"Oh yes, Willoughby mentions you often."

The telephone was silent a moment. "One of the scripts has been misplaced, I was wondering if Mr. Barnes had by any chance taken it home."

"Now let's see." The old woman lowered herself onto the wicker stool in preparation for a long conversation. "What does it look like?"

"It's in a soft green cover, gilt lettering, about eight by twelve."

"A green cover . . . I know Willoughby was home this afternoon. He could have left it in his room. I could look." The old woman liked playing games.

"Oh, would you?" the telephone sighed.

"Just a minute." The old woman got up and walked slowly into the hall. There was a stack of folders on the hall table. She picked them up, one by one, and considered the gilt lettering for thirty seconds. She returned to the phone. "*Belle's Last Ball,* is that the one you want?"

"No, I don't think so."

"Then how about *The Dancing Dybbuk* or *In the Bag?* It says here that *In the Bag* is a comic music-drama in two acts. Looks pretty turgid to me."

"Yes, that's the one." The telephone had raised its voice, as though speaking to two people at once. "Would it bother you if I came over and picked it up? Scripts aren't supposed to leave the library."

"Well . . . " The old woman hesitated. The idea of a prank intrigued her. On the other hand . . . "Nope," she decided. "Better wait till Willoughby gets back."

"But we need that script right away."

"Sorry, can't help you. I'm only the cleaning woman." With practiced pin-point precision, she dropped the receiver back into its cradle.

ALICIA VON HELSING DIES; AUSTRIAN ACTRESS
Anti-Nazi Songstress Agitated for Refugee Aid.
Oxford, Mass., June 16. Alicia von Helsing, one-term deputy chairman of the Austrian actors' and singers' guild and one of the most influential figures in that nation's inter-war theater, died today at the Eli University Hospital. Little known in this country, she was thirty-nine years old.

Miss von Helsing was in private life Mrs. B. C. Barnes.

Miss von Helsing, who introduced works of Strauss, Lehar, and Stolz to a worshipful public, had been bedridden for several weeks early last year with a blood ailment and was treated this year for a heart condition.

She was a key figure in the rebirth of Viennese operetta in the decades following the catastrophic destruction of the State Singspielhaus in World War I. An observer said recently that if one would number the most important Austrian light opera mezzo-sopranos on the fingers of one hand, Miss von Helsing would be among them.

An intimate of the German communist dramatist B. Brecht, Miss von Helsing introduced his "Salome of the Stockyards" in Berlin in 1934, after the playright himself had been forced to flee the country. The production was closed by the authorities, but Miss von Helsing became the heroine of European liberalism and resistance movements. Salome was her only non-singing role.

The part exemplified Miss von Helsing's "Method" approach to acting. It was said of her that when she played a part, she was the part, and during rehearsals she insisted that her friends and co-workers call her Salome. Reliable sources report that she answered to no other name, even going so far as to sign her bank-draughts "Salome." It went similarly with every other part, large or small. E. Bentley, a critic and translator, stated that her ability to "suspend herself and become the character" led to the uncanny realism of her performances.

In 1940 a Swiss magazine described Miss von Helsing as "a democrat, socialist, pragmatist, a full-blooded humanitarian." Miss von Helsing came to this country in December, 1941, having married Calder Barnes of Mount Kisco and Honolulu in 1926. This, her second marriage, took place in Paris. It is said that Ernest Hemingway, a novelist, was best man.

Alicia Caecilie-Marie Wilhansen von Helsing was born in Vienna on July 12, 1908. Her mother, a seamstress, had been a member of the Socialist Democratic party since 1899; her father, a barber, since 1888. The party at that time operated underground. She was the youngest of three sisters.

She attended elementary and secondary schools in Vienna and was head of Vienna's Socialist Pupils' Association. She was graduated first in her class in 1924 after having studied voice in Paris and acting in Moscow, under Marina Stanislaviska, step-daughter of the inventor of the Stanislavski method of acting.

Miss von Helsing then studied public administration in a Berlin school. There she met Helmuth von Helsing, artistic director of the Berlin Opera. They were married in 1925. In the early years of the Hitler regime, the von Helsings helped to establish underground Socialist organizations.

Politics were inseparable from Miss von Helsing's early stage career. International celebrity was hers by 1926, and greatly facilitated her access to high circles of state and finance. It is reported that she used many of her connections to aid socialist and liberal causes.

The last year before World War II, 1938, became an eventful year for Miss von Helsing. First, she withdrew from the stage and served as administratrix in a Berlin rubber goods factory, using business trips abroad to maintain contact with political exiles. Her assignment, communications work in Berlin, gave her access to files of arrested friends, and she became leader of the domestic operations of her first husband's resistance organization.

Mr. and Mrs. von Helsing were divorced in 1926.

In November, 1938, she was arrested by the Gestapo, the Nazis' secret police. She was able to conceal her high position in the Resistance and, to avoid arousing suspicion, consented to the demand of Minister of Propaganda J. P. Goebbels that she return to the stage and assume directorship of the Berlin Light Opera.

Miss von Helsing accepted the assignment because the company's tours permitted her to carry on her international activities. Detractors, however, dubbed her "the Nazi nightingale."

In 1940 Miss von Helsing escaped from Vichy France to rejoin her second husband in the United States. It was her first trip to this country.

In 1945 Miss von Helsing returned to Germany and Austria to aid refugees, many of whom she helped relocate both in this country and in South America. As a result of this work, she was recipient of many humanitarian awards and citations.

During the Nuremberg trials, it was alleged that Miss von Helsing had been Goebbels' mistress. The allegation was never substantiated, and the senior congressman from New Hampshire moved to prevent Miss von Helsing's extradition. Following her husband's death last year, she retired from public life altogether.

Miss von Helsing, as she preferred to be known, designed costumes for two Berlin Opera productions, *Die Walküre* in 1939 and *Götterdämmerung* in 1940 and for Rice Pudding Club Theatricals' *Say La La* (1945), *Achoo!* (1946), and *In the Bag* (1947). She is survived by a son, Willoughby Barnes.

Breeze folded the clipping and replaced it in the book. "I see she designed costumes for Langsam's show."

"She was very good at costumes."

"You wouldn't have photographs of the production?"

"We certainly ought to." She pulled out a drawer of the file cabinet. "Unless Mr. Barnes walked off with those, too." She lifted out a folder. "No, here we are." She spread the material on the desk. "That's the cast."

It was a glossy photo: four women, four men posed like fashion models on a settee against a white cyclorama. A thick noodle of typescript taped to the bottom of the picture identified the performers and the roles they played.

"Ah," Breeze said, "so that's Langsam." A little below average height, blond hair, clean sweatshirt, and pressed tennis trunks. "Looks hale and hearty."

"Very handsome, I'd say," said the secretary.

"What's that in his hand," Breeze asked, "a tennis recquet?"

She looked at him and seemed faintly astonished. "A squash racquet, Inspector."

"Oh, I see. Why is he carrying a squash racquet?"

"It's part of his costume. I expect he was playing a squash champion."

Breeze nodded and glanced down at the explanatory noodle. "Yes, it says he's playing the part of . . ."

She leaned close to Breeze's shoulder; her perfume was nothing special, but it was feminine, and it was pleasant. "Winnie MacAndrew," she said.

Breeze lifted the photo and angled it against the daylight. "Now who the dickens would have picked a name like that?"

"The author, I suppose. The real Winnie MacAndrew was a legend in his time—squash champ, Olympic team and all. The name must be a sort of in-joke." She pointed at another figure, a hefty Spanish woman in mantilla and hoops. "The author."

"Ah," Breeze said, "who's she?"

"He, sir. It's just a wig and costume. An old tradition at Pudding Theatricals." She produced a photograph of a young man, a portrait that might have come from a yearbook. "Ferdinand Fields."

Breeze took the picture from her and tried to imagine the black curls gray, the baby fat a little less firm. "I think I've met him. He was an Episcopal priest, wasn't he?"

"I really don't know. I could look it up in the files." She blinked her eyes apologetically. "I haven't been on the job very long."

"Maybe you could tell me what sort of role Fields was playing in that get-up. Was he some kind of fortune teller or Flamenco dancer?"

She pondered the photograph. "It was a female role, but more than that I couldn't say . . . without the script, I mean."

Breeze replaced the photo on the desk. "Say, Miss . . . "

"Gibbon, sir. Millie Gibbon."

"I ought to take a look at that script."

"The cleaning woman said Mr. Barnes isn't at home."

"But the script is."

"Yes, but . . ."

"That script is probably evidence," he said.

She blanched green against her cotton. "Evidence?"

"In the murder of Bertram Langsam. And the murder of Ferdinand Fields."

"Murder? I don't understand. The script hasn't been out of this office for twenty years, how can it have anything to do with a murder?"

"Miss Gibbon, what are you doing for dinner?"

She gripped the edge of the desk. "Why . . . nothing."

"When do you close the office?"

"Around five."

"Tell you what. Why don't you pick up that script, and I'll meet you in front of the building at five-thirty. And I'll explain this whole thing to you. Fair enough?"

Miss Gibbon sucked her lower lip, as though the decision were extremely delicate. Breeze gave her that smile again.

When the doorbell buzzed the opening bars of the "Hallelujah Chorus," the old lady jerked the television knob toward *off* and tiptoed into the hall. Behind her a young lady's twenty-inch-wide peppermint-fresh smile wobbled, then decomposed into stray electronic flashes. The machine gave a sound like a twang on a Jew's harp and rested in peace.

The cat followed its mistress down the stairs, though it could have as easily run figure-eights around her every step. But Tasha was a polite beast and had no wish to hurt the old lady with a display of superior agility. For her part, the old woman liked to think that the feeble, arthritic, tired-blooded creature depended totally on her charity, and Tasha was generous enough to allow her an illusion or two.

The old woman reached the door at the tenth hallelujah and put her eye to the peep-hole. An enormous cliff of chin surged up at her, head and limbs receding into a distant infinity. The caller looked something like a prenatal fetus dressed in a baggy tweed suit. The old lady shut the peep-hole silently and debated with herself.

"Should I, Tasha?" she whispered.

Tasha frowned.

"Why shouldn't I have a little fun?" The old woman put her hand on the door handle; Tasha pawed the rug and miaowed. "All right," the old woman yielded. "I'll play it safe."

She scurried up the stairs to her bedroom; the cat trailed skeptically behind her. The doorbell was still ringing. She dressed rapidly, then double-checked in the wardrobe mirror. She wasn't bad in a blue blouse and blue skirt and blue stockings—why, blue looked well on her!

At least, without her glasses, she thought it likely that it looked well.

She brushed her hair in front of the sink mirror. Not too many hairs fell into the bowl. She didn't want to be bald befor her time, so she went slowly, one hand pressing the hair down at the roots so it couldn't be tugged loose.

The brush was plastic with nylon bristles. The nylon left an electric charge that made each hair stand separate. Twenty brushstrokes produced a nice sort of continental beehive look that gave the illusion of three times as much hair—if you judged by volume. Stage-magic, she called it—a little stage-magic never hurt anyone. *After all*, she told herself for the millionth time, *life is theater!*

She had never been a small girl, nor had she been a small woman, but she had lately become something of a little old lady, and her skin had developed a few tell-tale sags; which was why she wore colored stockings, and which was why she wore colored arm-length gloves that met the arms of her dress, and which was why she wore low-hanging hats and kerchiefs and billowy scarves that blew up to her mouth even when there was no wind, and which was why she was more than partial to immense Italian-style sunglasses.

Not that she was vain or mourned a past beauty; she was merely a realist. When folks saw her, they didn't really see her, though they might have thought they did. They saw cloth and smoked glass. It was all part of the Big Charade. It was all Fun.

But . . .

There was always a *but,* sooner or later. Something had been happening lately; the Fun wasn't as much fun as it had once been; a little of the savor had gone out of the Charade.

True, she still had a wardrobe full of clothes, old, new, borrowed, and mostly blue; and she had props, like the wheelchair and the nun's habit and the Salvation Army drum and the meter maid cap; and she had the use of a car, and charge plates and charge cards, and the run of the neighborhood; and she could go almost anywhere she wanted and do almost anything she wanted. She had a little gymnasium in the cellar where she exercised and kept limber and strong, and she had a sauna in the garage where she sweated out her bodily poisons, and she had television and hi-fi and all the amusements.

But for all that, she rarely had much fun any more. In fact she had been wondering about psychoanalysis. She felt, lately, that she was losing touch with her Real Self, turning a little cranky (if not crackers). Maybe, she speculated, a shrink would be able to restore a little glue to her psyche, a little *joie* to her life.

The bell rang again, still the "Hallelujah Chorus."

The old woman wondered about the chair. She asked Tasha, and Tasha said yes, so she got into it and wheeled into the hallway. The bell was still going hallelujah as she drew the door open.

"Yes?" she asked.

The visitor looked frightened. "I phoned. I'm Millie Gibbon. From the library."

The old woman nodded her into the house. "Yes, I thought so." She wondered why Miss Gibbon let her graying hair hand like an unwrung floor mop; had the woman never heard of beauty parlors? And those rimless spectacles: they acted as a sort of equator, mercilessly emphasizing the distance between a forehead too high and a jaw too low. The features, compressed into the southern hemisphere, were set less into a recognizable expression than into a chain of miniature moun-

tains and craters. It was obvious that, given another decade at
the library, Miss Gibbon would be beyond redemption.

"Do come in." The old woman wheeled aside, let Miss
Gibbon pass, and studied the length of her skirt, the square-
ness of her shoes, the prominence of the tendons in her calves.
"Tash and I were just having our Postum—could we persuade
you to join us in a cup?"

"That's very kind of you," the visitor faltered, "but . . ."

"No trouble, no trouble. Won't you go in first, I'm a little
lame, paralyzed you might say." The old woman gestured toward the living room and noticed that the run in the back of
Miss Gibbon's stocking ran a little farther with each step.

"Here we are." The old woman wheeled in after her guest.
"You see, you can't refuse, we've already made a whole pot-
ful. Do you like yours strong or weak?"

Miss Gibbon seemed terror stricken by the little painted
tray, the steaming coffeepot, the two cups, and the cereal
bowl. "I really ought to pick up the script and run, you're very
kind, but . . ."

"Medium strong," the old woman said. "You can take the
comfortable chair. Tasha, get off the pillow, let Miss Gibbon
sit, she's walked a long way. You seem out of breath, my
dear." She handed her visitor a cup of Postum and offered
the sugar bowl. "Or maybe you prefer it without?" She returned the sugar to the little table. "I know how breathless
poor Willoughby is every day when he comes home for lunch.
Poor boy. Always running." She poured Tasha's bowl and set it
on the floor just beyond the carpet. The cat approached with
a swagger of boredom.

The old woman dipped a sugar lump into her Postum and
sucked it. She leaned back in her wheelchair. "Now tell me
about yourself."

"Myself?" The visitor's bifocals glinted in alarm.

"You're a friend of Willoughby's and you work at that library. How long have you known him?"

"Not long at all . . . I've only been there since Christmas."

"Does Willoughby tell you much about himself?"

"He never says much of anything, at least not to me." Miss Gibbon squinted at her enormous stained steel watch. "I really should pick up those scripts and . . ."

"Does he ever talk about his mother?"

"No." The cuff fell back.

"She was a great woman. Greatness like that . . . lives on. Tell me, what do people *really* think of Willoughby?"

"I have no idea."

"Come on." The old woman grinned. "You can tell me, I won't repeat anything to Willoughby."

"They like him, I suppose."

"Do you like him, Miss Gibbon?"

The visitor's head tilted left as though she could better gauge the old woman's meaning from the bias. "Of course I like him."

"No one even writes him any letters. He couldn't have a friend in the world outside of you. Though he does telephone people. Does he get his mail at the clubhouse?"

"I'm afraid I really wouldn't know." Miss Gibbon put her cup and saucer on the floor. "Would you excuse me, I must have those scripts back in the library."

"Careful, Tasha's going after your Postum!"

The warning came too late. The cat was tonguing the scum from the top of the cup.

"It doesn't matter, I don't really have time." Miss Gibbon slipped forward to the very edge of her seat. Her knees poked out from under the skirt like two fireman's axes. "Could I take the scripts now?"

The old woman dropped the unsucked sugar into her cup, where it floated a minute before deciding to sink. "Yes, of course." She wheeled into the hallway, making the act look a good deal more difficult than it was. She pointed her cane. "On the table there."

Miss Gibbon hurried into the hall. She gathered the booklets together and pressed them to her flat chest.

"Slam the door hard," the old woman said. "And do come back for Postum some time."

Without replying to the invitation, the visitor tripped through the doorway; the door slammed behind her.

"Here Tasha!" The old woman beckoned the cat away from the saucer of brown slop. "Now what was wrong with your own Postum—why did you have to go bothering Miss Gibbon's?" The old woman scooped the cat up. Tasha miaowed. The old woman stroked its fuzzy cranium, pinched its sharp little ears. "What do you think of our secretary friend, Tasha? Some number, eh? How'd you like to spend forty hours a week with *her?*"

The cat slept in a Sears Roebuck baby-blue pine cradle under the oven. "Here we are." Tasha bolted from the old woman's hands and snuggled against the foam rubber mattress. "Pleasant dreams, Tash."

The cat's scrawny body went limp, and the old woman could tell, though she was quite wrong, that it was sound asleep.

"Shit," Miss Gibbon muttered, standing on the corner. "He's a fag. A nut and a fag."

A tear bisected her field of vision. Clutching the scripts in one arm, she lifted her glasses and dried her eyes. The intersection wobbled back into focus—cars and pedestrians going dumbly, glumly about their itineraries. The people were heading home, Miss Gibbon supposed, and the cars to garages or parking lots or wherever they spent the night. People necked in parking lots, Miss Gibbon reflected, and something stabbed at her heart.

It was almost evening in the street, though she could see surviving glimmers of afternoon in the avenue where busses bright as lemons emptied laughing loads of students and co-eds onto the sidewalk. They were congregating for some purpose, some jubilation; and she realized that she would have to pass through them before she could return to her rented room and a bath.

A warm breeze blew down from the avenue bearing fragments of laughter. It swelled to a brief wind, and her skirt flapped as ridiculously as a sailor's pants. She felt as though she were stranded on the bridge of a diving submarine; she moved quickly out of the wind. Someone leaned on a horn.

She looked up, swallowed an apology to the truck driver, and pretending that she had a reason for being in the street, that she had been crossing to the other side, she walked (slow steps, now) to a doorway marked with a flashing, friendly sign: *Bar Grill.*

It was dark inside. She sat on a stool at the deserted bar and placed the scripts in front of her. The bartender moved them aside and set down a glass of ice.

"What'll it be?"

His voice was warm, manly; reassuring. She caught another tear on her wrist and sniffled. "Anything."

"Man trouble?" the bartender asked.

"Fag trouble."

The bartender poured a second shot on top of the first. "He doesn't dig you?" he inquired condolently.

"Six months, he never even looked at me. I thought maybe I was ugly or something—I was saving to go to beauty school. Fat lot of good that'd do."

"Gee, I hate to see a girl cry," the man said. "Someone should knock this fag's block off."

"Don't you dare! *I love him.*"

"That's a crying shame." The bartender refilled her glass, "When did you find out? Today?"

"Ten minutes ago. I went to his house. He was wearing a dress, and a big floppy hat, and lipstick . . ."

"A drag queen," the bartender said solemnly.

"He was talking in a high squeaky voice, pretended he was the cleaning lady. Didn't even recognize me. *Me.* I spend forty hours a week with him, I order his lunch for him when he doesn't go home, and I write all his letters . . . and he didn't even say hello."

"Sounds like a real louse to me."

"Maybe it's not his fault," she speculated without hope.

"He shouldn't mess with you, it's not nice to make a girl cry."

"Maybe it's that job in that theater, all those guys dressing up like girls, maybe it got to him."

"He should be locked up."

"Maybe he needs me. Maybe he needs me and doesn't know it."

"He needs a punch in the face."

A man was eyeing Miss Gibbon. More precisely, he was standing outside the bar peering in, eying her bundle. He was a fat man. The Tiparillo wedged between his lips gave off occasional damp smudges of smoke.

In the unbuttoned gap of his jacket showed a starched white collar and—sleeping halfway up the black tie—an immense gold worm that had twisted itself into the shape of the letters J. W. D. A gold turtle with a sizable emerald defect in its back clung to the middle finger of his left hand, and his left hand was twitching at a slender gold snake which had fastened fangs and tail into opposite pockets of his rounding abdomen.

He had come to town with a plan. He had watched the office from the delicatessen across the street, waiting for six-thirty when the secretary would scurry home and the employer would hurry to the squash courts. He had intended to go into the office, find what he wanted, and quite simply take it.

The plan had not worked. The employer had run off early, the secretary had disappeared two hours later, and when he sneaked into the deserted office at four o'clock in the afternoon, the thing that he wanted was no longer there.

He could see that the woman at the bar was weeping.

Just as luck had been against him that afternoon, it was inexplicably with him this evening. Turning a corner two minutes ago, he had seen her—the secretary—carrying something.

He had followed her.

His foot was tapping, a tap forward, a tap backward, taps right left and center, and his shoes were black mirrors unsmirched by rain or soot. He could have been whistling, for his cheeks, soft as pastry, pulsed with identical rhythmic tics; but no sound was audible. After a suitable wait, he went into the bar and parked himself on an empty stool next to the secretary.

She glanced at him without, he suspected, seeing him.

"Double Tanqueray martini on the rocks," he told the bartender. The secretary's hand rested on a stack of manuscripts. In the dim bar light, he thought he could make out the throb of her jugular. It was, perhaps, an optical illusion.

Miss Gibbon kept one foot hovering near the floor to make sure that she didn't fall from the stool. She blotted out the sound of the jukebox singing a love song and studied the dime-store mobile swinging in the fan breeze above the bar.

"More of the same?" the bartender asked.

She nodded. She couldn't remember what she had been drinking, but it tasted bad. She gagged.

The fat man next to her patted her on the back.

"I'm okay, thanks." She put five dollars on the bar and knocked over a glass when the bar tipped sideways. Her neighbor lifted the scripts out of the puddle.

"Can I take you home?" he asked.

"Why the hell should you take me home?" Miss Gibbon growled.

"Because you can't walk."

"I can walk," Miss Gibbon said, and tried to, but the juke box threw a flying tackle at her. Something caught Miss Gibbon gently beneath the shoulderblades and steered her toward the twilit door.

"Easy does it," a voice soothed.

The town was stormier tonight than any sea. The horizon could not even decide which way to tilt. The sun hung at the west end of the street like a red exit sign, and night was rushing in from the east. The hand that had been touching her vanished, lightly, as though a breeze had brushed her and decided to move on.

She stood there and wept. She was standing there weeping when the detective came up to her.

"Are you all right?" he asked.

"No," she said.

"Where's the script?"

She looked down at her empty hands. "I don't know," she said. "Don't ask me. I don't know anything."

Poor kid, Breeze thought; poor forty-year-old kid. The tears had melted her mascara into grit balls, and with her reddened nose and cheeks she had the face of a startled Kewpie doll. He put his arm around her to guide her off the street and was surprised how easily she sank against him.

"You need something to eat," he said. "Sop up a little."

"I don't need anything to eat, I need a drink." Her breath was freighted with rye.

"You've had a few of those already."

"So what."

"You were supposed to meet me."

"I was busy."

He eased her into the car and started the motor. "Where's a good place to eat?" he asked.

She pointed across the street. "There." The finger swept out an arc of ten restaurants. They got out of the car again, and he walked her to the nearest. She had trouble balancing at the table. The menu looked Mexican. Breeze wondered if that would cheer her up, or if chili aggravated sniffles.

"Ever had a margarita?" he asked her.

She lifted her face out of the menu. "I've never had a margarita." She sniffled. "It sounds pretty. Would it go with my dress?"

"Why not." Breeze snapped his fingers. A waiter swooped in their direction, a tray clinging by some gyroscopic miracle to his upstretched palm. Breeze ordered two margaritas. Miss Gibbon looked disappointed when the waiter brought two drinks.

"Tequila," Breeze explained. He toasted her.

"Tequila," she replied, lifting her glass. She sipped the drink, then took her napkin and carefully wiped the salt chunks from the rim.

"Know how they make tequila?" Breeze asked. She shook her head. "From the century plant," he said. "They roast the stems."

"Is the century plant pretty?" she asked.

"Related to the amaryllis. It blooms once, then it dies." Breeze regretted the words the minute they were out. For all he knew, Miss Gibbon was related to the amaryllis, too.

"I don't like to hear about things dying." She sipped her drink cautiously, as though she sensed the alcohol lurking beneath the sweetness. "I should think a century plant would bloom for a hundred years."

"It's a misnomer," Breeze said.

"It seems a shame to grind up a plant for liquor."

"Sometimes they even put a worm in the bottle—for flavor."

"Then I won't drink it." She planted the glass on the table. "I'd like a cream soda, please."

The waiter brought cream soda on the rocks with the main course.

"Where's the script?" Breeze asked Miss Gibbon.

Her eyes glazed over. "The script?" A chunk of chili rolled off her fork into her lap.

"You went to Willoughby Barnes' house to get a script."

She retrieved the chili between her thumb and forefinger and placed it on the tip of her tongue. "There were three scripts in the house."

"Did you find the one we wanted?"

She looked around the table, then peeked under the tablecloth. Her knee banged Breeze's. "Maybe I forgot it."

"Miss Gibbon . . . has something upset you?"

She took a long swig of cream soda. "He was there."

"He?"

"Mr. Barnes was in the house. It was horrible."

"What was horrible, Miss Gibbon?"

"When I phoned, this voice answered and the cleaning woman said I shouldn't come over. I guess I shouldn't have. Because when I got there Mr. Barnes was in the wheelchair, using the same voice. Pretending he didn't know me."

"You mean he was pretending to be the cleaning woman?"

Miss Gibbon began crying. "He was dressed . . . like his mother. Like Alicia von Helsing in those old photographs. I knew he worshipped his mother, but getting dressed up in her old clothes . . . I wanted to scream, I wanted to run. But he made me sit down and started asking me questions . . . as though he was her. And then the cat, this cat put its nose in my Postum . . ." She turned away and hid her face in her hands.

Breeze gave the sobs a minute to subside. "Why the wheelchair?" he asked. "The cleaning woman wouldn't be in a wheelchair."

"It wasn't the cleaning woman. A maid doesn't wear floppy hats and long lace gloves when she's cleaning the Venetian blinds!"

"So why the wheelchair?"

"Because it's part of the mother thing. Mr. Barnes' mother was an invalid before she died. And he's pretending to be be her."

"Why is he pretending?"

He had never seen a human being look so hopeless. "I don't know," she said, and her stare dropped to the tablecloth.

"How do you know it *was* Mr. Barnes?"

She pointed her fork to her breast. "I felt it."

"You felt it," Breeze said respectfully, though dubiously.

"I spend forty hours a week with him, I order his lunch for him when he eats at the office, and I write all his letters . . . I ought to know."

"Be reasonable, Miss Gibbon. All you have is a *feeling*. Now feelings are fine, but they can be irrational. Let's be rational for a moment. What if Willoughby Barnes was a hundred miles away when you went to the house? What if it turned out . . . oh, say he had an appointment somewhere else this afternoon?"

"But he didn't."

"But say he *did*. Would you still have this 'feeling'?"

She squinted. "He wouldn't have kept that appointment."

"What appointment was that?" Breeze asked.

"The squash date. Mr. Barnes doesn't play."

Breeze lurched forward, his elbows almost landing in the guacamole. "*Squash?*"

Miss Gibbon nodded.

"Someone asked him to play squash tonight?"

"On the Higginson House courts," she said.

He put a five-dollar bill on the table. "Come on." He pulled her by the hand. "Take me there."

When they reached the squash court stairs they could hear shouts and screams from a crowd gathered somewhere above their heads. Breeze signaled Miss Gibbon to wait on the landing.

"Maybe you should stay here," he said.

"I don't want to stay here. If Mr. Barnes is playing squash I want to see him."

"I don't think you'd better."

"I have a right to!"

"I'm afraid Mr. Barnes may have hurt himself."

"Huh?"

"It won't be a very pretty sight."

"What's happened to Mr. Barnes?" she shrieked.

"Please, Miss Gibbon . . . Millie . . . stay here."

"He needs me!" Miss Gibbon lunged forward and up. He caught her by the hem of the skirt. She wrenched loose.

"It's too late, Millie . . . Miss Gibbon . . . don't you hear the noise?"

"What? What noise? What are they screaming about?"

"Miss Gibbon . . . Millie . . . get a grip on yourself."

She grabbed his arm. "I got a grip."

"Mr. Barnes . . ." he began.

"Yes?"

"That shouting up there . . . it's quite possible that Mr. Barnes . . ."

"Oh *crap!*" She pushed him aside and ran up the stairs.

"Miss Gibbon! Millie!" He tore after her up into the shrieking crowd. Upstairs, it was like a Roman circus.

The hotel smelled of frying fish. The lobby was deserted except for the clerk staring at her over the rim of a sexy paperback. Frieda ignored him and thrust a forefinger at the elevator bell. Chains clanked and an engine growled and the metal doors slid open.

The old Negro asked her what floor, neglecting to put a "ma'am" to the question. There was a sullen anger in his voice, as though she and she alone caused him to run the elevator endlessly up and down its cable.

She found her room key. "Seven," she said. She did not thank him when he let her off, but hurried down the dim corridor. A figure was waiting against the light of a half-opened door. As she approached she thought she could make out shirtsleeves, the glint of a belt buckle, the shine of a bald head. The door slipped shut without a sound. She slid her key into the lock of the door beside it and entered the room.

I'll get the visa, she promised herself. *The delay is only a formality. They always delay. Just to make themselves important.*

She kicked off her shoes. They landed with distinctly different thumps: one on a thick patch of carpet, the other on a spot where the rug had worn thin. She massaged her aching feet and rolled off her stockings. They would have to be thrown out. They had runs to hell and back.

The suitcase was propped on the luggage stand by the wall.

She snapped it open and searched for fresh nylons. There were a good many hairnets and bobby pins, leaky powder boxes, mouthwash bottles, slips and night gowns; but nothing was in order, nothing that she needed was where it ought to have been. She wondered if someone had come into the room during her absence and stolen her nylons.

Through the wall came the sound of a glass being set down.

She went into the bathroom and ran a hot bath, then sat on the rim of the tub and soaked her feet. Relief began seeping up through her legs.

I'll make it, she thought. *I've made it this far, Paraguay's just a little jump after all I've been through.* She had a catechism of such optimisms, one for every situation. They cheered her up.

Through the tiled wall came a sound like that of a glass being set down. This time the noise caught her attention and held it long after the reverberation had died. When she returned to the bedroom, the glass was set down again.

The wall, she realized. *Someone's holding a glass to that wall, listening.*

She opened the door to the hall. An instant later, like a telegraph signal, a click reached her ears, and a slice of light fell onto the opposite wall, slowly broadening into a rectangle. She closed her door and packed her bag.

No, she reconsidered. *The bag would be a giveaway. He'd follow me again.*

She slipped her toothbrush into her purse, put on the one untorn stocking she could find, and went out to the elevator. Behind her, she was dead certain, an eye was watching her through the slit of a partly opened door. She kept the presence of mind not to turn around.

A veritable Roman circus, Willoughby Barnes thought, surveying the squash match from his seat in the bleachers. The spectators were screaming and throwing paper streamers, leaping about so wildly that, squint as he might, Willoughby could nowhere in the churning sea of undergraduates make out the man who had invited him to a game of squash.

A game of squash, Willoughby laughed to himself. It had been a ruse, of course. *Just as well Duchamp didn't show up. I might have slugged him . . . or worse.* In fact he had kept the date on the off-chance of slugging Duchamp, or worse. But Duchamp had not even reserved a court. Today was the day of the house tournament, and all courts, Willoughby had discovered, were taken. Beneath him, someone won a match, and he joined in the applause, then rose from his seat, squash racquet in hand. He was dressed in his playing clothes, his T-shirt and shorts still crisp as an advertisement.

As he reached the stairs a hand caught at him. It belonged to Miss Gibbon, his secretary. Her face was ashen.

"We were looking for you," she said.

Willoughby eyed the crowd around, looking for the other half of the plural pronoun. Perhaps, he decided, she was using the journalistic *we.* "Well," he smiled: "here I am. Anything the matter?"

She went down the stairs with him, her eyes fixed with what seemed unnecessary caution to the steps. "We were wondering about the scripts. The ones you took this morning."

"Oh, yes?"

"They should really be kept in the library."

"I suppose they should, really."

"The cleaning woman said . . ." She cut herself short. They were at the bottom of the stairs, inside the entrance. "I'm glad you're well, Mr. Barnes."

She turned, bumping into a sophomore, and made her way out the door. Willoughby had the impression that a short figure in black accompanied her out, but in the crowd it was hard to be sure.

Odd of her, he reflected, *to track me to the squash courts.* As he walked along the street to his car, he saw her again, very definitely in the company of a short man, setting off in the opposite direction. The man appeared to be holding her up, as though she had had a stroke.

Willoughby threw his racquet into the back seat and climbed into the car. He drove the long way home, past the river and the towering porticos of the business school. When he reached Constitution Avenue it was after eight. He parked the car in the street and let himself into the house.

The stale air swept up around him. *Home,* he thought, with a twinge of hatred.

Directly across the street from Willoughby Barnes' house stood another dwelling in an even greater state of disrepair. A sign tacked to the door read *Roms,* amended with a carat and a second *o.* To the ruin of tilting pillars and sagging roof a riot of vines added a note of peaceful havoc. Whether they were pulling the structure down or holding it up would have been difficult to ascertain, especially in the unreliable moonlight of June.

At the rear of the house, behind windows patched with cardboard, was a kitchen; within the kitchen, an old and leaky gas range; stooped over the range, a nearsighted creature, a woman making tea with tea bags that were not virgin.

The brew prepared, she set it on a tray, with tea cup, milk pitcher, and sugar, and fumbled her way down an ill-lit hallway and up a treacherous flight of stairs. Turning to the third door on the left, that under which a bar of light gleamed, she rapped on the wood.

"Tea," she announced.

"Leave it on the floor," a voice replied.

After she had stumbled back down the stairs the door opened, and Rabbi Blake stooped to lift his tray. He closed the door and took the tea to the table by the window, where he had erected a small telescope. He sipped without tasting and from time to time pressed one eye to the lens, tracking young Mr. Barnes through the windows of his home.

Breeze took Miss Gibbon home, and on the steps of her rooming house he kissed her goodnight on the cheek, like a college boy on a first date.

"He acted as though nothing had happened," Miss Gibbon marveled, though the marvel was clearly not a happy one. "He looked me straight in the eye . . . after *that!*"

"Not surprising," Breeze said softly. "After all, there are mass murderers who claim they'd never hurt a fly."

She looked up at the moon. "I suppose it's exactly the same," she said. "It all depends what you want to believe about yourself."

"It all depends," Breeze agreed, and he kissed her again, on the lips, lightly.

He was sorry about Willoughby Barnes, very sorry. That night, abusing himself in his hotel bed, he dreamt of Millie.

Saturday, June 24

In the morning Breeze brushed his teeth, spat out the taste of a night's salivation, and took a cab over to county records. The same building housed City Sanitation and Public Libraries Management, and it took him three elevators and five corridors to find the little back room with the desk and the sign *Mrs. Forsyth* and the girl, who couldn't have been Mrs. Forsyth, filing her nails.

As he shoved the door shut, the glass rattled, and she laid down her file and put on her eyeglasses to look at him. She was young, she could have been a drum majorette last season, but now she was just a bit too chubby for the uniform. She wore a tight sweater with nothing underneath and the two top buttons open. A tarnished golden cross, the kind that might have come out of a box of Cracker Jacks, caught occasional window light and sent an SOS out of the crevasse. Her glasses were studded with rhinestones, and her eyes were big and wet, green in the irises and pink in the whites. She had been crying.

"Yeah?" The word came out clogged, and she cleared her throat.

"I'd like to look up a death certificate."

"Mrs. Forsyth isn't in yet, can you wait till she gets here?"

Breeze reached for his wallet and waved the badge at her.

"Whose certificate?" she asked.

"The name would be Alicia von Helsing or Alicia Barnes. She died about twenty years ago."

"How do you spell it?"

He had written everything down, and gave her the slip of paper. She looked at it, looked at him, looked at it, looked at a filing cabinet accross the room, and looked at her nails.

"If it's in the closed stacks I can't help you. Mrs. Forsyth has the keys to those."

"Maybe it's not in the closed stacks," Breeze suggested.

She gave him a dirty look, got up and walked carefully— her skirt was so tight it could have ripped with one false move—to the cabinet. She searched, found the drawer marked *B,* and opened it. She flipped through the index cards, looked again at Breeze's bit of paper, flipped back. She went to the *H* drawer and repeated the operation, and then the *V* drawer.

"Not there." She wiped her nose on the sleeve of her sweater.

"What's not where?" Breeze said.

"It's not in the closed stacks."

"Then you can show it to me."

"I guess so." The girl pushed open a door marked PRIVATE AUTHORIZED PERSONNEL ONLY. Breeze followed her down a corridor. The records were kept in steel cages like dangerous animals. She stopped at the end cage and nudged it open with her foot.

"Somewhere in there." She pointed in an evasive sort of way at the rows of leather bindings crowding the shelves from floor to ceiling. Breeze nodded, and she left him alone.

Breeze snapped on the electric light and read down from the top row of bindings until he came to the typed card *Babbington—Bartlett* that someone had wedged under the cellophane window in the binder. He stood up on a chair and reached for the book. The volumes were packed close together, and he practically took the skin off his fingers prying it loose. He climbed down, sat on the chair, and opened the volume on his knees.

There were some Barneses in the book, but none of them were called Alicia. He double-checked, then took down *Hellman—Herscholt*. There were no Helsings. *Vincent—Wilson* yielded no Von Helsing.

Breeze replaced the books, closed the cage, and pushed open the glass door with

PRIVATE\AUTHORIZED PERSONNEL ONLY

gilded across its middle. The girl was sniffling at a postcard. When she saw Breeze, she slipped the postcard under the blotter and put on her glasses.

"You sure you got everybody in there?" he asked her.

"Everybody that's dead, mister," she said. "Everybody that's dead from around here."

"Your records go back to the Second World War?"

She nodded. "And we got them on microfilm back to the Civil War."

"Okay," Breeze said. "Thanks." He called Miss Gibbon from a pay phone in the street. Her voice was husky when she answered, as though she had a sore throat. "If Alicia von Helsing Barnes died in this country," Breeze said, "I'm a monkey's uncle."

Miss Gibbon gave a little gulp before protesting. "But she

died at University Hospital. I showed you the obituary."

"Somebody *said* she died at University Hospital," Breeze corrected.

Her voice was tight. "Wht do you mean, she died somewhere else?"

"Maybe she did, maybe she didn't."

"Inspector, I have a hangover, I'm not up to riddles."

"I don't blame you. Get back to work, and do me a favor, will you? Keep Willoughby Barnes busy. Don't let him go home."

"If I see him I'll try to." She sounded worried. "Could you tell me why?"

"I'm going after that script—*In the Bag*—the one you forgot. I'm also checking a hunch. So don't be surprised if that little old lady you saw in the wheelchair . . ."

"I'd rather not talk about it, Inspector."

"Look, Miss Gibbon, for all I know the wheelchair's a fake, in fact it sounds like a fake. But I have a tingling little suspicion that that little old lady *is* a little old lady."

"I wish I could believe you," she said. "But I guess I just can't believe things any more."

"Look, Miss Gibbon, you had a shock and you had a lot to drink. I don't blame you for feeling the way you do. But something tells me you've got another shock coming, and I wouldn't be surprised if it cleared the air."

"Another shock," she said, "is the last thing I need."

1346 Constitution Avenue was a very off-white house on the edge of the college district. A two-storied, wood-shingled, wood-framed affair, it looked too new to be quaint or historical, too old to be comfortable. Breeze would have put its years at three score and some.

The shingles were cracked, missing in whole patches. The paint was peeling, like the skin off a tramp who had dozed too long in the sun. The shutters, hanging crookedly, lent a giddy touch that was more ominous than rakish, as though the house occasionally went on benders. Breeze paused on the sidewalk, then turned in at the gate.

The fraction of an acre lawn matched the house; it had not seen a mower in months and was beginning to develop a Vidal Sassoon look. The little pathway leading to the front door was weed-infested and more dirt than gravel. Breeze kicked his shoes clean on the step and put his finger to the doorbell.

Inside the house, something rang, faint-hearted and far away.

After two minutes, Breeze was about to turn away when the door opened. A pair of dark glasses stared up at him. "I'd like to speak to Willoughby Barnes," he said.

The old woman smiled. "He won't be back for a while."

"Perhaps I could wait for him?" Breeze suggested.

The smile clicked off. "Not here you can't. I got a whole house to clean."

"I wouldn't be in the way," Breeze promised. He wished she would open the door farther so he could see if she was a big lady bending down or a little lady sitting up.

"Strangers are always in the way." Her voice was gravelly.

"All right, but could I leave a message?"

"If it's short."

"Tell him I came about the young lady."

"What young lady?"

"He'll know."

The old woman's eyes narrowed on him, and Breeze knew he had caught her interest.

"Hold on." She opened the door; she was sitting in a wheel-chair. "You better come in and write it down." She steered him into the hallway and handed him a pad and pencil.

"Nice house," he observed.

"We like it. Now what's all this about a young lady and Will?"

Breeze tilted his head somberly. "If you don't mind, ma'am, it's personal."

"Why couldn't she come herself?"

"That's the trouble . . . I mean that's what make it personal."

The old lady shifted her shawl forward and knotted it under her chin. "You make it sound like this young lady's in traction."

"I'd rather not say, ma'am."

The hallway was dark, crowded with incongruous furnishings, as though Willoughby Barnes, ever mindful of living on the economic precipice, never let any particle of furniture—hand-me-down moose head, fake Moorish ottoman, Swedish-style Yugoslav sofa—escape his household. Either that or he had moved his attic down two flights.

"I think I've got a right to know, considering . . ." There was gravel in her voice again, a whole pitful.

"No soap," Breeze said. The words echoed, and gray silence swallowed the echo.

The old woman looked at him coldly. "In that case I have to get back to my cleaning." She gave the wheel such a vigorous spin that she almost fell out of her chair. Breeze helped her back into the seat. She was far sturdier than she looked. What appeared to be scarves and shawls billowing about an old skeleton had more the feel of solid flesh and muscle.

"You'd better be careful," Breeze said. "It can be dangerous to go cleaning in a wheelchair."

"I don't clean in the wheelchair." Her voice was defiant, almost boastful. "This chair's to get around in, that's all." She flicked a switch on the arm rest. A hum like a hive of subdued bees rose in the neighborhood of the wheels, and slowly, jerkily, the chair began to move in widening, nonconcentric circles. As it brushed the knick-knack-laden table, she pulled the brake. "Takes a load off my heart."

"I'm sorry to hear you have heart trouble."

"Me—heart trouble? Not on your life."

Her denial struck him as a shade too insistent. Since the subject appeared to irritate her, he pursued it. He had found that irritated people were apt to sputter, and sometimes they sputtered the truth.

"All the same," he suggested smarmily, "it wouldn't hurt to have a doctor take a look at you."

"He *did* take a look at me. Fit as a fiddle, he said."

Breeze became even cozier. "Maybe if a *specialist examined* you . . ."

"Sonny, I was in the University Hospital and they electro-cardiogrammed me for *two weeks,* and if Dr. Evan Jones isn't a specialist, well . . ." She seemed to lose her train of thought. "Well, I'm Marie the Queen of Romania."

"Who's Evan Jones?" Breeze asked.

"No one," she said with icy and swift finality. "No one *I* ever heard of."

"What's Romania?"

"Where pastrami comes from." She brought the chair to a stop at a door, deliberated, and thrust the door open with her foot. "Gotta clean this library today. Books attract dust."

Something was off-center, Breeze decided, though here, in the center, he could not tell quite what it was. He usually relied on reflection, retrospection, to distill these interviews; for the moment, it was only an imprecise feeling. Who could say?

The house, he realized.

The house could say. This very room where the old woman whittled away her afternoons dusting and rearranging unread books, this room could have told. For it was here that mother and son had lived, and spoken, and whispered. The floor-boards had bent beneath their footfalls; the bookbindings had felt the touch of their fingers. The plaster had witnessed their movements, muffled their secrets. If rooms remembered, this room knew.

"What a beautiful library," Breeze lied.

"We like it."

"Yes, it's so . . ."

Again, Breeze let the words die. He felt an awareness, a

premonition, perhaps nothing more than a draft on the back of his neck. She had closed the door behind him, and as he stood waiting for her to break the silence, he realized, without looking around, that he was alone.

It was odd, he thought, that she had left him alone.

But that was not all: something began to take shape among the shadows of the bookcases. He squinted and would not have been suprised to make out an actual, animate presence, holding its breath, observing. A pet, perhaps; but it did not move.

And then there was a gurgling, a mournful, constricted attempt at sound, as though something, someone, were trying to call out to him through the very plaster of the walls. "Twenty-four hours," it could have been sighing. Then, "Protection."

He remembered that Kennedy had criticized his tendency to leap at conclusions.

His eye caught a movement, so slight as to be imperceptible, there in the corner, where potted palm and globe of the world cast their blackness across the shelves. More than a movement, a light . . . as though a page in a book had caught fire.

"When emotions are at a peak," the voice said, "so is perspiration."

Breeze recoiled as the door opened behind him. The chair propelled itself over the doorjamb, and the old woman held out a cup of brownish liquid. "Postum." She glanced at the mysterious corner. "Ah, television's warmed up." She wheeled herself to the machine. "I always watch while I clean."

Breeze was disappointed. Somehow, before the picture had come on, it had seemed more than a television set.

"Now, about this young lady." She put her chair into low gear and passed along the shelves waving a feather duster at invisible motes.

"I'm sure you've seen her," he said.

"Will never has anyone to the house." Her voice was stern.

"Not even his girl?"

She seemed to gather herself together. "I never heard of any young lady, unless it's that woman at his office . . . she has a name like a monkey, what is it, Miss Gibbon? She didn't seem like much of a lady to me, and she's certainly not young, and well, frankly, I don't think Will would bother with her. He just wouldn't bother with a woman like that."

"Does he bother with any women?" Breeze asked.

"Not the way you mean. Why should he waste his time?"

"Is it a question of time?" Breeze approached the chair and laid a hand on each arm, staring down at her. "Or is there something else?"

"What do you mean?" she said.

"Maybe he has some other interest? Perhaps he's already engaged, or going steady?"

She loosened the chair from his grip and took a book from the shelf. "Certainly not." She blew dust from the top of the pages. "Will's not engaged, and I don't think he ever took any girl out more than twice—and that was years ago, just after the war, when he was very young. Will's settled down now. He has his career to think about." She slapped the book shut and put it back.

"Or maybe it's just sour grapes," Breeze said.

"I beg your pardon?"

"Maybe no woman would want Willoughby," Breeze smiled. "So he figures, why bother with them."

She dropped a book. "That's a vicious canard. Why, Willoughby Barnes is a very attractive man, attractive to women I mean. A lot of women would give their eyeteeth for a chance to . . ."

Breeze knelt to retrieve the book. It was a scrap album. He wondered if she had dropped it on purpose.

". . . a chance to take care of him." The woman was watching him. "And cook his meals for him. And see that his clothes are cleaned and pressed. A lot of women would be *flattered*."

"I suppose," Breeze nodded. Page one of the album was a

photograph of Alicia von Helsing, her name gold-lettered beneath it. "Did you know Willoughby's mother?" he asked casually.

She resumed her dusting with fresh energy. "A little."

"Tell me about her," Breeze said.

One thing the woman did not require was coaxing. She told him about Alicia von Helsing for two hours, as though there were nothing or no one in this life she loved more.

Greg breezed into the office without knocking. "Mrs. Forsyth," he announced, "you're a doll."

Behind the desk, a droop-lidded matron with tiger-lily eyeshadow and many chins pressed a finger to her lips, indicating that times had changed, things had altered since yesterday; her assistant, a rosy little dumpling, was standing by the file cabinet, appropriately enough, filing her nails.

"Any time, Professor," Mrs. Forsyth said with a stagey formality that seemed to cloak many layers of mischief. The phrase could have had any of several meanings; remembering that there's no time like right now, you should never put off till tomorrow what you can do today, Greg followed her through the door (PRIVATE AUTHORIZED PERSONNEL ONLY) down the corridor to the cage where the records were kept.

"You got what you want?" she asked.

"Yes indeed." Greg handed her the manila envelope. "Two Xerox copies, a little co-ed did them on the library machine."

"Little co-eds can be convenient."

Greg grinned. This gal, he decided, was a swinger. He had never had any grudge against maturity; why, a dynasty of mature women had seen him through some of his leanest days.

Mrs. Forsyth took down the Babbington—Bartlett volume and inserted the death certificate in its proper place. "You're doing a study on Mrs. Barnes, Professor?"

"Confession," he said. "I'm not a professor."

"Ah ha." She poked a finger at his tummy, and he quickly

sucked in. "I didn't think so. You look too . . . ah . . . impetuous."

"Right," he nodded.

"Then . . . ah . . . what are you doing with Mrs. Barnes' death certificate, or shouldn't I ask?"

"Well, it's sort of semi top secret."

"I'm disappointed." She pretended to pout, and pretended charmingly. "Here I thought I was going to be whisked up in some sort of skulduggery."

"It's sort of skulduggery," Greg admitted.

"Now that you've got what you want, what do I get? Not even a slice of the conspiracy?"

"Er," Greg deliberated. He hated to leave a lady disappointed. "I'll tell you a different secret." He leaned toward her and plunged his tongue into her ear.

Mrs. Forsyth whisked herself into the dry and slapped Greg. "Fifteen dollars," she said.

"What?"

"Give me fifteen dollars."

"Mrs. Forsyth, I've never paid for it."

"Fifteen dollars or I report you for unauthorized removal of county documents."

The picture slid into focus. "Ah ha," Greg mumbled. He peeled a day's wage out of his wallet.

Mrs. Forsyth opened the cage door and held it for him, something in her stance suggesting that the quicker he left the premises the better. "Any time," she smiled.

At five thirty Breeze awoke from a nap in his hotel room. Dressing was easy, since he had slept in his clothes. He put on a tie and went into the bathroom to see whether he could postpone shaving. He decided to ignore the gray upper lip and chin; he brushed his teeth, massaged his gums for two minutes, and spat energetically.

Breeze rinsed his mouth twice and combed his hair. He had been needing a haircut for over a month. When he grew too shaggy, he began looking like a raven. Breeze did not like birds.

He walked the three flights to the street. The sky was blue, and early evening was cool. Birds were chattering in the little park, and traffic was stirring. He decided to look for a barber shop; he always thought better with someone fussing over him.

"Haircut, sir?"

"Just a trim."

The chair was as comfortable as a Pullman seat; Breeze settled in and pretended he was on a trip. The barber pulled a lever and he fell backward. The murals on the ceiling reminded him of an opera house. He was in Ravenna, he decided; he had always dreamt of taking a vacation in Italy.

"Nice day."

"Mmm-hmm," Breeze said.

He closed his eyes and mentally reviewed the day's findings. First, no script. That didn't surprise him; it was hidden, he'd have to search. Second, the woman in the chair: she was not paralyzed, not if she could lift her wheelchair up the four front door steps or the three at the back door; and since there was no bathroom on the ground floor, she would have to get upstairs from time to time to pee, unless she carried a chamber potty under her seat; and unless she had an extension on her feather duster, and Breeze doubted that dusters came with extensions, she would have to stand up in her chair to dust the top bookshelves—and the top shelves were dust free. No, she was not paralyzed. Of course, he remembered, she had told him as much. That seemed odd when he thought about it.

"Haven't seen you here before, are you new in town?"

"Mmm-hmm," Breeze said.

The barber pulled another lever, and Breeze sailed up and forward and into a bowl of steaming water. Strong fingers worked over his scalp, and suds stung his eyes, and then he was lifted backward.

"Just a haircut," he said.

"Yes sir."

And she wasn't a next door neighbor, for the simple reason that there was no house next door; just a garage on one side and a grommet factory on the other. He wondered what the hell grommets were. And she wasn't a back door neighbor, because the family that lived in the house behind Willoughby Barnes' had no grannies; in fact, the little boy had told him that the only old woman on the block lived in Barnes' house. Breeze tended to believe the boy, not that the kid looked trustworthy, but the story made sense.

"Staying long?"

"Maybe," Breeze said.

She wasn't paralyzed, and she wasn't a neighbor. Now whether she was old, or a woman, remained to be seen.

There was a stropping sound, and Breeze felt something cold and sharp at the back of his neck. His eyes blinked open; the barber was grinning at him.

"It's very much the style, sir."

"What is?" Breeze said.

"Razor cut."

"Just a trim, I said."

"I can't trim, sir, your hair's wet."

Breeze glared at the barber. Without awaiting his consent, the razor swooped down to begin its work.

Miss Gibbon had to knock a long time on Inspector Breeze's door before it opened. He apologized that the bed was in disorder and his clothes lying around. His hotel room was larger than the place she lived in. There was room to walk, room to be alone in, even room to share with someone else. The inspector gathered up his shirts and socks and began stuffing them into his suitcase.

"I knew something nice was going to happen to me today," he said.

Miss Gibbon sat on his bed, noted the ridges under the

spread where the sheet was bunched up. She supposed he had taken a nap. "How is it coming?" she asked. "Have you found anything?" She took a cigarette from her purse, lit it. She had taken up smoking, though she could not yet inhale.

He closed the suitcase on what was probably an entire week's laundry. He fell into the chair and stretched out his legs. "Didn't do much today."

Nor had she; at noon, when Mr. Barnes hadn't shown up, she had bought a pack of cigarettes from the machine in the corridor. She had spent the rest of the day lighting them, one by one, and puffing them down to the filters. She wondered if the inspector had seen Mr. Barnes; she supposed he would tell her. She hoped he would.

"I got a haircut," he said. "Thought it was about time— I was beginning to look like a student demonstrator."

Miss Gibbon smiled in spite of herself at the idea of Inspector Breeze looking like a student. There were traits in a personality, in a face or a smile, that nothing could obscure, not even long hair, beard, sandals, picket posters. She was grateful to him, to his ordinariness, to his pink cheeks and the clean smell of his hair. If she reached over and touched him, he would be there, solid, like the furniture or the four walls.

"Yes, you were looking a little like a student demonstrator," she agreed.

"I made the mistake of all time and went to a barber down the street—cost me practically five dollars. That's two meals."

Five meals at Miss Gibbon's standard of living.

"This very afternoon I was thinking . . ." He was staring straight at her, the way he had when he kissed her. "How perfect it would be if I were having dinner with a girl this evening."

He paused for a moment, she supposed to permit her to wriggle out, to announce another commitment. She wondered why he thought she had come to his room if not to spend the evening with him. Well, with someone.

"Will you have dinner with me?" he asked. Under his smile he looked as though something depended on her answer.

"You took me out yesterday."

"Then I'll invite you out two nights in a row."

"I'd love to have dinner with you two nights in a row."

"Or three?" he smiled.

A panic shot through Miss Gibbon's stomach. She mastered it, blew out a line of smoke, and tried to look as though she were very relaxed.

"There's a nice-looking restaurant walking distance from here," he said. "Lots of mirrors and chandeliers. Don't know how the food is."

"That sounds fine," Miss Gibbon said.

The street they took was familiar, the walk to the restaurant brought back echoes of other walks; she was afraid that she had eaten in Breeze's place before, a business lunch with someone she had loved. She did not look around the dining room, but watched his feet, brown leather, and hers, green leather, cross the floor. They sat at a table, and she lit another cigarette.

"Do you mind smoke?" she asked.

"Not at all. If you'd like to give me the matches, I'll be your gigolo for the evening. It looks strange, you know, a young lady lighting her own cigarettes."

A *young lady*, he had said. Earlier he had called her a *girl*. She wondered what was wrong with him. She had seen herself every day of her life, and never once had she looked young or like a lady. She didn't dare turn to the mirrored wall to see if some magic had lengthened her nose and straightened her hair and made it dark again and brightened her eyes.

"Then let me look strange," she said. She put the matches back in her purse. They were useful to play with, to turn over in her hand. Like the little wooden hand of a scarecrow whose touch reminded her that she was not alone.

They had cocktails before dinner and wine during the main course. The alcohol relaxed her—it always did, which was why she avoided it. She knew they must have been talking about something, but she could not remember what. With the fourth glass of wine her headache, legacy of the night before, vanished. For an instant she felt cheerful, kooky; she seized the instant.

"Inspector," she said, "talk to me."

"What shall I talk to you about?"

"Anything. I just want to hear you talk."

"I'll tell you about . . . my apartment in New York. Does that interest you?"

"Super," she said. She lit the wrong end of a cigarette, and it tasted awful. Still she smiled.

"Across the way," he said, "there's a tiny park, and my window looks out on a fruit stand. I have a convertible bed and I'm very comfortable in it—I can roll over at night without falling onto the floor, I can stretch out my arms and legs and feel nothing but cool sheets—if I've remembered to get the sheets back from the laundry. There's a fireplace, a desk, a bookcase with all sorts of dull books, given to me by relatives, naturally. A big ugly standing lamp, a horrible-looking but very comfortable chair, my favorite chair in the whole world, in fact."

She had had no idea he could be so talkative. The words were meaningless, but the voice—like a little schoolboy reciting at assembly—fascinated her.

"There's a rug on the floor, but only a little rug, because I enjoy looking at the parquet. It's not good wood, but the pieces are laid in an interesting pattern: diagonally."

"Diagonally," she repeated, to catch the inflection.

"Diagonally," he said. "And I love crossword puzzles."

She decided on another cigarette and took out her matches. He took the book from her, struck a light for her. "Do you live alone?" she asked. She wondered if he knew she wanted to kill herself; of course she wouldn't kill herself, not till vacation.

"Yes."

"Inspector . . ."

"Call me Stan, or Breeze, for God's sake."

"I was hung over when you talked to me this morning. You said something about Alicia von Helsing?"

He nodded.

"You said she didn't die in this country?"

"I said she didn't die."

The waiter brought double brandies, though Miss Gibbon did not remember ordering one. The first sip made her head even clearer. "I was trying to think all day what you meant by that. You don't mean she's still alive?"

"If she didn't die, she'd have to be alive, wouldn't she?"

"But the obituary . . ."

"All that's printed is not truth."

"Why would anyone lie about her death?" she asked.

"Any number of reasons. Maybe she was a Nazi. Maybe she had to disappear. Maybe she's hiding in Willoughby's house, maybe she's that little old lady in the wheelchair. Miss Gibbon, I don't want to raise any false hopes in you . . ."

"No," she agreed. But she could see that he had raised false hopes in himself. He thought Willoughby had spent the day in the office. His whole theory rested snugly and neatly on a falsehood. She wondered whether to be cruel.

"Let's just say there's a little more to that little old lady than what you saw yesterday or what I saw today," the inspector smiled. He was a schoolboy, performing in front of the class. "She seems a bit too familiar with that house to be just a neighbor, and she seems a bit too maternal about Willoughby to be just a housekeeper. I'm checking the hospital records tomorrow."

"Why?"

"To see whether they jibe with the announcement of her death. I have a hunch they'll tell another tale. Just a hunch. Now don't get your hopes up, I don't want to raise any false hopes."

Miss Gibbon smiled, not because his ideas were funny, but because they were so impossible. "Thank you for the brandy," she said. "And dinner."

Walking in the street, he took her hand. His touch did not feel intimate. It gave her far less sensation of life than her book of wooden matches. She hoped she had not left them in the restaurant.

"I think you're wrong," she said.

They were passing through a triangular park, and a breeze was crooning in the trees. "Why?" he asked.

"Maybe I'm just a defeatist. This morning I was thinking, Alicia von Helsing couldn't be sitting in that wheelchair. Why I've called Mr. Barnes' home a hundred times, and no old lady has ever answered. But that's not so: I've never called Mr. Barnes' home, not till yesterday. And I've never gone there. I don't think anyone goes there. So she could have been in the house all the time. Still it seems strange. Don't you think she'd at least hide or something?"

"Do actresses ever hide?" the inspector said.

"I mean if anyone could just barge in and discover her, then she wouldn't stay there, would she?"

"Possibly not."

"And anyway, you're not interested in Mr. Barnes or me or Alicia von Helsing, you're interested in a murder that happened in New York that none of us had anything to do with."

"If none of you had anything to do with it," the inspector said, "I wouldn't be here."

Miss Gibbon broke the hand clasp. The matches were in her purse after all, and he lit the cigarette for her. The smoke filled her; she floated, felt her head rise, buoyed up on a white cloud. She kept the cigarette in the hand he had been holding, so now they walked side by side without touching.

"Do you like me, Inspector?"

"Of course I like you."

"Thank you, Inspector."

"There's a bottle of brandy in my room," he offered.

The word *bottle* made her think of a worm. She pushed the thought aside, but it swam back: a caterpillar, suspended in a transparent jug of formaldehyde.

There was no worm in the bottle he showed her, only an amber water filling it halfway to the top. He poured her a little in a cup, a little too much, and she took a tiny burning sip. She had drunk too many drinks this evening, and she felt her stomach squeeze shut against the liquor.

"Is it that awful?" he asked.

"No, no." She sat on his bed, up by the pillow. He took the chair and poured himself a drink in something that looked like an eyecup. He took it in a single swallow and poured another. He was nervous. He had been all evening. She wondered if it was her fault.

"I've depressed you this evening," she said.

"No you haven't." He turned the eyecup around in his fingers.

She sipped the brandy again, realized that she couldn't take it, and set the little cup on the shelf that hung over the head of the bed, right between his plastic soap tray and his toothbrush. When she had made sure that the cup was not going to fall and turned back toward the room, she saw first that the chair was empty, and then she saw that the inspector was crouched at the bed, one knee raised against the mattress. His hand was in the air, guilty, caught in the act of moving to touch her shoulder. He looked frightened; that seemed incongruous for a policeman.

She closed her eyes and lay back on the pillow.

His hand was on her throat. She rather hoped he would turn out to be a madman, a strangler; that would simplify things. She managed to open her arms, and his face came down beside hers, against hers. The bay rum flooded into her nostrils, and she had the sensation of alcohol eating into her. She felt his heart bumping against his ribs like an angry, imprisoned animal.

"You're beautiful," he said. His voice came from on top of her ear, and it was mostly a brandied warmth. When you heard a voice in one ear, she thought, it was like listening to stereo with one of the earphones dead.

"I'm beautiful," she said.

As he went on she noticed that she felt nothing but that she was reminded of something and of someone she had once loved.

Halfway through the 11 P.M. rerun of *The Slasher* Gwennie's phone rang. When it didn't give up after twenty rings, she saw there was no use and answered. "Gramercy Market," she said in a heavily disguised voice.

"You didn't answer my letter."

"I didn't get any letter," Gwennie lied.

"This is Mo Jackson, at the rest home."

"I know who this is. I happen to be busy at the moment. I'm in conference." It looked like the best part of the movie: the two co-eds had just gone into the shower, while outside, in the shrubbery . . .

"I just called to warn you. Winnie did it again. That minister on the railroad."

Gwennie turned down the volume on the television. "That's not possible," she said.

"Worse yet, he's planning to break out of here some time tomorrow. Just thought I'd warn you."

When Gwennie hung up, she had lost her appetite for television.

Sunday, June 25

FROM THE TROLLEY STOP it was another ten minutes to University Hospital. The stone building was wrapped in a high concrete wall that could easily have contained a penitentiary. But inside the wall were flowerbeds and a surprisingly green lawn. A few students were sitting on benches, perhaps waiting outdoors for their appointments. They did not seem to notice Breeze as he walked along the path. He sensed a quiet about the place that went beyond peacefulness, as though everything, even the birds, had been artificially tranquilized.

Inside the door a secretary in white took his name and asked him if he would care to sit down. He would have preferred to pace, but he sat anyway. Across the corridor a little boy stared at him. He smiled, but the boy did not smile back.

Breeze took a magazine and tried to read it; a woman's magazine about knitting.

"That's him," Breeze heard the little boy say to his mother.

"You mean, that is he," a woman's voice corrected.

"That's him," the little boy repeated. Breeze glanced up and was surprised to find the boy pointing at him.

"That is whom?" the mother asked, refusing to look up.

"He," the boy screamed. Breeze felt his face redden for no reason. He raised the knitting magazine between himself and the boy.

"Dr. Miller will see you now," the secretary said in a manicured voice. Breeze replaced the magazine on the stack, carefully avoiding the little boy's eyes, and followed her.

He arrived at a door with Dr. Miller's name on it, knocked, and when there was no reply, went in. His first impression was of a green room—no bookcases, no window curtains—green rubber-cushioned chairs and a green rubber rug. A plump, unsmiling man sat behind a greenish formica desk and chewed the rubber eraser of a pencil. A sheath of papers was spread on the blotter before him, and he said, "Good afternoon, Mr. Breeze, won't you sit down?" without looking directly at Breeze. "Graduate student?"

"I'm not with the university." Breeze sat.

"Ah?" The doctor seemed interested.

Breeze laid his wallet on the desk. The doctor glanced at the badge. "How can I help?" he asked.

"I'd like information on a patient," Breeze said. "Alicia von Helsing. I believe she was treated here for heart trouble some time ago."

"What information would you like?"

"I'd like to see the records."

"Ah." The doctor picked up his telephone. "Records," he said; his voice was flat, as though he were giving instructions to a machine. "Alicia von Helsing." He covered the receiver with his hand. "Who was the physician?"

"Evan Jones."

The doctor uncovered the receiver. "Dr. Evan Jones. Thank you." He hung up and smiled at Breeze. "Retrieval is faster when we have two or more factors in the parameter."

Breeze was not certain he followed, but he nodded. In a moment there was a light rapping on the door—Beethoven's Fifth—and a boy in white pushed a supermarket cart into the office. He handed the doctor a manila folder.

"Now, let's see." The doctor opened the folder and flipped pages. "What precisely did you want to know about Miss von Helsing and her doctor?"

"Everything."

The doctor, lips pursed into a prune, nodded, skimming what looked like charts and small print. "In a word, angina." He shoved the folder across the desk.

"Angina?" Breeze asked.

"Seven years ago. Old fellow, not surprising. Health service was understaffed then, he probably worked a sixteen-hour shift till the day he died."

"I was wondering about Miss von Helsing."

"Massive blood clot," the doctor said. "June fourteenth it looked like pneumonia, June fifteenth it looked like cancer of the lymph. Diseases are chameleons, Inspector, they're like very clever criminals. Imagine, they were running cancer tests while the clot was heading straight for her brain."

"I don't understand," Breeze apologized.

"She died," the doctor said. "June sixteenth, 1947. Sad business. She was a Nazi, wasn't she?"

"I don't know." Breeze reached for the report. "Could I borrow one of these pages?"

"Which page?" the doctor asked, as though it made a difference.

"The description of her death." Breeze removed the sheet from the folder.

"You're . . . ah . . . investigating Miss von Helsing?"

"Indirectly." Breeze pondered, with some uneasiness, her death. "Do you know psychiatry, Doctor?"

"In a pop sort of way."

"I'd like to ask you about something . . . someone. Off the record."

"Certainly." The doctor leaned back comfortably in his chair, hands clasped over his stomach.

"Imagine the son of a famous woman, a celebrity."

The doctor closed his eyes. "I'm imagining."

"She lives in Europe, he lives in the United States."

"Broken family," the doctor observed.

"Not really. She has a career . . . she's an actress. He has to go to school, so his father has brought him home. All he knows of his mother is the letters and postcards she sends him."

"Absence," the doctor remarked, "makes the heart grow fonder. Does he idealize this woman, worship her?"

"Maybe," Breeze said. "Until she comes home and moves into the house with him. In a few months his father dies."

"Oedipus," the doctor nodded. "Agamemnon—Clytemnestra."

"Not that she has anything to do with his father's death . . . so far as we know. On the other hand, it turns out that she *is* a criminal. Her career was a front. Now, assuming her crimes were public knowledge, I want you to tell me how the boy would react."

The doctor unclasped his hands and began softly tapping his pencil against the blotter. "What do you mean, *react?*"

"Well, does he have mixed feelings? Does his old love for his mother survive side by side with his hatred?"

"Why on earth should he hate her?"

"Assuming he did. Is it possible he'd turn into a . . . you know . . . split personality?"

The doctor smiled. "You mean *schizophrenia?* Lordy me, I haven't heard *that* word since Forty-three.

"Assuming the groundwork for schizophrenia is there, when his mother dies . . ."

"He succumbs to guilt feelings for having hated her."

Breeze nodded.

"In fact . . ." The doctor's eyes were shut again, as though he were seeing it. "Half of him refuses to accept the fact of her death. He creates a fantasy that she's still alive. He begins acting out her role, even wearing her clothes."

Breeze nodded again.

The doctor's face lit up with an inspiration. "And he even takes a *knife* or a *hatchet* or something and cuts up a few of the people who offend the mother-half of him."

"That's very close," Breeze admitted. "I'm not certain in what way the victims offended his mother-half."

"Oh, that's easy," the doctor said. "The dead mother had a criminal past. These victims were her accomplices. The son is afraid they'll give Mumsy away—spoil her reputation."

Breeze snapped his fingers. It fitted. "Doctor, do you know of a case like this?"

"No," the doctor said, "but I saw the movie. And, psychiatrically speaking, it's a load of horse-guano."

Breeze returned the folder.

"You'll take care of that page, won't you Inspector? We haven't microfilmed that year."

"The certificate says blood clot, complicated by cancer and pneumonia. But the records say . . . well, see for yourself."

His newest conquest, Miss Owen from the hospital, craned her head at the document and almost lost her nursing cap. "The record doesn't say anything," she observed, her brown eyes large with apology. She sipped her root beer through the candy-striped straw, thumb and forefinger pressed gently around the flow. "Maybe a page is missing."

"I doubt it," Greg said. "See the signature?" He licked the hot fudge off his spoon and tapped it against the Xeroxed death certificate. "Dr. Evan Jones' signature." He tapped the spoon against the little stack of purloined papers. "Dr. Jones' hospital records, June, 1947. Same signature, same doctor, right?"

"Right," Miss Owen nodded. A policeman strolled into the soda fountain, and she threw a paper napkin over the documents.

"It's okay," Greg promised, his hand touching hers under the napkin.

"I just don't want to get fired again," she said. "It'd kill my mother." The policeman loudly ordered a black and white malted and took a seat at the counter; he spun on the stool, then settled down with his back toward them, a revolver handle jutting up from his hip. "I shouldn't have taken the papers," Miss Owen said. She sucked miserably at her root beer. The straw gave a slurp of finality.

"You need another one of those." Greg nodded to the waitress.

The second root beer seemed to calm Miss Owen, and when the policeman left she was able to smile. "These records aren't on microfilm yet," she apologized. "They're kind of valuable. In fact I had to lie to get them."

"I know," Greg smiled back. "You're a great gal Friday. And you've helped me uncover a little homicide."

She must have taken some root beer into her lungs, because she began coughing. Greg laid the relevant documents side by side for her inspection. This time he got fudge on the death certificate.

"Dr. Jones filled in a death certificate for the county, but he didn't keep a record of Alicia von Helsing Barnes' death for the hospital. Doesn't that seem a wee bit peculiar?"

She swallowed; her face was white. "It seems against the law."

"I suspect that Dr. Jones was very much against the law in his treatment of Mrs. Barnes."

"Wait a minute, wait a minute." Miss Owen snapped her fingers. "The death certificate's a fake, she didn't die."

"The death certificate's a fake," Greg corrected, "and she *did* die."

"You mean she didn't die the way he said?"

"Right." Greg spooned the last marshmallow and fudge out

of the dish and let it dissolve on his tongue. "That blood clot and cancer and pneumonia crap might go down with the politicians, but no first-month medical student would swallow it. Solution to Dr. Jones' dilemma: omit Mrs. Barnes from the hospital records. No record, no embarrassment."

Miss Owen shuddered. "You make it sound like she was murdered or something."

Greg reached for the check.

"Who did it?" Miss Owen asked. "Dr. Jones?"

"Let's say that whoever did it, Dr. Jones lent a professional helping hand." Greg replaced the records in their folder. "Now why don't you just sneak these back where they came from, all right?"

Miss Owen looked a little let down. Greg leaned across the table, planted a kiss on her sweet little nose, and left a twenty-cent tip.

It wasn't so much that Breeze wanted the script; he needed another hour in that house, alone. But Miss Gibbon was the kind of woman who needed explanations, and so he told her he was going back to find the missing script.

"It has a soft green cover," she said. "Gilt lettering, about eight by twelve."

"Probably upstairs," he said. "In the bedroom."

"But what if he . . . she catches you?"

"Not a chance. You're going to stall Willoughby here at the office. If he leaves, you telephone the house—ring three times, hang up, then ring again—so I'll know it's you. That'll give me time to get out."

"I don't like this," Miss Gibbon said. "It doesn't seem fair, breaking in."

"It'd take a week to get a search warrant—and I'd just as soon keep the local police out of this," Breeze said. "Relax, there won't be any problem. I'm very good with a penknife."

The screen door was locked. Breeze used his penknife to lift the latch. The blade split the wood, and he pushed the bits back into place, just in case anyone had sharp eyes.

The kitchen was dark. A raw roast of beef was sitting on the table, bleeding onto a sheet of waxed paper. A driblet of blood had inched its way down the table leg toward the linoleum. There were vegetables in the sink, soaking in a puddle of warmish water. Breeze tiptoed into the hallway.

The house was silent. He passed the deserted library, the living room, the dining room. At the foot of the stairs he felt a vibration in the air, regular and recurrent, like the sound of an air conditioner. He hesitated, a foot on the first step, and after a sniff decided to take the risk and let the devil take the consequences.

The first room at the top of the stairs must have been Willoughby's.

It was a cheerful room, considering the condition and character of the house. Willoughby—or someone—had decorated the leak-stained walls and pennants, plaques, school photos, pin-ups of movie stars and singing groups, travel posters, and record jackets. The bookcase was filled with knick-knacks that must have dated back to Willoughby's—or someone's—childhood: some tattered but obviously beloved dolls, to count the stitches and bandages that had been lavished on them, and a sprinkling of school books and paperbacks. The bed and overstuffed chair were piled with clothes, suggesting either that the cleaning woman had not done her duty, or that Willoughby threw off his togs at night and got into the first thing he stumbled over in the morning.

On the table was a phonograph, one of those ingenious ersatz leather units that sell for forty dollars and develop pitch wobble within two hours, never to be the same again. A rock and roll record was spinning off-center on the turntable, the needle trapped in the last groove. Willoughby or someone must have forgotten to turn the machine off; Breeze did not disturb it.

The phonograph shared the table top with a framed photo of Alicia von Helsing in operetta regalia, a Nordic sugar-plum fairy with idiot blue eyes and a corrosively sweet smile. Breeze studied her a moment and was certain that he would not have enjoyed her performances. He sifted through the articles in the bookcase, found no green script, then on a hunch searched Willoughby's bedclothes, mattress, and pillow. Plenty of stains, but no script.

A bell rang.

Breeze dropped the pillow and followed the sound across the hallway into another bedroom. The walls were papered with yellowed views of Venice, and a crazy quilt lay smooth but askew on the bed. At the second ring he located the source of the noise: a lime-chiffon extension telephone on the bedside table. It rang a third time and lapsed into silence.

The house seemed to be holding its breath, and when the phone rang again, treble and coquettish, he felt an exhalation in the air about him. He snatched up the receiver and pressed it to his ear.

"I think he caught on." The tremble could have been in the wires rather than in her voice. "He asked me why I was working in the office on Sunday. He always works Sundays, but I never do. So I guess it looked funny."

"Goodness yes, very funny," the phone said in a distinctly different voice, a sort of androgynous rasp. Breeze frowned as the receiver continued to talk to itself.

"The phone here was tied up, so I couldn't get to you right away. He took a taxi. He'll be arriving any minute, he might even be there now."

"You mean Willoughby," the phone said.

"Yes." Miss Gibbon sounded a little baffled. "Willoughby."

"Good. I'll put the kettle on. Thank you so much." There was a click. Breeze squinted his ear and was certain he caught a sound in the downstairs hallway: a telephone replaced in its cradle and the faint whirring of a motor. He lowered the receiver as quietly as he could, tiptoed to the door, and peered down the stairs.

He glimpsed a shadow sliding off the front door, receding

toward the floor and out of sight. A swinging door banged open, and in the kitchen water ricocheted in a kettle.

He calculated at least ninety seconds for the old woman to put the tea on—enough time for him to scoot down the stairs and creep out the front door. He had taken three steps when he heard footfalls.

He hesitated, listened. The silence seemed a trifle ominous, and he decided to retreat. He crept back to the bedroom. The footsteps followed, and he found himself smiling, faintly amazed, at the rapidity and lightness of the old woman's feet.

It was only after he had backed into the doorway that he realized the stupidity of his position. If she were coming upstairs, it was almost certainly to go to her own room, precisely where he now stood. He considered hiding behind the door, or in the closet, or in the bathroom.

As though wondering whether or not to enter the room, the feet paused outside the doorway, giving the inspector time to duck down beneath the bed. He squeezed beneath the box mattress, wincing as his elbows dislodged a dust storm. His fingers caught his nose in time to stifle a sneeze.

In a mounting agony of suppressed coughs, he peered to the side; the unevenly hung quilt afforded a wavering slit of a view toward the door. His stalker entered—a zebra-striped cat with a bulging waistline which dragged on the carpet. The animal sniffed, then waddled toward the bed and thrust its eyes, brighter than jaundice, against Breeze's. He tried to push it away, but the cat planted its claw on his hand. At that moment a pair of slippered feet shuffled into the room.

"Now now Tasha," an old voice croaked, and the animal waddled to its mistress. A gloved hand dipped into view and lifted the cat out of sight. There was a squeal—it could have been human or feline—and an enormous pair of Italian sunglasses fell to the floor. Breeze twisted to remove himself from the old lady's sightline.

His shoulder hit an obstruction, and looking to the side, he saw two books lying by the leg of the bed, placed there

perhaps for easy reach—though he remembered seeing a bedside table with nothing on it but a phone—or perhaps, hidden
there.

Inching forward like a nascent fetus, he closed one eye
and brought the bindings into focus. The top book, a small
one, was Kahlil Gibran's *The Prophet*. The other, with no
title on the binding, had a soft green cover.

Careful not to grunt, Breeze hunched onto one shoulder,
slid *The Prophet* aside, and since he seemed to be engaged
in a waiting contest with the old lady, began studying the
green book. The title, *Eli College Class of 1947, Vigintennial
Report 1967*, indicated that the work was probably not a musical. He opened it nevertheless.

A blue slouch hat, blue elbow-length gloves, and a blue
scarf drifted to the rug like props in a striptease. He glanced
at them, decided not to consider their implication, and read.
An item caught his random eye:

Byron, James Evarts, 111: English Horn Specialist. Office
address, Hotel Esmeralda, 13 Rue du Dragon, Paris VI, France.
Graduated in June, 1947, I took a post in one of New York's
larger advertising agencies. After several years of this I left to
inscribe myself at the Peabody Conservatory of Music in Balti-
more, Maryland. Taking a summer of study abroad I came to
France in May, 1958, and have been here ever since. As of April,
1961, I confined my too-crowded schedule of musical pursuits to
the study of the oboe, but decided to specialize on the rarer but
inaptly named English horn, and am now the student of a capable
and very famous teacher. As for the condition of the country, not
wishing to endorse the cause of either political fringe, is there not
more than sufficient proof of its decline in the eyes and attitudes
toward us of the civilized world?

Breeze wondered. He turned his eyes from the report in
time to see one foot step out of its enormous slipper; the other
foot followed suit, and both stood in white ankle-length athletic socks. With a skill reminiscent of the soccer field, the left
foot kicked first one, then the other slipper across the room.

From the tinkle of little bottles it sounded as though they had fallen on the dressing table.

Silence again. Breeze returned to the report, skipping over several pages.

Fields, Ferdinand Euclid, priest. Home address, Paris house, Saint Mark's Episcopal Church, Syosset, New York.

Apart from administering the sacraments to the Episcopal and other wildlife population of the parish, I pass the residue of my time battling deacons, acolytes, archbishops, and the yentas of the altar guild. These bouts distract me from anxieties consequent to sharing a house with (a) Father Justin, (b) poltergeists, and (c) squirrels with snowshoes who live in the attic. I would greatly appreciate correspondence from a qualified exorcist. Last month, upon Father J's retirement, I became head, i.e., Rector, of Saint Mark's.

The last sentence was circled in red, with the note *N.B.* penciled in the margin. Breeze scratched his chin. His eyes drifted to the side in time to catch a blue blouse as it fluttered to the floor. Hoping she was not preparing for a nap, he skipped another handful of pages.

Kincaid, Francis Griffes, 111, Lawyer. Home address, 2536 Veronica Lane, Butte, Montana. Married, Mitzi Bukopfzer, June 2, 1947.

I entered Law School in September, 1947, and graduated a bachelor of law though no longer a bachelor in 1950. I then returned to Butte, and was admitted to the Montana State Bar in September, 1950. In July, 1950, I became associated with the firm of Lawrence and Mills, where I still am. In the fall of 1953 I was one of three counsels appointed to defend a nationally famous killer on eight counts of first degree murder. We were successful in obtaining a change of venue. In April, 1956, I was elected president of the Young Democratic Club of Patterson County. In November I ran as candidate for State Representative, placing third out of eleven Democrats in a county where no Democratic legislator has been elected since 1950. I was assistant to the coordinator of the Kennedy for President Campaign in Montana, and was fortunate enough to be among those who personally greeted Vice President Lyndon B. Johnson on his trip to Butte. I am now Regional Director of the College Young Democratic Clubs in America. My athletic drives are channeled into brisk noon-hour squash sessions at the local YMCA.

A blue skirt dropped to the rug, leaving a pair of sturdy legs encased in athletic shorts. Breeze pursed his lips. The cat jumped to the floor and stared at him balefully. He licked his fingertip, ignored the animal, and on a hunch turned to the L's.

Langsam, Bertram Amadeus, Musicologist. Office Address, School of Music, Manhattan University, New York, N.Y. 10043.

Little to report of interest in the last twenty years. As this report goes to press I am about to be appointed head of the Musicological Department of the School of Music of Manhattan University, a post I shall assume next week. A pleasant enough task, coupled with a raise in pay!

The entire article was circled in red and an arrow pointed to the letters in the margin, *N.B.*

"Come on Tasha," the voice rasped, "time for a walkie walkie!"

But Tasha, disobedient and perverse, wandered over to Breeze and parked her rear three inches from his face; intentionally, he felt.

"Come on, kitty," the voice coaxed.

Tasha dug her claw into the rug.

"Attagirl, Tash."

A thumb almost dislodged Breeze's left eyeball as a hand dove down and grabbed the cat. Tasha fought, freed herself, and dodged under the bed. Breeze drew his legs up into a ball and wished he were invisible.

"Here girlie, here we go."

A face appeared at the edge of the quilt. The brown hair and chubby cheeks were not those of a gaunt old lady; they were not even those of a woman.

"Come on, baby." The hands whisked Tasha away, and the face disappeared.

Breeze did not think Willoughby Barnes had seen him. All the same, he waited till the front door slammed before he crawled out from under the bed.

"What a busy little girl, you never take a rest, not even on Sunday?"

Again, Miss Gibbon did not know how long the blond man with the mustard-stained vest had been standing in the doorway. He was smiling; she was unable to return the smile.

"Hi," he said, "remember me?" He sauntered in and took a seat just as he had before. "I don't suppose that script has turned up yet?"

"*In the Bag?*" Miss Gibbon shook her head. She had the oddest feeling—a certainty, really, that he was annoyed to find her there on a Sunday; he had exepcted to break into a deserted office and have his way with the archives.

He was scratching his chin. "Do you have any posters from the show?"

"We ought to," she said coldly.

"Could you let me see one?"

Miss Gibbon felt instinctively that it was the wrong thing to do, but she could think of no reason to refuse him; after all, it was her job to show people the memorabilia they wanted. She went to the file and located the poster for him.

He spent several minutes cluck-clucking over it, copying down names and credits in a little pocket notebook. After he had gone, she studied the poster. She wrote down the names of the composer, the lyricist, and the librettist, and then she went to the cross-reference file to see if there was any information on them.

"Greg?" Gillian's voice was staticky. "What a surprise, you're not calling collect."

"Forgot to," he said. He wedged the pay-phone door shut

against the clanging of a streetcar. "Get a pencil and write
down this name: *J. Whittaker Duchamp.* He's a musical comedy lyricist, bumming around New York. I want to meet
him."

"Do I have to give a party for him?"

"Or get me invited to one of his."

"Will do. Who the hell is he?"

"He seems to be the only living lead we have. And he may
not be that for long."

"Sounds like fun," she said. "I'll get cracking."

Breeze pushed the buzzer a third time. Miss Gibbon came
to the rooming house door in her bathrobe. She smelled clean
and fresh, as though she had just come from a bath, and she
was chewing an apple. She looked Breeze in the eye.

"I was right," she said. "Everything I told you was right,
wasn't it. Everything I was afraid of."

Breeze nodded.

"You don't need to say anything," she said. "I knew it anyway."

"Can't we go to your room?" he asked.

It was a small room, beautifully neat. She couldn't have
made much spending money off that job at the club, but still
there was a vase of fresh roses on the table. The sofa had already been turned into a single bed, and a book was open
on the pillow, Kahlil Gibran's *The Prophet.*

"I have a feeling we're not going to find that script," Breeze
said. He closed the door behind him.

She sat down on the edge of the bed and stared bleakly
across the room. "Why not?"

"Because the murderer needs it for a prompt-book. Each
time he kills someone he's playing a role the victim played in
the original show." He took her hand and interlocked fingers.
"Who was the third man—the lyricist?"

"Whittaker Duchamp," she said in a monotone. Her hand
was limp.

"Where's he living?"

"New York."

He kissed her again, lightly, this time on the lips. "What doing?"

"Writing shows. At least the last thing we have on him in the files says he's writing shows."

"Duchamp played a role in *In the Bag*, didn't he?"

"He was in the chorus." She sighed. "He was up here, you know. He made the squash date with Mr. Barnes."

"Interesting," Breeze said. They were sitting on the bed, and she did not move when he slipped an arm around her. She did not even seem to notice.

"That man came to the office again," she said in a glazed voice.

"Who's that?" Breeze asked.

"The biographer—the one who's working on Bertram Langsam's life story. He wanted to see the script: *In the Bag*."

"Figures."

"He looked at a poster and left. Do you think he's really a biographer?"

"Why not?"

"I don't know. Something . . ."

Nor did Miss Gibbon object when Breeze began making love to her.

On the other hand, she showed no particular enthusiasm, either.

Breeze caught the 3 A.M. milk train to New York and got back to his apartment in time for a phone call from Kennedy. He had almost forgotten the voice.

"Where the hell have you been for three days, Breeze?"

"Out of town, sir."

"I'd appreciate your keeping me informed. I'd also like to know who authorized your going out of town?"

"I was following a lead."

"I don't like things going on behind my back. I expect to

be informed and treated with a certain degree of respect. I'm
not an old fool, you know."

"I know."

"Well stop treating me like one. I don't like being told I'm
a washed-up old has-been."

"You said it, sir, not me."

"What was that, Breeze?"

"Nothing, sir."

"Didn't sound like nothing to me. So help me Breeze, if
you don't wrap this up this week, you're off the force . . .
you hear me?"

"I hear you."

"Well, what are you going to do about it?"

"I'll wrap it up, sir. And tie a pink bow on it for you."

As if the movie on television wasn't terrifying enough, there
was a crash in the downstairs hallway. Gwennie turned down
the sound. "Emelina?" she called. "Are you all right?"

There was no answer, and the movie was pausing for a deodorant commercial, so Gwennie went investigating. From the
top of the stairs she could see that the hall table was smashed,
caved in as though someone had struck it with an ax. Gwennie
gave a little gasp and hurried, her feet clad only in slippers,
down the steps. She stooped to gather up the bits of broken
cup. She recognized the pattern of little roses and regretfully
dropped the bits into the pocket of her housegown; she could
try to glue them together some rainy afternoon.

"Emelina," Gwennie called, "what has happened?"

The trail of china bits led through the dining room. Gwennie stooped to study them, sighed as she remembered flora'd
saucers and fauna'd cups, imitation-Dresden nymphs and
shepherds. They were beyond repair. She opened the door to
the pantry and dropped the pieces into the wastebasket. They
rained like sleet against the metal.

Gwennie took a small glass from the sideboard and poured
herself a wee bit of vodka from the decanter. She sipped,

then turned at a whirring sound in the kitchen. It sounded
as though Emelina might be whipping up mayonnaise. The
vodka warmed Gwennie's throat, her stomach, her mind and
soul. Something inside her was happier . . . calmer . . . less
perturbable.

"Emelina?" she called.

But the whirring sound was too loud. Gwennie poured herself a second glass and took it in two swallows. For an instant
she felt almost enthusiastic. It was good being alive, sipping
vodka, listening to your maid whip up mayonnaise. Except . . .

Gwennie took her glass, empty, into the kitchen. There was
no eggbeater, there was no mayonnaise. The rotary knife-
sharpener was clamped to the edge of the table. Gwennie
touched the stone. It was burning hot. She almost dropped
her glass.

"Emelina!"

She heard a banging and saw that the wind was slamming
the kitchen door. Luckily her heart slowed down after the
initial thump. She never knew whether her heart thumped
because she was scared or whether she was scared because
her heart thumped. The fright and the thump always came
simultaneously.

"Emelina!" she called, angry now. The lights flickered, and
abruptly the kitchen was dark. The television set upstairs faded
with a sputter into silence. She gripped the edge of the table
and fumbled in the drawer for the flashlight.

The beam wavered, but it guided her to Emelina's door.
She knocked, then went in. The beam scanned the room: one
bed in disorder; tacky nightgown thrown across the chair;
stockings heaped on the floor; a mountain of grayed and
yellowed blouses, rotted with deodorant, rising beside the
chest of drawers; a bulletin board of clipped-out photographs
of athletes, weight lifters, and Marilyn Monroe nailed—yes
nailed—to the closet door.

"Of all the . . . " Gwennie muttered.

She went into the bathroom. Towel on floor. Talcum powder

on bathmat. Shower dripping. Toothpaste tube without top, paste oozing onto the glass shelf. Gwennie glanced into the medicine cabinet to see what sort of tranquilizers Emelina took. She found a roll of dental floss, an aerosol of contraceptive foam, and a stick of chewing gum.

"Will you turn the goddamned electricity back on?" Gwennie shrieked.

No one answered. She tried to remember where the main switch was, for clearly the whole thing was a main switch job, calculated to give her a heart attack. Just the sort of thing that happened in that nasty French movie to that sweet Vera Clouzot . . .

The flashlight showed up cracks in the plaster and floor that Gwennie had never seen before. She went up the back stairs to the second landing and kicked open the door to the hall. The window at the far end outlined four squares of cloudy night sky.

"Who is there?" Gwennie enunciated. Not that she had heard anyone; but it was best to suggest that she was aware of whoever it was, whatever it was.

At that moment the heavens burst open with the sound of a firecracker, and rain splattered across the roof like machine-gun bullets. Gwennie dropped the flashlight.

She heard it roll away from her. She felt her way to the front stairs. She crouched and probed each step. The light was resting on the fifth. It wouldn't work when she pushed the button.

"Damn."

She wanted to hurl the flashlight through a window. But she told herself to be rational.

"Somebody is up to some hanky-panky."

She made a face in the dark. She couldn't think of anyone but Emelina, and why should Emelina play tricks on her? What had she ever done to Emelina except pay her a good salary and put up with her dry roast beef? Gwennie reviewed her life and tried to think what she had ever done to anyone. Very little in fact that was good or bad. She had always tended to leave people alone.

But in the dark of the upstairs hall, by the anemic light of a stormy night sky, the unlikely seemed more likely than ever. Gwennie's heart thumped at the thought.

"Be quiet!" she told it.

She decided that she would be safest in her own bedroom. She tiptoed down the hall and pushed open the door, wondering who had closed it in the first place. The room was dark. She could see nothing but the outline of a far window cut in half by the bedpost. She inched toward the bed, careful not to bump any tables or chairs.

The phone rang.

Gwennie scratched her nose with the glass end of the flashlight. She picked up the receiver.

"He's escaped."

"I beg your pardon?" Gwennie said.

"This is Mo Jackson, at the rest home."

"Yes, Mr. Jackson."

"I just called to warn you, Winnie is loose."

"It's not possible," Gwennie said. Though, with the electricity off, the impossible looked more possible than ever.

"He said something peculiar yesterday."

Gwennie sat on the bed. "I don't think I want to hear it."

"He said he was warmed up and ready to go for the jackpot."

"You're joking," Gwennie said.

"Uh uh. *He* might have been joking, I'm not."

"What jackpot?" Gwennie said.

"Good-bye." Mo Jackson was gone.

Gwennie double-locked her bedroom door. She turned back the bed covers and slid her feet between the sheets. Her toes struck something wooden. She stiffened. No, she refused to believe that there was a foreign body in her bed. She explored the thing with her foot. It was about three feet long and seemed to have a sharp, cold, metallic head.

"Winnie," Gwennie said. "Winnie, are you in this room?"

Monday, June 26

AT 10 A.M. Breeze was strolling to work through the park. The fountain had not yet been turned on; yesterday's overflow was still seeping through the cracks in the cement pond, and a child's plastic sailboat had run aground on Neptune's stomach. Three dozing drunks, daytime shift, occupied the benches in the playground that were supposed to be reserved for children and their escorts. Breeze recognized two of them, the regulars. A newspaper hid the face of the third.

NO LEADS IN AXINGS, the headline blared in three-inch black letters, but the hand that lay across the headline was clean, no black under the nails. The fingers were young, not yet arthritic; the brown suit was rumpled, but not filthy. Ordinarily Breeze would have envied the hoboes; the only souls with a franker stance against life were the suicides. Breeze had from time to time thought he would like to have their courage; and their height.

But today he was an hour late and cheerful. He struck his finger into the granite mouth of the lion crouched before the public library. Someone had chalked on the pedestal the word *stoned,* and a rumpled, home-rolled cigarette drooped from between the sculpted incisors. Breeze flicked it out, sniffed his fingers, and thought he smelled something illegal.

As he pushed through the swinging doors of the station the day sergeant, a big redheaded fellow, smiled at him and asked what was new.

"The lions at the public library are on pot," Breeze said. The sergeant's frown followed him all the way down to his office.

Kluski was standing by the window, tapping his glasses against his palm. "Kennedy wants you," he said.

"Yeah?" Breeze leafed through the advertising circulars and most-wanted criminals in the morning mail.

"By the way," Kluski's face was flushed with accomplishment, "I located J. Whittaker Duchamp. The Securities and Exchange Commission has a fat file on him."

"What's he done?" Breeze asked.

"Fraud. Him and his producer go around raising money for musicals that never come off. Matter of fact he's throwing an audition tonight and another this Wednesday."

The phone on the desk rang.

"That's Kennedy," Kluski warned.

Breeze let it ring four times more. "Listen, you half-pint flatfoot," Kennedy croaked.

"I'm all ears."

"If you don't get this bag off my back you're going to rue the day they waived the five-foot eight minimum for cops. Get down to my office."

Breeze hung up and took his time arranging the mail into

a neat little pile. "Kluski," he said, "get me the address of that J. Whittaker Duchamp audition Wednesday."

Breeze entered without knocking. Kennedy was hunched in his chair staring with an envious expression at his desk-top Laocoon. Gwennie MacAndrew, barely visible under the shade of a white Floradora hat, was sitting on the metal stool usually reserved for recalcitrant suspects. There was nothing recalcitrant in the way she was talking to the police chief.

"I think you ought to know something about those murders." Her glance swiveled from Kennedy to Breeze. Her eyes had the fiendish sparkle of those models in subway posters pushing nonprescription tranquilizers.

Big-jowled and probably hung over, a nerve twitching under the right lens of his dark glasses, Kennedy flashed a grimace at Breeze. "Like what," he growled.

"In the first place," Mrs. MacAndrew stated, "Bertram Langsam was not murdered on the squash court at the Eli Club. He was murdered in the Yale Club, and the pieces were brought over in a brown paper bag."

Kennedy emptied an envelope of white powder into a cup of water and stirred, then swallowed the foam in a gulp. Something like an epileptic froth remained clinging to his lips. "Okay, you got that, Breeze? Thanks a lot, ma'am." Slowly, with effort, Kennedy rose from his desk. He must have weighed close to three hundred pounds.

"I'm not through," she said. "I know who killed Langsam and Father Fields."

Kennedy fell back into his seat and rested his forehead in his palm. "You listening, Breeze?"

Breeze nodded.

"My husband killed them," Gwennie MacAndrew said.

Kennedy made a face as though he had foreseen as much. "Is that the husband in the oxygen tent?"

"Mr. Kennedy, there are no locks on those tents." Mrs. Mac-

Andrew raised the brim of her hat, her eyes taking a direct bead on his. "And if it's proof you want . . ."

"A little proof never hurt," Breeze said.

"I have plenty," she said. "You see, last night my husband tried to murder me. He's insane."

After the meeting Breeze phoned Millie Gibbon at her office. "Can you do me a favor?" he asked her.

The voice had a hard edge, as though she had been reconsidering a few things. "All right," she said.

"I want you to put out a press release to the wire services and all the papers. You're going to say that J. Whittaker Duchamp has just been made head of something—I don't care what—some organization, some club, anything. Just make it big."

"How about theatrical music division of the American Society of Composers, Recording Artists, and Publishers?"

"Great. And be sure you use the word *head.*"

"*Head.* All right."

"And mention that Duchamp's auditioning a show this Wednesday at the Pocket Theater on Fourteenth Street."

"His producer sent us a leaflet about that; I'll write it up in the release. Anything else?"

"One thing. Don't forget, Miss Gibbon—I love you."

She must have hung up without hearing him. Breeze stared at the mute black receiver; his stomach went sickeningly empty.

Rabbi Blake came across the item in the evening paper quite by accident. He had been about to fold the *Oxford Pilot* and drop it into the waste-basket beneath the table when his eye was caught by a grinning face barely recognizable in the photogravure. He read through the accompanying squib rapidly, then read it a second time more carefully.

"ASCRAP," he wondered. "What the hell is ASCRAP? A pill?"

He clipped out the article and folded it into his wallet. After watching the house across the street, counting the comings and goings and faces, he was certain, altogether certain of himself. There was little need to spy in windows when he could now see two days into the future.

"Heads of the theatrical music division of ASCRAP," he cantillated softly to himself. "Well well. How we rise in the world."

Sometimes, he reflected, a person who rose too far too fast had to be cut down. The Lord, always a democrat, had a way of evening things out—or so it seemed to the rabbi's admittedly idle speculation. He dismantled his little telescope and began replacing it in its case.

"Supper!" the landlady sang out. She was standing in the doorway with a tray of pot roast and mashed potatoes.

"I won't be staying," the rabbi apologized. "How much do I owe you?"

She set the tray on the bureau and counted on her fingers, her eyes avoiding his and circling the floral wallpaper instead. "Twenty-two fifty," she said hopefully. "That includes hot water."

"Fine," the rabbi said, and he paid her. She was a thief, but he paid.

He took the night plane to New York, and a taxi from John Fitzgerald Kennedy Airport to Congregation Beth Rico. He let himself in the back door and went down a coal-dusty flight of stairs. Behind a pink bedspread strung across the cellar the janitor trembled in his sleep on a pile of newspapers, his swarthy face mouldy with whiskers, his snores hoarser than the noise of a ship's engine.

Without waking the man, the rabbi lifted the ax from its nail on the wall. "I'll be needing you," he chanted softly to the tune of "I'll be seeing you." *For an audition . . .*

Not being a musician, Rowena Bishop had difficulty deciding which was worse, the words or the music. The music was

loud, which could have been part of the problem; the lyric
was like something out of a college show.

> *Though I've sometimes slipped,*
> *I get my balance again—*
> *When I'm not stripped,*
> *I top the best-dressed ten!*

The chorus girls were several years beyond being girls,
and they didn't sing in chorus, but they bawled the number
with an approximate rhythmic consensus that brought ap-
proving nods from the well-liquored audience. Probably half
a dozen or so of the women in diamonds and suntans who had
piled their minks in the master bedroom thought that the
lyrics were witty, incisive, devastating—the music helped the
illusion along by stopping short and allowing the three singers
to smirk a couple of *a capella* syllables before picking up again
with a whorehouse thump.

Unamused and pinched in the rear by the wood slats of
the caterer's chair, Rowena leaned across a softly snoring blue-
haired lady and sneaked her thirty-fifth Vienna sausage from
the silver platter on the window ledge.

> *I've counted counts among my beaux,*
> *I've bopped with barons when I chose,*
> *And now I jig with—gigolos!*

Rowena had seen the rhyme coming thirty syllables away
and did not even pretend to join in the merriment and applause.

> *But I'm still a lady at heart!*

The three harridans clasped arms and attempted a few un-
synchronized kicks of can-can as they exited around the piano
into the kitchen. When the clapping died down, Rowena could
hear them behind the door, opening tonic bottles and sloshing
the stuff in their gin.

"Delightful, don't you think?" the blue-haired woman asked.

"Needs work," Rowena said.

"You can't deny it has potential."

Rowena covered a burp with a thirty-sixth sausage and dropped the yellow toothpick onto the carpet, a wall-to-wall mauve thing that glistened like spun glass beneath a scattering of ashes and torn synopses. The producer, a thin man by the name of Monty Saint-Michael, had asked the audience out of consideration for the singers to refrain from smoking, and then he had told a joke about Julie Andrews and a cigar. The audience had smoked anyway. The room—a low-ceilinged living-dining area in one of those gadgety new apartments in one of those glass and cinderblock buildings built for ten-year obsolescence—had about as much breathable oxygen left in it as a gas chamber.

Rowena bit into her thirty-seventh sausage, decided that she had done her duty, and pushed up from the chair. With the merest glance at pink hairdos and blue hairdos and slicked-back gray hair she whispered, "Excuse me, please," thirty times and forced her way through a makeshift aisle blocked by shantunged knees and sequined purses. She reached a clear space by the punch bowl, and just for the road, helped herself to a cup.

"Well?" the composer asked her.

Rowena gagged back a mouthful of champagne, caught it before it sputtered into the room, and swallowed. "Needs work." She forced her lips into a smile.

Rowena felt a kinship with Whit Duchamp that was probably based on their being the same age, disliking a great many of the same people, and both weighing close to two hundred pounds. At six-foot-one, Whit had an eight-inch advantage over her, and though he did not need to resort to Rowena's beltless, baggy clothes, he bore his flesh with a smiling, gesturing energy that she recognized as her own favorite camouflage. In his lively, rather self-pitying eyes she saw something of herself, and she suspected that if they ever got down to a few drinks, they would understand each other much too well to be friends. Under his questioning glance her smile wilted into a condolence.

"It stinks," she said between sips.

He nodded.

"Maybe it would help if you got some decent singers," Rowena suggested. "Those dykes with the can-can . . ."

Whit refilled Rowena's cup. "Yesterday we raised thirty thousand." Success did not noticeably cheer him.

"It's a nutty world." Rowena shrugged, and the beads and baubles around her neck jingled. "Maybe this is next season's hit. But those lyrics, Whit . . . they're worse than a college show. Can't you change them?"

Whit gestured with his paper cup toward the thin man profiled in the kitchen doorway. "Monty says don't change a thing."

"And the book—that head in the bag on the squash court —ugh!"

"I need the advance." Whit drained his cup, crunched it, and dropped it on the carpet. Rowena touched his dark sleeve.

"Whit, I know you have it in you to do great shows. This just isn't one of them." She gauged the arc of his sway and estimated that he had had at least a dozen cups of the champagne mix. "Next time *will* be better."

She clasped his hand and smiled into his eyes. He lurched forward. For an instant she was afraid he was going to fall on her, but he merely planted a kiss on her cheek.

"Walk me to the door?" Rowena slipped a guiding arm through Whit's. She still wondered about taking him on as a client: New York was full of hard-drinking whiz kids, ten or fifteen years out of the Ivy League, wheeling their musical comedy careers along the cocktail party circuit. She decided to reread the copy of the show he had given her.

"Don't forget," she reminded him, "lunch next week."

She gave Whit a friendly poke in the side, provoked a burp, and slipped out of the apartment into the hall. She moved down the softly carpeted, dimly lit corridor, past steel doors painted to simulate wood and alphabetized *P* through *A*. Over the not-very-muffled din of Whit's audition she caught spattered gunshots and canned laughter from various television sets and stray whiffs of the roast beef and boiled artichokes that the building's caterer must have been serving to the entire twenty-ninth floor. She was glad not to be living in one of the Bauhaus beehives that seemed to be erupting like a disease over the entire island of Manhattan.

A youngish man in a tweed vest was waiting at the elevator. He smiled at her and indicated with a tanned hand that she was to get in before him.

"Thank you," she murmured, and—pretending to study the floor indicator that flashed numbers in italic stencil above the door—she squinted at his profile and noted that it would be pudgy in a year or so. He turned toward her, an affable smile on a not unhandsome face.

"You were at the audition, weren't you?" he asked.

Rowena felt her face flush. "Yes, I was." She debated how best to find out whether he was thinking of putting up money. "Very unusual show," she said brightly.

"Unusual," he nodded. He turned his gaze toward the floor indicator and whistled several bars of a tune that was not Whit's. You could never tell with these people, Rowena reflected; he could be rich—or he could be an audition bum.

"You can't deny it has potential," Rowena said. "Are you a friend of Whit's?" She used her coziest voice, her follow-up already prepared: one of two laugh-getting anecdotes about Whit's capacity for liquor, the time he swiped Billy Rose's limousine, his hilarious flirtations with two of Broadway's leading Lesbian producers . . .

"Never met him," the man said, as though he would be happy to forego the pleasure. The number 1 flashed on the indicator, and the doors slid open. He stood aside for Rowena. She was halfway across the imitation marble-floored lobby when she heard him call, "Heading downtown, Miss Bishop?"

Rowena stepped out of the line of reflection of the mirrored pillar and waited for the man in the vest to hold the glass door for her. "East thirty-third," she smiled.

With a gallantry as clearly habitual as it was devoid of

implication, he stretched an arm behind Rowena's head and
pushed the door open for her. The night air hit like a blast
furnace, and she almost recoiled into him.

"My car's across the street," he said.

Rowena had no doubt that the ride, or whatever he was
about to offer, was an act of charity. All men had their char-
ities; Rowena knew the fact full well and often exploited it.
This man's charity was probably fat women. Maybe his
mother had been one.

He unlocked a battered MG and held the door for her.
Pretending to gather her skirt, she sucked in her stomach
and managed to squeeze into the car. He slid into the driver's
seat and offered her a cigarette with a recessed filter. By the
flicker of his lighter he seemed less pudgy and a little hand-
somer. Rowena tried to move away, but she was already tight
against the door and overflowing the bucket seat.

"The name's Archibald." His smile was off-tilt in a kind of
debonair way. "Greg Archibald."

"Oh," said Rowena.

His hand plowed into her thigh when he slid the gearshift
forward. She tried to cross her legs away from him, but the
dashboard intervened.

"You're very kind to give me a lift downtown," she said.
"It's impossible getting a taxi in New York."

"No trouble," he said.

At the green light he shifted into what Rowena suspected
was an unnecessarily high gear. They sped south past dark
tenements suspended in the process of demolition and empty
skeletons of apartment houses going up.

"You're a theatrical agent, aren't you?" he asked without
looking at her.

Rowena did not blush. She never blushed in the dark. "Yes,
I am." She wondered how he knew the name of someone
who had been in the business less than a year. He was after
something, she knew; and she had the ridiculous feeling that
he was after *her*. Maybe he had a thing for fat lays.

"I'm an investor," he said. This time Rowena found the smile charming.

She hesitated, clearing her throat to focus her voice on a bright, casual plane. "I take it you were at the audition on business?"

"I had hoped it would be for pleasure as well." They were silent on the crosstown blocks; when he turned downtown on Park Avenue, he smacked his lips and shook his head. "Then again, it was such a damned lousy run-through—for all I know, the book might be brilliant."

"It is," Rowena said.

He turned toward her, his face even tanner in the glow of the red stop light. "Do you have a copy?"

Rowena nodded.

"I'd like to see it . . . very much."

The apartment disturbed Greg; it was as chatty and chic and glacially unfucked as a page of *Harper's Bazaar*. Miss Bishop's sleeping alcove was gardened off from the living room by pots of elephant-eared plants and vertical poles supporting house-broken vines and oddly spaced shelves of modernish tiny sculptures and colored porcelain nothings. Miss Bishop, or her decorator, had placed orange-filtered lights under the pots and above the vines and in a cavity in the wall, and the porcelain sparkled as though in sunlight. So, oddly enough, did her teeth.

They sat on the edge of the bed, brandy snifters in hand.

"This is his script," Miss Bishop said.

Greg accepted the green-covered mimeographed script, opened it at random, and smiled at the first bad joke that caught his eye. He flipped back to the title page. *Rice Pudding Club 1947 Competition. In the Bag.*

"Who's Ferdinand Fields?" he tested. The name was right there, topping the others.

She took a quick swallow of brandy. "I suppose he had a hand in the original, but Whit's reworked it into a . . . completely new concept. You're coming to the audition Wednesday, aren't you?"

"Sure," Greg said. "Wouldn't miss it."

"Two P.M., the Pocket Theater, West Fourteenth Street. Everyone'll be there."

Greg nodded. "What are those two other scripts?"

"Those aren't Whit's," she said. "He gave me all three in a box—I really don't know what they are."

Greg opened the yellow script to the title page. *Rice Pudding Club 1947 Competition. Belle's Last Ball. Book by Willoughby Barnes, Music and Lyrics by Fritz McCoy.*

The only difference between this title page and *In the Bag*, Greg noted, was that *In the Bag* had a gold star pasted above the title. He glanced around the alcove, avoiding Miss Bishop's hungry eyes.

The decorator or Miss Bishop had hung a 7 by 6 unframed canvas at the deep end, 42 square feet textured in burlap and sand and inch-deep in oil paint, a huge red amoeba with safety pins and old French francs stuck in it. He supposed she had picked it up in Paris.

He opened the orange script. *The Dancing Dybbuk. Book and Lyrics by Erwin Blake. Music based on traditional Hassidic themes.*

"Blake," Greg said.

"Something the matter?" Miss Bishop asked.

"Very much the matter," Greg said. And he saw just what it was.

Tuesday, June 27

"Your wife," Breeze said, "has accused you of trying to murder her."

The old man drew his Mohawk blanket tighter around his shoulders. "She never came to visit me," he said. "She always had a movie on television, she always had to stay home. Once in a while she'd drop in at 2 A.M., if the Late Late Show wasn't any good. She never came Sundays, or afternoons."

"Do you have any idea," Breeze asked, "why she'd accuse you?"

"Sure," the old man said. "She was frightened. Frightened people will blame anyone sooner than themselves."

"What was she frightened of?"

"Hard to say, exactly. Mo's theory is . . . that's Mo Jackson, that fellow over there . . ."

Breeze glanced in the direction of the pointing finger, and an attendant tipped his beret. MacAndrew, Breeze noted, was in a rocking chair, not a wheelchair; and he seemed to be doing well enough, for the moment, out of the oxygen tent.

"Mo's theory," the old man said, "is that those horror movies finally got to her, she began believing them, you know how people get? Well, one day she said she was coming up here; it was urgent, she had to talk. She said she'd be here at 8 P.M. Well, I sat waiting for her till one in the morning. You can bet your life I was boiling mad. Horror movies were her excuse, too good to miss, she said. Then she wanted to know if I'd cut some fellow's head off."

"And what did you tell her?"

The old man smiled. "I evaded the issue. I figured, she puts me off, I'll give her some of her own medicine. So she asked Mo there if I cut this fellow's head off. Now Mo's clever, cleverer than me and a hell of a lot cleverer than Gwennie. He said sure I cut the fellow's head off."

"She believed it?"

"She'll believe anything if it's gory enough. Then one of the nurses found a story in the newspaper, some minister got his head cut off. So Mo got in touch with Gwennie, told her I'd done it again." The old man smirked. "She was running around like a headless hen, phone calls here, phone calls there. Why she even skipped her horror movies she was so damned nervous."

"Something happened to her last night," Breeze said.

"Last night we really topped it off. It was Mo's idea. We bribed the maid, telegraphed her a hundred. During the Late Late Show, she cut the electricity. Can you imagine Gwennie without her Late Late Show?"

"I believe some furniture was destroyed."

"Well, we had to set the scene. Anyway it was my furniture."

"And the ax in your wife's bed?"

"Nice touch, don't you think?"

"Your wife is very upset."

The old man sipped his tea. "She should spend more time looking after her old man and a little less watching television. And you can tell her that for me. And something else you can tell her."

"What's that?" Breeze asked.

"Tell her if she doesn't shape up, last night might be just the beginning."

When he left the rest home, Breeze knew who had killed Langsam and Fields.

"In recognition of works beneficial to mankind, the Brothers of the One Book award their annual citation to Ferdinand Fields, Alicia von Helsing, and Erwin Blake." Dr. Wharton-Steinman pressed a finger to one finely arched nostril, as though stifling a sneeze, and leaned closer to the parchment. *"The eleventh day of Av, the year five thousand seven hundred seven."* He looked up. His hair was neatly trimmed and combed, his young face evenly tanned, but his eyes had the blue sparkle of antique crackle glass gone berserk. "Where, Mr. Archibald," he asked, "did you get this?"

"From Father Fields—indirectly."

"This is a scandal," Dr. Wharton-Steinman said.

"It's not a fake?" Greg asked.

"No, unfortunately not." Dr. Wharton-Steinman drummed tobacco into his pipe and held a lighter to the bowl; an expensive smell filled the study. "It's an error—a serious error."

"You're certain Rabbi Blake's name is on that citation?"

"Mr. Archibald, I do read Hebrew. The consonants *B, L, K,* are ambiguous, to be sure, but the nikkud leave no room for doubt."

"The nikkud?"

Dr. Wharton-Steinman tapped them with his pipe stem. "The nikkud, these little points, are a system of dots and marks placed under the Hebrew consonants in order to indicate the vowel sounds. There are two sets of nikkud: one for the short vowels . . ."

"I'll take your word for it." Greg leaned his elbow patches on Dr. Wharton-Steinman's desk. "How did Rabbi Blake happen to be associated with Father Fields and Miss von Helsing?"

"He was one of my predecessors," Dr. Wharton-Steinman said. "From some time in the early 1940's to 1947—whenever von Helsing died—he was chaplain of Jewish students here at Eli University. Then came Milton Lubavitcher, and then . . . me."

"Do you know for a fact that Blake worked on a refugee project with Fields and von Helsing?"

"Yes He . . . collaborated with them."

"And *The Dancing Dybbuk?*"

Dr. Wharton-Steinman tapped his pipe bowl on the manuscript. "Hassidic shmaltz. Blake always wanted to mix the two cultures. Perhaps he thought he could turn the Rice Pudding Club into a national conference of Christians and Jews."

"Did you personally know Erwin Blake?"

"Not personally, but I know about him," Dr. Wharton-Steinman said. "But I'm afraid I have a student waiting."

Greg made no move to rise from his chair. "If you could tell me a little about Blake."

Dr. Wharton-Steinman considered his guest a moment. "I can tell you a little, Mr. Archibald. But this must be strictly off the record."

When Dr. Wharton-Steinman had told the tale of the rabbi's decline, Greg asked about the doctor who had tended Alicia von Helsing in her last illness.

"Dr. Jones?" Wharton-Steinman smiled, as though remembering a personal joke. "An idealist, they tell me. Also an excellent bridge player."

"Any connection with Blake?"

"Of course."

Which brought them to Bertram Langsam. Wharton-Steinman had a theory on Langsam's concentration camp days; only a theory, of course, and strictly off the record.

"And Ferdinand Fields?" Greg asked.

"His activities were well known."

Off the record again, Dr. Wharton-Steinman outlined a few of them. By the time he left Wharton-Steinman's office, Greg knew who had killed Langsam and Fields.

Frieda sat on the upholstered bench, folding and refolding her newspaper, her eye falling without interest upon a line of advertisement, a smidgen of news, a meaningless photograph.

He was waiting for her, of course. Probably he had sighted her through the French window and was standing on the avenue, outside the metal fence. She knew he had been trailing her ever since New York. There was something elephantine about the rabbi's persistence. But she could, at least, get on a plane; an elephant couldn't.

Around her, they were talking Spanish. Her ear caught an occasional cognate. "Passport . . . the chief . . . the president . . . airport . . ." They scurried past her like hound dogs on a scent, the men with their pin-striped suits and their vaselined hair, the women with their olive skins and imperious eyes, hurrying to destinations and intrigues she could only guess at

She was no longer afraid; at least, her heart had stopped accelerating at unexpected backfires in the day and thumps in the night. Awareness of danger was merely part of her daily calculation now, like remembering to put her stockings on straight. She had bought a new pair, cheap, at a sale at Garfinckel's department store.

They'll give me the visa. It's been four days. Four days is all it takes to get a visa anywhere.

"Miss Langsam," a voice called. She glanced up at a gray-haired man with a Sunkist complexion and a movie star accent. "We'll be with you in a moment," he assured her, disappearing; and abruptly she was alone in a marble room, at liberty, if she wished, to punch electric typewriters and adding machines and to ransack filing cabinets. On the desk, a phone rang and went unanswered.

Then she noticed the news item: a paragraph, reprinted from an earlier New York edition. She read it three times, and each time her pulse beat faster.

"Bastard," she muttered. "Auditions yet . . ." The announcement itemized the score of a musical comedy: she recognized nine of the song titles and had a feeling she would recognize all of the tunes. "They take your life, they take your music—what next?"

She was on her feet, low heels clacking across the marble, before she was even aware of having consciously made the decision. *First things first:* her brother's honor before her own safety. After all, he was the genius of the family.

"Miss Langsam," someone enticed through an open door.

"Later," she said. "I got business."

Greg sat in lotus position on Gillian's double bed, the Olivetti balanced on his knees. While he typed on her Tiffany stationery, she proofread and clipped the monogram off the pages.

MEMO TO PLIMPTON DANIEL

Let us review the evidence at hand to see what conclusions we may, indeed must, logically draw. On June 16th Bertram Langsam, Eli '47, was found beheaded on the squash court of the New York Eli Club. The victim was born in Latvia, during that country's years of independence; during the Second World War, he found himself in Germany in a camp for Jewish prisoners. A refugee organization, One Book or Sefer Ehad, brought him from that camp to this country and arranged for him to complete his education at Eli. In his senior year he contributed the score to a Rice Pudding theatrical.

We know that Langsam's murderer was fair-haired, about five foot eight, of medium weight, and apparently in his late twenties. He reserved the squash court in the name of Winston MacAndrew. (The *nom de guerre* is of utmost significance, for in his musical of twenty years ago, Langsam himself played the role of one *Winnie MacAndrew.*) The results of the squash match speak for themselves!

Three days later Father Ferdinand Fields, a classmate of Langsam's, was beheaded on the Long Island Railroad while returning from Langsam's funeral. The murderer, a Spanish-speaking woman, dressed in traditional Andalusian skirt and blouse, of mature but indeterminate age, vanished in the confusion following the discovery of the murder.

The second crime casts a new light on the first.

Fields and Langsam, while at Eli, worked together on a Rice Pudding show, Fields supplying the book to Langsam's score. Like Langsam, Fields took a role in the production, that of a Peruvian sun priestess, Malagueña la Cha Cha del Amor. So far as can be ascertained, Fields and Langsam drifted completely apart after college. Yet they both died by the ax, beheaded by the very incarnation of the roles they had respectively played two decades previously in the same college musical.

The odds against this happening accidentally allows us to rule out coincidence.

In 1947, three musicals were submitted to the Rice Pudding competition: *Belle's Last Ball,* book by Willoughby Barnes, music and lyrics by Fritz McCoy; *In the Bag,* book by Ferdinand Fields, lyrics by J. Whittaker Duchamp, and music by Bertram Langsam; and *The Dancing Dybbuk,* book by Erwin Blake, music based on traditional Hassidic melodies. To the belated misfortune of its composer and librettist, *In the Bag* won the contest.

We come now to a curious tie. Alicia von Helsing Barnes, a continental actress of no small repute, designed the costumes for three Rice Pudding shows, including *In the Bag.* Mrs. Barnes also served as adviser to the organization One Book or Sefer Ehad responsible for the rescue of Bertram Langsam. She was thus in the remarkable position of being both Bertram Langsam's savior and his costume designer.

We must now touch on a perhaps still sensitive point. Though Mrs. Barnes worked with anti-Nazi organizations and received Jewish citations for her post-war service to humanity, the most recent scholarship indicates that she was in fact a Nazi sympathizer. Her humanitarian work, in the retrospect of the Nuremberg trials and subsequent revelations, takes on the color of camouflage. That Mrs. Barnes was Goebbels' mistress has been established beyond any doubt (their love letters are preserved in a Vienna archive). Under her administration, Sefer Ehad or One Book became nothing less than a conduit of Jewish funds to Nazi survivors.

Mrs. Barnes died in 1947 at Eli Hospital. Though a death certificate is filed at County Records, attributing her demise to an improbable combination of ailments, there is no mention whatsoever of her death in the hospital records themselves. The reason for omission, I believe, is that Mrs. Barnes, with the cooperation of her own physician, was medicinally murdered.

To return to the other victims: the most reliable sources now indicate that Bertram Langsam was not *interned* in any Nazi concentration camp. On the contrary, his original birth certificate, at present in the files of an organization in Vienna, indicates that he was the son of the chief administrator of the camp from which he was purportedly "rescued." In all probability, he assisted his father.

Finally, Ferdinand Fields, as an undergraduate and later, upon ordination, acted as Protestant adviser to the Sefer Ehad.

Let us now consider the murderer. Did he change sex between crimes? Far from it. The murderer changed costumes, not gender. We can even pinpoint where the costumes came from: the warehouse where old Rice Pudding props are stored. Why did the murderer wait twenty years between the first crime and the second and third? Because for those twenty years he was *in no position* to deal with Langsam and Fields. Do we know anything else about the murderer? Yes.

The murderer was at Langsam's funeral.

While the killer had to make a squash date to lure Langsam into the open, *no appointment* was necessary to get at Fields. The murderer merely followed him from the funeral.

Who is this murderer?

I regret to say that he is Rabbi Erwin Blake.

Mr. Blake, chaplain of Jewish students at Eli University in the 1940's, misguidedly joined with Mrs. Barnes in sponsoring the Sefer Ehad and its activities. Grossly overestimating the philo-Semitism not only of this organization but of the Rice Pudding Club, Mr. Blake submitted a musical based on Hassidic themes to the 1947 contest. It was rejected. Mr. Blake detected, perhaps, a whiff of betrayal in the triumph of Fields, Langsam, and Alicia Barnes with *In the Bag.* Discouraged, he quit the university scene to become rabbi of a wealthy Brookline congregation. His tenure was brief.

Late in 1947, a witness at the Nuremberg Trials hinted at Mrs. Barnes' Nazi connections. Sefer Ehad immediately became suspect, and with it Mr. Blake's well-intentioned work. Mr. Blake was fired from his temple.

Mrs. Barnes' doctor, on record as virulently anti-Nazi, was a bridge partner of the rabbi's. The hospital records, as I have indicated, show signs of omission. It is hardly beyond the realm of probability that the rabbi and doctor conspired to dispatch her.

Rabbi Blake then fled to South America. A downhill trail led from the better congregations of Buenos Aires to the Jewish enclaves in Ecuador, Nicaragua, Guiana. Three months ago, Rabbi Blake returned to this country, broken so far as we can judge in body and spirit, to preside over a mongrel congregation of his own devising—Congregation Beth Rico, never accredited by the American Board of Rabbis.

It is my opinion that the Rice Pudding Show's summer tour stirred ancient antipathies in the rabbi's soul and prompted him to complete the vengeance he had begun two decades earlier. He arranged to meet, murder, and bury Langsam; he then followed Father Fields from the last rites and dispatched that gentleman as well.

The rest of this lamentable incident is merely a matter of costume changes.

Our opposition, the New York City Police, have set a trap for the murderer; it is to be sprung tomorrow. The trap will not work. The bait, Mr. J. Whittaker Duchamp, is of no interest to the rabbi; though Duchamp wrote lyrics to *In the Bag*, he is unconnected with Sefer Ehad or the Nazis.

I recommend, in the interest of god will and religious harmony at Eli, that we consider this a closed matter and leave Rabbi Blake to heaven.

Breeze stopped off at the station to leave an interoffice memorandum for Kennedy. As he typed, he could imagine the old fool's fat face.

Memo to Kennedy: URGENT from Breeze.

I want six (6) plainclothesmen at the Pocket Theater, West 14th Street, tomorrow, 2 P.M. They are to mingle with the audience and backers, but to stay close at all times to the composer-lyricist, J. Whittaker Duchamp. At some time during the audition, the murderer of Bertram Langsam will attempt to behead Mr. Duchamp. The murderer will be wearing a straw boater and an "old school" blazer and tie and should not be difficult to recognize or apprehend. Please have two police photographers present to get the murder attempt down on film. This should spare us a lot of haggling in court.

Gotta do something about the bureaucracy in our department: it cost me a good week in solving this case. I refer to the beheading of Ferdinand Fields on the Long Island Railroad. Since the crime took place in Mineola, i.e., outside of our precinct, I was not allowed to investigate. This second murder, as luck would have it, is our single most important lead in the solution of the first.

I don't suppose you caught the gory pun in the deaths of Fields and Langsam. Both had recently been promoted to "head" of their respective departments—Langsam, head of musicology in his university, Fields rector of his church. And both were immediately beheaded.

If you're squawking that Langsam was killed by a man and Fields by a woman, hold your horses.

Langsam was murdered in the Eli Club the night that the Rice Pudding troupe was performing there. The murderer used the name and adopted the appearance of the character Langsam played in the 1947 musical. (N.B.: there's an actual man with the same name, squash champion 1892. The use of his name in the show was an in-joke, so far as I can gather.) Likewise, Father Fields' killer adopted the appearance of the character Fields played in the same show.

Both killers were the same person; two people couldn't be that nutty.

The murderer, then, had to have an intimate knowledge of the 1947 Rice Pudding show; he had to have access to the scripts and costumes; he had to know about Fields' and Langsam's promotions; and he had to have a grudge against them both.

That spells Willoughby Barnes.

Barnes lost the 1947 script competition to Fields and Langsam. People have killed for less. In Barnes' case, natural resentment was probably heightened by the fact that he had a theatrically prominent mother and thus felt his failure all the more acutely.

Barnes traveled with the touring company and was in the Eli Club the night of the murder. This explains why the murderer was not seen leaving the building. Mr. Barnes just went to the dressing room and changed back into street clothes with the rest of the cast.

It sounds screwy, but I have personally observed Barnes to be a schizophrenic. When he's not dressing up like musical comedy characters, he's dressing up like his dead mommy. In fact, I suspect, he's under the impression that he's assuaging mommy's disappointment at his own failure by chopping off all these heads. The psychiatrists will have a field day with him.

As for tomorrow: I planted a press release that Duchamp has been promoted to head of the theatrical musical division of the American Society of Composers, Recording Artists, and Publishers. It's a load of baloney. However, Duchamp wrote lyrics for the show that ousted Barnes, and he also played a part in the chorus, a society boy. I'm 99% certain Barnes wil get out the old ax again, follow his pattern, and change into costume and, taking advantage of the crowd tomorrow, try to lop off Duchamp's head in some unguarded moment. So let's for once try to avoid unguarded moments.

P.S. I'd appreciate a vacation and a raise, and I'd appreciate not being assigned to cases like this any more.

Wednesday, June 28

Greg found two seats in the fourth row. The theater was small, but still inexplicably full—maybe because the drinks after the show had been advertised as gratis. "Can you see?" he whispered to Gillian.

She slipped out of her gloves and grimaced affirmatively. "It's the same bunch you get at pop art openings," she whispered, "a lot of forty-year-old teeny boppers."

"I guess they go to anything free."

"Like us."

"Beautiful crowd." Rowena squeezed Whit's hand—it was damp. "Everything'll be okay, don't you worry."

"You've been an angel," Whit said. "I mean it."

"Let's just hope they'll be angels, too." Rowena kissed him

on the forehead and gave him a gentle shove toward the piano. The audience applauded as he took his place next to the drummer; the singers, seated on stools on the stage, stopped shuffling their sheet music. Whit lifted his hand to give the downbeat; Rowena threw another kiss, and the audience stopped chattering, and the drums banged into the beguine that began the overture.

Breeze peered over his shoulder and mentally counted the plainclothesmen in the audience, the bored faces that didn't even pretend to smile, the five-o'clock-shadowed jaws trying to stretch a stick of gum into a five-minute chew. Four. Four wash-and-wear jackets with four bulges under the left shoulder. Four in a row, like blackbirds baked in a pie. At least they could have had the sense to sit separately.

Breeze turned to whisper in Kluski's ear: "I told Kennedy to give me six plainclothesmen. He only sent four."

Kluski shrugged and leaned perceptibly forward, out of whisper range, as though he actually enjoyed the show. On stage, a Marlboro man with much gray at the temples was courting a starlet with a blond streak.

Love, love, he was singing, *when you're in love,*
     The world's an old devil balloon—

That milky way above, she chimed in,
     Drips popsicles in June.

Breeze tugged the elbow of Kluski's tweed sleeve. "Where are the other two?"

"The cameramen," Kluski whispered.

Breeze glanced at the cameramen, crouched at either end of the stage, popping bulbs now and then just to look busy. There were bulges under the left shoulders of their wash-and-wear jackets.

"How the hell does Kennedy expect them to aim a gun and take pictures at the same time?" Breeze whispered.

A tiara'd lady in front turned around and said in a loud voice, "Wouldja shut up and let 'em sing?"

"Question of economy," Kluski whispered. "Kennedy says this case is running over budget."

I look like a stupid chorus boy, he thought; *well, not stupid, but a chorus boy most definitely.* He tried to analyze his reflection in the little glass pane over the fire extinguisher. It was the boater that did it, he decided. Nobody wore boaters these days unless they were hoofing in revivals of *The Boyfriend* or Rodgers and Hart. In a way, the boater was becoming; corny, but becoming. He wondered how it would look at a more roguish tilt and eased it slightly to the side with the edge of the ax. That was more like it.

> *Get the hang of love, love,*
> *The bang of love . . .*

The song was upbeat with a vengeance, and the little pane trembled in time to the drums.

> *Some rainy afternon,*
> *Over the rainbow, love,*
> *We'll fly in that balloon . . .*

He lowered the ax carefully, as though it were a delicate precision instrument, and leaned it against the corridor wall.

> *Love, love, we'll make love*
> *In that old devil balloon.*

Like a good and faithful servant, the ax stayed exactly where he had put it. He made sure his legs hid the blade handle. Then, adjusting the hang of his blazer, he listened to the applause on the other side of the door and braced himself for a wait.

The applause was warm, friendly, generous—maybe twenty thousand dollars generous. They were smiling; Whit smiled back and winked at the drummer to keep the beat going, keep them clapping.

"Hey Whit—sing another!" someone called. A few of the others took up the cry and a woman stood up in the third row and shouted, "Aw come on, Whit, sing!" She looked like an aged version of a debutante he had once known. The performers were standing and they were clapping, too.

Home free.

"*Sing Waterloo!*" someone shouted, and the little theater echoed with the shout. Whit riffed an introductory chord.

> *The length and breadth and height of you,* he crooned,
> *Total up to quite a view . . .*

The drummer was following him warily with the swish cymbal.

> *A single glance and I'm askew . . .*

Whit motioned to the audience: "Come on, join in!"
You, you, they sang in rising unison, *you, you, you,*

> *You—are my Waterloo.*

Whit riffed a dominant seventh to take it up a key and really slam it home:

> *My defenses crumble at the sight of you . . .*

They weren't following him: he'd have to tighten up that line.

> *I capitulate to the utter delight of you . . .*

He gave it a leer, but the voices were thinning out. He was losing them. And then, the last thing he needed:

"*Goniff!*"

A woman—gray hair flying like a frizzled wig—was climbing through benches and people and wooden chairs; her skirt caught and there was a flash of ham, garter, and lacy pants before she lost her balance and clutched a cameraman. A flashbulb went off and she was standing at the piano, lips trembling, eyes blazing lava and destruction.

"Goniff!"

Whit did a double take to the audience, as though she were part of the show. She grabbed the music paper off the stand and rattled the pages at him.

"Thou shalt not steal!" She flung the words with all the contempt and spittle a human being could muster. "That was Bertram's music! My Bertram's music! You stole it! You two-bit crumb-bun *lyricist*—you hack, you maggot!"

Grin in place, Whit riffed the loudest chords he knew and signaled the drummer to beat up a storm. She turned to the audience, as to a court of last resort.

"That was my brother's music," she shouted. "That was Bertram Langsam's music, every note of it! That was *In the Bag*!"

So what, Whit thought, he wasn't going to let her ruin the audition. His chords were covering her until she whirled around and slammed the piano lid down on his fingers.

"I beg your pardon," he grimaced. His right hand was bleeding. "Madam . . . you have wounded me." He nodded to the drumer to take the piano, and with a smile at the audience he tottered across the theater to the side door.

It was a relief to hide himself in the hallway, where the noise was a little less loud, where there were no eyes to watch him. He closed the door carefully, as though sealing a box, and took a deep, calming breath.

"So . . . you got the score after all."

Whit turned and peered into the darkness from which the voice had spoken. "I beg your pardon?"

A familiar face emerged from the shadow, smiling like a bust of the god Pan. "You never could compose worth a damn. You needed Langsam twenty years ago, and you still need him now."

"Need him?"

The figure shrugged. "Well, you stole his music, didn't you?"

Whit took a step backward. Why, after twenty years, was everyone calling him a thief *now?*

"I didn't actually *steal*," he fumbled. "We needed a script and a score. We had to show the backers something . . . we couldn't go on improvising and telling jokes about Julie Andrews." Whit straightened his bow tie. "So I borrowed. As a matter of fact I got some other scripts, too—*Dancing Dybbuk* and *Belle's Last Ball.* It's ridiculous to say I lifted everything from Langsam . . . I took a little bit from everyone . . . even you."

"I know."

"The old tunes sound pretty good, don't they?" Whit flashed a little smile. "The years haven't dulled them a bit."

"The only thing the years have dulled, Duchamp, is your brain."

"Well." Whit waved his bleeding hand as though it were a safe-conduct into the bathroom. "Sorry you feel that way . . . though there's not really much anyone can do about my brain now, is there?"

"There's always a cure for everything."

"Well . . . yes . . . I daresay." Whit was about to turn his back when his eye was caught by a glimmer at the baseboard of the wall, behind the white bucks of the shadowy figure. At first he assumed it was a lit match, dropped by accident, and he was about to call his friend's attention to it. But the cold steadiness of the glint cut his words short. It was no flame, he realized with a shrinking of the stomach.

It was absurd of the ax to be there at all, as though this were a carpentry shop or a woodshed; but the thing was there, scarcely five feet from him. He could see nothing except the narrow, unmistakable slice of light, yet he knew the ax was standing on its head, leaning against the wall like some malignantly playful baboon. He sank back slowly, careful to avoid any sudden movement that might bring it upon him. His tongue went dry, and a drop of sweat crawled down his cheek.

When Breeze opened the door, they were standing like two old friends at a cocktail party who had run out of small-talk—Whittaker Duchamp, mashed against the wall, slack-jawed and perspiring; Willoughby Barnes, watching him, whistling.

"Oh," Willoughby said, glancing up at Breeze, "hi there."

"Hi there yourself," Breeze said. He motioned the plain-clothesmen past and pointed at Willoughby. "Him."

Willoughby tried to shrug them off, not angrily, but distastefully, as though they might spoil the press in his blazer. Four pairs of handcuffs came out. Willoughby held out one pair of hands.

"I hope you know what you're doing," he smiled.

"I know what I'm doing." Breeze glanced at Whittaker. "Are you all right?"

Whittaker raised a bleeding finger. "A-a-ax," he stuttered.

Breeze patted him on the back. "I know. It's all right now. Get in there and rinse your hand off."

Whittaker nodded and stumbled into the bathroom and made a retching at the sink. Breeze peered after him just to make sure he wasn't going to pass out, then followed Willoughby and the plainclothesmen back into the theater. Kluski cleared the way through the babbling crowd.

"You know," Willoughby said, "you're making a mistake."

"We just don't like seeing people get their heads cut off," Breeze said.

"Who said I was cutting anyone's head off?"

"A little bird." Breeze snapped his fingers. "Kluski, get the ax, will you? Careful of the fingerprints."

Whit completed his dry retching and wiped the sweat from

his chin. A chorus boy came into the bathroom, and Whit moved aside to let him have the sink.

The boy whistled a bit of *Waterloo* and smiled at Whit. Whit smiled back, pressed the electric dryer, and flapped his hands in the warm breeze. He took a comb out of his pocket and turned back to the mirror.

The boy was standing behind him with an ax. Whittaker saw him and whirled just as the ax cleaved the mirror in two. An ear was hanging from the blade.

"My God . . ." The buzzing in Whittaker's head half drowned out the boy's giggling. The ax swung again, and Whittaker ducked. There was blood on the floor, with sparkling bits of mirror strewn through it. Whittaker dove for the toilet stall and bolted the door behind him.

Whittaker began screaming for help. Then he saw the man crouched in the back of the stall with the ax.

Greg steered Gillian out of the theater up the sidewalk toward the avenue. "I'm glad that's over," he said.

"I kind of liked it," Gillian yawned. "That Waterloo song, I mean it's awful, but it has a sort of relentless naïveté . . . I mean it's almost catchy."

"So's syphilis," Greg said.

"Cynic, can't you ever be sentimental about anything?"

Greg whistled for a taxi. "I can be sentimental about plenty of things, under the right circumstances."

"What are the right circumstances?"

He held the cab door for her. "Your apartment."

"Here he is, boys," Breeze announced. "Here he is, world—the headsman." He gave Willoughby Barnes a shove into Kennedy's office. Willoughby regained his balance and dropped comfortably onto the stool. He lit himself a cigarette.

"What's your name?" Kennedy asked gruffly.

"His name is Willoughby Barnes," Breeze said.

"Let him talk," said Kennedy. "You killed Bertram Langsam?" he asked the suspect.

"And Father Fields," Breeze added.

"Leave Fields out of this. I'm asking Mr. Barnes if he killed Langsam."

Willoughby exhaled and brushed a thin lock of brown hair from his eyes. "No. I didn't kill Langsam."

Kennedy looked over at Breeze. "He says he didn't."

"For Chrissake, of course he says he didn't. We happen to have caught him *in flagrante* with an ax, threatening Duchamp."

"Who's we?" Kennedy said.

"Kluski. He'll be here in a minute."

"I'll admit there was an ax," Willoughby said, "and my fingerprints are on it, but it's not mine."

"Whose it is?" Kennedy asked.

"My mother's."

Kluski heard screams as he opened the door. There was no ax in the hallway, but there were two in the bathroom, and the rabbi and a chorus boy in a straw hat were swinging them at one another.

"Stop!" Kluski shouted.

They were making too much racket to hear him. Kluski fired two warning shots—one at the rabbi's kidney and the other at the chorus boy's neck. The rabbi doubled up over the sink, and the chorus boy collapsed against the electric dryer.

Something odd about the chorus boy held Kluski's attention. The boater slid from the boy's head, taking the blond Beatle wig with it, and a coil of gray hair spilled down to his shoulder—rather, it spilled down to *her* shoulder, for as the blazer slipped open, the two breasts beneath the shirt bulged sufficiently into evidence to indicate her true sex. She was not only a woman, she was—the make-up running in sweatstreams down her face left no doubt—an older woman: the impersonation of a boy one third her age had been nothing less than a cosmetic and athletic miracle.

Kluski was so caught up in the transformation that he hardly noticed when the door to the toilet stall swung open and Whittaker Duchamp stumbled out, trailing a stream of scarlet toilet paper from the hand pressed to his ear.

"You crook," the woman snarled, her voice a harsh contralto. Her eyes followed Whittaker. "You cheat."

"Nazi," the rabbi rasped.

"You shut up," the woman said. "I was talking to Whittaker Duchamp."

"I was talking to you," the rabbi said.

Kluski snapped out of his paralysis and stooped to pick up the two axes by their handles. Whittaker was huddled in the doorway. "Get a doctor," he whispered, his free hand clutching Kluski's leg. "My ear . . . she took my ear."

"The doctor'll give you the tin ear you deserve," the woman gloated. Kluski ignored her for the moment and slapped the rabbi on the cheek and got him to open his eyes. "What the hell are you doing here?"

"I came to kill her." The rabbi pointed at the woman.

"And what are you doing here?" Kluski asked the woman.

She pointed at Whittaker Duchamp. "I came to kill him."

"Don't ask me where she got the ax," Willoughby sighed. "We don't keep axes in the house, or long carving knives for that matter. I forbade her all weapons, from pistols to pinking shears. She must have stolen the ax from somebody, a neighbor perhaps. It looks . . . you know, used."

"You're saying your mother killed Langsam?" Kennedy asked.

"She hated Langsam and Fields . . . and Duchamp, for that matter. Ever since their Rice Pudding show beat mine. She felt they'd plotted against me. And when the class report mentioned their promotion, she went into a dither. Far worse than when Sefer Ehad was exposed . . . but that's another story. Only this time she disappeared for days on end. I was busy with the tour, so I didn't think much of it, at first. Mother was always going out . . . in costume, of course. I never let her appear in public as herself, but there were lots of costumes in the Rice Pudding warehouse, and she's always been good at quick changes. And she always managed by herself—she had the use of the car, and the credit cards; I wouldn't let her charge at the hardware store, because she would have bought an ax there, and she was always saying that some day she would ax Langsam and Fields—and Duchamp—just the way they'd axed me. She said it so often I stopped taking her seriously. There didn't seem to be any reason for me to worry."

Kennedy lifted his ballpoint pen from the doodle. "I asked if your mom killed Langsam."

The man nodded. "And Fields, too. After Fields I saw the pattern and I realized mother was living up to her word. There was no doubt; I found the alumni report where she'd put checks by Fields' and Langsam's names. Then came the announcement of Duchamp's promotion. She disappeared again. This time I had a pretty clear idea where she was going, so I came here today." Willoughby glanced at Breeze. "Just in case Inspector Breeze had figured out anything, I dressed the way I knew mother would dress . . . in this blazer and boater. I wanted to keep him confused till I could get her to safety. And, if possible, I wanted to keep her from killing Duchamp. I got her ax away from her." Another glance at Breeze. "But then Inspector Breeze interrupted."

"There's only one problem," Breeze interrupted again. "Your mother died twenty years ago."

Willoughby shook his head. "No. I never knew the truth about Sefer Ehad until it was exposed, but then I realized she was in danger. The papers those days were full of reprisals against Nazis. She was my mother, I had to protect her. The

simplest thing was to fake her death, pretend she had died
. . . which we did."

Breeze shook his head. "Uh uh. You think you pretended.
Your mother's been dead twenty years."

"Then who's that woman living in my house?"

"That woman living in your house," Breeze said, "is you,
kiddo."

"Why would you want to kill a nice woman like this?"
Kluski asked the rabbi.

"Because sooner or later justice must be done."

"That blabbermouth," the woman said, "doesn't know what
justice is."

"Justice," the rabbi cried, pointing, "will be that woman's
execution."

"I'd expect something stupid like that," the woman said,
"coming from a third-rate rabbi like Blake."

"Third rate I may be, stupid perhaps, but not as stupid as
your friends who pay me a thousand dollars for an echt-
Jewish funeral, not as stupid as your friends who send me
an uncircumcized corpse and tell me the dead man is a Jew."

The woman tossed Kluski a shrug. "I never gave him
money, I never sent him a corpse."

"Frieda did," he said.

"Frieda's a fool."

"A fool she may be, but she opened my eyes!"

The woman sniffed. "Cataracts."

"Even through cataracts a man can see darkly! I saw Fields
at the funeral, didn't I? And I knew he had cheated me, and
I followed him, didn't I?"

"Don't ask me," the woman said. "Did you?"

"I did! I followed him! And what did I stumble upon but
a wretched, *sixth-rate,* Bavarian operetta imitation of a
gypsy . . ."

"Peruvian!" she cried.

"Gypsy!" he shot back. "Gypsy hatchet woman!"

"Peruvian sun priestess!" Her face was pastrami red, and the veins stood out in her neck. "It was a brilliant performance —I spoke with an Andalusian trilled *r*, I had lemon in my hair—I *was* Malagueña! Just as I was Winnie! Just as I was Bertolt Brecht's immortal Salome of the Stockyards!"

"You were an overweight wiener hausfrau on *pep* pills and I daresay marijuana and I thought you were *laughable!*"

"Bullshit!"

"Bullshit yourself, Miss von Helsing! It was laughable and *I recognized you!*"

"Impossible. No one recognized me."

"I wasn't a hundred percent certain," the rabbi granted. "Who could be certain after twenty years. You've aged, Miss von Helsing. *Aged.* I'll admit I had to double-check—I told Frieda the corpse had no circumcision—before I could be sure. She ran scared, and then I knew. I knew that silly *zigeunerin* had to be you, Miss von Helsing. In an old costume from that old show."

"You knew," she laughed. "You didn't know from peanuts!"

"And I knew Langsam was one of your Nazis. And I knew *all* your refugees were Nazis—all the old accusations were *true.* I knew, this time I was certain. And I knew you were alive. And I watched your house, and I followed, and I caught you, Miss von Helsing, I caught you!"

To Kluski it was worse than Greek, it was Armenian. "Why the hell," he asked the woman, "did you want to kill Duchamp?"

She waved an accusing finger. "Because *In the Bag* was a lousy show. *Belle's Last Ball* should have won . . . it would have, if those three hadn't rigged the votes. They killed my boy's career."

"Which of you killed Langsam and Fields?" Kluski asked.

"They were Nazis," the rabbi said. "They deserved to die."

"Nazi shmatzy," the woman cried. "They hurt my boy! Nobody hurts my Willoughby, you hear me? Nobody!"

"Which of you," Kluski repeated, "killed Langsam and Fields?"

The woman's eyes shone with a fierce pride. "I did. Of course."

"I caught one of your quick changes last Sunday," Breeze said, "under the bed."

"I staged it," Willoughby said. "I had to throw you off Mother's scent."

Breeze smiled.

"So I pulled that schizophrenia crap," Willoughby shrugged.

Kennedy smiled. "I'd say you fell for it hook line and sinker, Breeze. And I think your report's a load of insolent bull. And I think you're a bad cop, Breeze. And I think the mother did it."

"There is no mother," Breeze said.

"Then who's that?" Kennedy lifted his sunglasses and nodded toward the doorway. Kluski was standing there holding an ax, and a woman in a college blazer was handcuffed to him arm.

Willoughby rose from the stool. "Mother," he said. "Oh, Mother."

She threw her unfettered arm around his neck. "Willoughby."

Breeze lit a cigarette. "It's an act," he said. "Where did you find her, Kluss?"

"In the men's room," Kluski said. "She was trying to kill what's-his-name."

Breeze gagged on a cloud of cigarette smoke. Kennedy was smiling like a big happy spider. "She really did it, hey?" Kennedy said.

The woman ignored him. "All our lives," she said, "we are part of a tradition."

Willoughby hugged her. "Yes, Mother."

"What I did, I did for you, Willoughby. It was only justice."

"Let's not talk about it, Mother."

"What else could I do, when they're promoted to the top, and my boy is stuck in the library?"

"I like the library."

"They ruined your life."

Willoughby sighed. "Yes, Mother."

"And you must promise me," she said, "after they have hanged me . . . promise me to be happy."

"Yes, Mother. I'll be happy."

Thursday, June 29

"Congratulations," Plimpton Daniel said, half rising from behind his desk.

"Congratulations?" Greg echoed.

"Your report." Daniel waved the manila envelope. "Brilliant. How would you like to be head of our new public relations department?"

"That's very good of you, sir, but . . ." But Greg had read the newspapers, and he knew that his report, however brilliant, was far from accurate.

"Virtually a shoo-in. The board of directors votes today. I'll see that you get the job. Needless to say," he smiled, "there'll be a slight raise in pay." He laughed and rose.

A viciously strong slap on the back sent Greg reeling into

the anteroom. The secretary was sucking a Coke bottle, staring at him.

"I hope you don't mind," she said. "I retyped your report." She waited till the door to Daniel's inner office had clicked shut of its own weight. "I changed a few things."

"Thank you," Greg said, wondering why her hair was orange.

"I got a friend who works on *The New York Times*. He's a printer. He gets me the early edition."

"I suppose I should thank you *and* your friend," Greg said.

"Aw, don't worry about Barry." She smiled a smile subtler and more insinuating than the Gioconda's. "He doesn't mind helping."

"You're both very good," Greg said, moving toward the door.

Her fingers reached the handle before his, immobilizing it. "My name," she whispered, "is Lulu, like Little Lulu in the comic strips? Lulu Bernkrandt, B-e-r-n-k-r-a-n-d-t. I'm here till five, and I'm in the book."

Her lips tasted of Coca-Cola.

"Breeze?" said the voice on the telephone.

"Yes sir?"

"I've been rereading that report or memorandum or whatever you call that letter you sent me. You know what I've decided, Breeze?"

"What, sir?"

"I'm sick and tired of you. I don't understand you, I don't understand the way you think or the way you do things. I'm highly dissatisfied with the way you handled the Langsam business."

"May I ask why?"

"Because you fingered the wrong man. Because your assistant Bernard Kluski brought the killer in while you were sitting on your sawed-off butt. Because of that sassy note you sent me. You're unsubordinate, Breeze. You're uneffective and you're unastute and you're unaccurate."

"I feel my solution was relatively close to the mark."

"In this department we hit the mark or keep our mouths shut."

"I still feel I was on the right track."

"No use being on the right track if you haven't got the steam to get to the station."

"I did my best."

"If you can't do better than that, you better get off the city payroll. Matter of fact, that's what I called about. Until I can get you fired, you're demoted. You'll be patrolling the Staten Island coast."

There was a click; after a while Breeze hung up the phone. He went out and bought all the day's papers. The *Post* said Austria was suing for Alicia von Helsing's extradition; the *Daily News* said she was under observation at a Rockefeller research institute. The rabbi, according to *The New York Times*, was serializing his story for *Life*, and Frieda, according to the same unnamed but reliable source in the *Times*, was in Paraguay.

Breeze sat and watched the news on television. The phone interrupted; it was Millie Gibbon, long distance, barely audible.

"I just want to thank you for everything," she said.

"You're welcome," Breeze said.

"We're in the Virgin Islands . . . Mr. Barnes and me. We're married."

"Congratulations."

A while later a telegram came from Kluski: SHAKESPEARE HAD A WORD FOR EVERY OCCASION. "YOU ARE NOT THE FIRST NOR SHALL YOU BE THE LAST TO SUFFER CALAMITIES SUCH AS THIS." HAVE PATIENCE, THEY KNOW NOT WHAT THEY DO.

Breeze propped the telegram on the mantelpiece, settled down in a chair, and began a crossword puzzle.

Greg felt fifty pounds lighter and took the steps two at a time. A little breathless, a little dizzy, he let himself into the apartment. It was a day of miracles. Someone had cleaned up.

The bed was made, the scatter pillows were stacked in a bright jumble. The carpet was freshly vacuumed, the ashtrays were empty, the windows washed. He ran his finger along the edge of the desk; it came up clean. He whistled, as he would have whistled fifteen years ago at a pretty girl. It was an admiring, rhetorical whistle. He did not expect a reply.

A whistle answered him from the kitchen.

"Gillian?" he called.

"Mmm?"

"If Hindus have angels, you're one."

He slipped out of his jacket. Out of deference to the state of the flat, he did not toss it on the bed but hung it in the closet. "Today," he called, "I start a new life."

"Hmm?"

"I'm reborn. I've got a future, a job . . . and you."

"Mmm-hmm."

He sniffed. A pungent current was drifting from the kitchen. His nose analyzed: raisins, roasted almonds, onions, fried apples, fresh grated coconut, curry.

"Gillian, you magnificent bitch goddess, you must have heard about the promotion!" He peeked into the kitchen. She was bent over a recipe book, her back toward him. "No more debts, no more laundromats, no more evictions!" he chanted. "Whoopee! No more cockroaches, no more *Wall Street Journal* or *Village Voice* for john paper!" He approached. "Smells like a royal celebration, a real high wind in the Spice Islands. Mind if I peek?"

She shook her head, he thought in the negative, but he tiptoed to the stove anyway and lifted the lid off the pot. Huge chunks of veal were bubbling in a thick brown broth. His mouth turned to water. After one delirious inhalation he replaced the lid.

"How did you know they made me head?" he asked.

"Hmm?" The book snapped shut.

He reached out to touch her, then stoped. She was dicing scallions with a cleaver. The down-slap of the blade bounced shards of light off the copper-bottomed pots on the wall.

I don't know her last name, he thought. *She could be anyone, anything.* He couldn't remember if he had given her a key or simply forgotten to lock the door. *Langsam was the head of musicology, and Fields was the head of Saint Mark's. And now I'm head of public relations . . .*

His collar felt very tight. She was whistling, a piercing stab of a Hindu tune. He backed off, but not in time.

"The phone's been going all morning," she said in an inexplicably sour voice.

He knew that cooks were temperamental, jealous of their domain, and irritated at interruptions, but he was completely unprepared for the jagged snarl that whirled on him.

"Who's Mrs. Forsyth?" she demanded.

"Mrs. Forsyth?" he stuttered.

"And Rowena Bishop? Who's she?"

"They helped me," he fumbled. "They helped me break the case." But before he could elaborate, the cleaver, trailing scallion, struck him across the forehead. "Come on now, Gillian!" he cried. "Cool it, will you? I can explain!"

He couldn't explain though. His tongue wouldn't work. The words were there, bright and disarming, but the room streaked red with a burning sting, and he could not get them out. He fell to one knee.

"And Lulu Bernkrandt?" she shouted. "B-e-r-n-k-r-a-n-d-t— who the hell is she?"

The question was clearly rhetorical, for the cleaver flew at him again. He tried to dodge, but an uppercut caught him under the chin, lifted him, and flipped him off his shoulders.

He never reported for work at the Eli Club; his debts were never paid; and Lulu Bernkrandt never saw him again.

The telephone gave a peremptory jangle, but Breeze let it ring thrice before picking up the receiver and very slowly tucking it under his chin. "Mmm-hmm?"

"Breeze?" Kennedy barked. "We can't make head or tail of this mess."

"Mess, Mr. Kennedy?" Breeze counted the empty squares in 34 across and wondered about a seven-lettered Hittite deity.

"These damned ax murders."

"I thought those were solved to your satisfaction," Breeze said.

"Well they're not. There's been another. Head of public relations at the Eli Club."

"Sounds intriguing." Breeze gave up on the deity and tried 27 down, a three-lettered revolutionary government. CIA? he wondered. "I wish you luck."

"It's not intriguing, damn it, it's a nuisance. We have to clean this thing up. And don't tell me that old lady did it, we've got her in jail. And don't tell me her son did it, he's off on his honeymoon."

"I wish I could help, but I'm busy with a crossword puzzle." Breeze hung up, mixed himself a cup of instant coffee, and stretched out on the comfy chair. He let the phone ring twelve times.

"Mmm-hmm?"

"Breeze, if we haven't got a killer for this guy we may not have a killer for the others. That shit about the crazy old actress just won't jell."

Breeze stared at his crossword, tapping the pencil against his teeth. "Was the victim by any chance recently promoted in his job?"

"He was made head of public relations at the Eli Club the day it happened."

"Curious. Very curious. The case is solved, but the pattern continues . . . with a life of its own."

"Breeze," Kennedy said, "I'm sorry . . . what I said."

"What you said, Kennedy?"

"About firing you, demoting you, whatever I said."

"Am I back at my old job?"

"You're back at your old job."

"With a raise?"

"I'll file for a raise."

"Expense account?"

"Screw it, Breeze, let's not haggle. Just get on the job."

Breeze replaced the receiver and got into his shoes. He was knotting his necktie when Kluski knocked on the door.

"Welcome back on the team," Kluski said. "We're supposed to get over there and fingerprint."

"What's the hurry." Breeze sipped his coffee to the bottom of the cup.

"Any theories?" Kluski asked in the squad car.

"Funny business," Breeze frowned. "You know, I'm wondering about Winnie MacAndrew, the real Winnie, that old man."

Kluski look politely dumbfounded. "You think he did it?"

"No."

"So what are you wondering about?"

"I'm wondering how it feels to be that old."

"What do you think about the case?" Kluski prodded.

"The case?" Breeze sucked his lips. "My hunch is, this might be one of those ten percent."

Kluski squinted at Breeze. "Ten percent?"

"The insolubles," Breeze said. The word dissolved into the air-conditioned cool of the car. "Insoluble," he murmured, and nodded at the idea. "They're on the increase, you know."

Kluski stared at Breeze, and Breeze stared out the window at the city.

"There's no such thing," Kluski announced, "as an insoluble case."

"An interminable case," Breeze said, "is by definition insoluble."

Kluski harumphed and crossed his arms. "*Cherchez la femme,*" he said. "The woman did it."

Breeze turned to consider Kluski. "The woman?"

"You know, maybe there's some other woman . . . like a girl friend . . . or a jilted fiancée."

"Kluski," Breeze smiled, "you're beautiful, but you'll never make a detective."